The LIGHT through MY EYES

CINDY KUPINSKI

Copyright © 2019 Cindy Kupinski
All rights reserved
First Edition

PAGE PUBLISHING, INC.
New York, NY

First originally published by Page Publishing, Inc. 2019

ISBN 978-1-64424-967-3 (Paperback)
ISBN 978-1-64424-969-7 (Digital)

Printed in the United States of America

DEDICATION

In Loving Memory of my Mom. Even with all the craziness, she planted the seed of God in my life.

I WANT TO THANK ANNA AND Sheryl for all they have done for me. All the hours of counseling and helping me with different parts and stages of my healing.

Especially Mark—there will never be words to describe how grateful I am for you, and for keeping your promise from so many years ago. It's been a such a crazy, long hard road, but with God's help, I was finally able to receive true healing from all this craziness and be truly healed.

Thank you to Lisa, Brandon and everyone else that I didn't mention but you know who you are.

To Kathy, for all the hours and hours on the phone with me for my really bad days. When my panic attacks were so, so bad, I felt like I couldn't live anymore.

To Sergeant McFadden, for saying enough is enough, for changing my life forever, for giving me the courage even on the really bad days to keep moving forward and to finally stop the cycle of abuse.

To Colleen, for being such a huge support in my last stages of healing, for believing in me and this book.

To my girls, for being there with hugs and love when you had no idea what was going on during all my panic attacks and horrible memories.

To my wonderful boys, for growing up with a dissociative mom. I know it wasn't easy. But you guys were the only reason I had to live, to get up every day and keep moving forward on my healing.

But most of all, I want to thank my wonderful and amazing husband. You believed in me so many years ago. Words can never express how I feel about you and how thankful I am for you. With all the craziness, you showed me what true love is. I know down deep in my heart, I would never be this healed without you.

FOREWORD

HELLO AND WELCOME. CINDY'S BEEN waiting for you. At least I think it is you she's been waiting for. You see, the whole time she spent writing out her story, she knew that there was a particular person out there who needed her story, who would better be able to understand his or her own story by hearing hers. So if this is you, welcome. Cindy has been waiting for you. Get comfortable; you are in for quite a read. However, if you're not the person we have been waiting for, if you are not the person she knew she was writing to, welcome anyway. Feel free to eavesdrop on an amazing conversation. And before the story comes to its conclusion, you might just find that you are the one we've been waiting for, that Cindy's story does help you better understand your own story or the story of someone important to you. So get comfortable because, as I stated, you're in for quite a read.

One other note, and that is regarding the word presented here as *hap-pened*. It is a very important word when encountering a memory that upsets a person. It is important to remember that it is a memory; it is the recollection of something that hap-pened. Past tense. Not hap-pening now. That is why the ending of the word is separated out to show its significance, to remind someone that the thing he or she is bothered by is not hap-pening in this moment. Recognizing this is a huge step toward healing. You will see this throughout Cindy's story. So be prepared to read about what hap-pened to an amazing woman and how she went from not remembering to feeling overwhelmed when she did remember to allowing her mind and body to accept the reality of what hap-pened and finally find healing.

My counseling colleagues, Mark and Anna, and I have had the privilege of accompanying Cindy throughout this process. Now it is your turn to walk alongside her. You will note times where she is hesitant to continue her story. She wrote as she was working through things, so you will see where she struggles, and you may even find yourself struggling with her. Other times you may find yourself wanting to say, "Whatever you're about to tell me, just tell it!" And once or twice you may say, "Wow, I wouldn't have wanted to tell that part either." I was honored to go through the telling with her, to encourage her as she processed and wrote all at the same time. As I was helping Cindy prepare this book, I was struck by how her story echoes the words of Psalm 139. That is why passages from that Psalm are included at each chapter break.

I trust you will recognize that it is an honor to be invited to hear, read, and struggle with her story.

—Sheryl

CHAPTER ONE

> You made my whole being;
> You formed me in my Mother's body.
> I praise you because you made me in
> an amazing and wonderful way.
> What you have done is wonderful.
> I know this very well.
> —Psalm 139:12

HERE IT IS, ANOTHER OCTOBER. October has always been a horrible month. I never knew why because, otherwise, I have always loved the fall months—the leaves changing a wonderful warm color, the cool crispness in the air, a time to cuddle under a blanket, walking holding hands, walking through the leaves. A wonderful time for change.

I never thought that October would change my life so much. A time that would change my life forever. So here it is, another October. It has been my best yet. As I was told over the years, each October would be easier and easier, which it has, but it still is October. As many times as I told myself it is just another month, it still is October.

CINDY KUPINSKI

Back in September, about eighteen years ago, I got stung in the arm by a bee, the same arm that my mom broke when I was a child. I worked in a hospital. I was in so much pain that they took me down to the emergency room to be checked out. They must have thought that I was having an allergic reaction to the beesting. Boy, I wish that was the case. Fortunately, or unfortunately, that was not the case—far from the case. Actually, there was nothing wrong with my arm but all the memories that came with it.

When I was a teenager, early teenager, I always wanted to die. I remember walking in the middle of the street, not understanding why nobody in their cars would hit me. I would just keep walking and walking, but the cars would never hit me. I could never understand why I was *always* in so much pain. But God would always give me the strength to get through whatever I had to go through no matter how bad it was. God would always give me the strength or coping mechanism to get through everyday life. Yes, coping mechanism. It's amazing how the mind works.

One day, I must have been in tenth or eleventh grade, my girlfriend was over my house. My mom and I were in a terrible fight; we were yelling at each other, and she was hitting me. It was horrible, but it was the norm at my house. After my girlfriend and I left the house, I went from crying uncontrollably to walking out the front door and being totally fine. A coping mechanism. I always have hated it, but as I grew older, I really had to thank God for it.

Like I was saying, it's another October. As much as I love October, it has always been the hardest month for me. You are probably wondering what's wrong with October. After all these years, it is still hard for me to talk about it and to truly know that it *hap-pened*.

One day, when I was driving down the road with my two youngest boys . . . Robby is the older of the two. He has dark-brown hair, deep dark-brown eyes, and a really sweet smile. He is very quiet and easygoing and has a great personality. Joey is only nineteen months younger than Robby, but he is very different. Joey has blond hair, almost like dishwater blond, and bright blue eyes. He is more outgoing than Robby. You always know when Joey's awake from all the noise. I remember that when my cousin Kathy would call in the evenings, she would always know if the boys were there because of the noise in the background and that it was more than likely Joey's. Robby was very calm and quiet, very easygoing, always went with the flow. As good as Robby was, it is sad to see what role he was to play as a child.

Like I was saying, I was driving home from work one day after picking up the boys when I started seeing visions of my dad, visions that made no sense. First I saw my dad's headboard of his bed. My mom and dad didn't sleep together. My dad had his own bed on the front porch. You heard it right. My dad's bed was on the front porch. It was an enclosed porch, but still it was the front porch. My mom had her bed in the living room. That's right. Her bed was in our living room. There was no couch, only her bed, a black-and-white TV, Dad's chair, a red recliner, and one end table. We had dark-brown wood paneling that was falling off the walls, and every time Dad went to nail it up, Mom would yell. There was dark red carpeting that was never actually laid out. One day, Dad bought carpeting, brought it home, laid it out on the floor, unrolled some of it, then left the rest of the carpet rolled up on the back of the wall. The other end of the living room, which was the dining room, had a dining table up against the wall with three chairs. The table was always a mess; there was so much stuff on the table there was only barely enough room for two plates. One spot for me and the other spot was for my younger sister, Mary.

Mary is almost five years younger than me. She has beautiful blond hair, big blue eyes, and has such a kind, sweet heart. She would do almost anything for anybody. I miss her dearly. It is so sad what our family has done to us.

Also in the dining room was a china cabinet in the corner and a baby dresser next to the table that was dark-brown with pictures of baby bears on it. On the other wall, there was another dresser. It was a golden oak color, a big dresser with a lot of drawers in it. On the last wall, there was our heater, a stand-alone heater. When it turned on, boy, it would blow out a lot of warm air. I would stand there, just trying to warm up. The warm air was so comforting to me. The only thing that gave me relief, took the pain away, the only warm mother's arms I would experience. What someone would get from a mother, I got from a heater. I remember how many times I felt scared and alone and just freezing, a cold that you would feel from your insides out, so cold you could have a hundred blankets on but you would still be freezing. You can't warm up because you're cold and alone and freezing, shaking internally. Horribly cold and alone. Yes, then that heater was my friend. Little did I know that when I grew up, that heater would be my only friend. That through my adult life, everyone—I mean everyone—would betray me. Not just a little betrayal but a betrayal beyond belief. As I look back and think about everything and everybody, who would like to believe it? Yes, that heater would be my only friend.

As I was saying, I had visions of my dad that made no sense. The view in the vision would be as if I'm on my father's bed, which doesn't make sense because his bedroom (the front porch) was taboo. I wasn't supposed to go into his room, mom always said that it was "dirty" because "bad things" happened there. But I see the headboard so clearly—white with little pellets going around it. The angle would be as if I were on the bed on all fours, looking straight at the headboard. I do not want to tell you the feelings in my body that came with those visions.

Having the vision was horrible. When it happened while I was driving with the boys, I slammed on my brakes in the middle of the road. Even these words do not explain how bad it was.

As I'm sitting here writing after all these years later, it is so hard to believe. I always said that knowledge is power, and as much as I have healed, it is still so hard. As hard as it is to write, as hard as it is just to remember everything, the very hardest part is letting my oldest son, PJ, read this. PJ is twenty-three years old, my baby. Oh, how I love this kid. PJ is very much like Robby; he has the same dark hair and same deep brown eyes, the same warm, sensitive, loving heart. PJ has touched so many people's lives. The calling on his life is amazing. The reason that it is so hard to let PJ know is that he is close to my dad. PJ thinks the world of my dad and PJ finding out the whole truth. If I can't believe this and this hap-pened to me, what is PJ going to think? PJ loves his mom (Ma) with his whole heart, and I know he would do anything, I mean anything, for me. I know this is going to hurt him so much. I have always tried to *protect* him. But I know with my whole heart that God will and always has taken care of him.

I guess that's the same way with my grandma. She always, I mean always, tried to protect me. I don't think I will ever honestly know what my grandma knows of my past. Grandma was always there for me, or so I thought.

When I was little, my mother was very abusive. What I remember was Mom hit me. I would end up in the hospital, go to a foster home, then back to Grandma's. Mom and Dad would get better, or I suppose they just did what the courts believed meant that they were better. I would go back home, and it would be the same thing all over again and again and again. That went from when I was about two days old. Yeah, it started when I was two or three days old.

The day my mom brought me home from the hospital, I did not go home. I went to Grandma's house. My dad is Grandma's oldest son; she had four. She had my dad, then about a year and a half, she had Uncle Hank, then another year and a half later, she had Uncle Don, then ten years later, she had Uncle Ed.

I had a very different relationship with each of them. My uncle Hank was married once and had no kids; they were married for a couple of years, I think. After the divorce, my uncle Hank moved back home with my grandma and grandpa. My uncle Hank was my favorite uncle and PJ's favorite too. He is my and Robby's godfather. What I remember was, he was always good to me and all three of my boys, perhaps especially since Hank never had kids. He always made a special point to take care of all the kids in the family.

My uncle Don was so different. He was in the Vietnam War when he was seventeen or eighteen. I'm not sure exactly; I wasn't born yet. When he got back, he married Bonnie, who was my godmother. They had three kids. Uncle Don and Bonnie got divorced, and he married Carol. They had two kids. I would baby sit for them a lot.

Around the time that I was babysitting for them, the movie *Sybil* came out. I couldn't figure out why I had to watch it, didn't know why my insides would shake, didn't understand why I felt sick, but I still had to watch it. Come to find out, Sybil's life was my life too.

I remember when I was little I loved stuffed animals. But there was a slight problem, well, no, a big problem. Because my childhood was so bad, I would pluck out all the fur on stuffed animals, actually, anything that I could get my hands on, even the bed that was in my front room at Mom and Dad's house. I did not have a place to sit, so I would lie in front of the bed on the floor to watch TV. There as a small hole in the bed. I guess it was the box spring, and there was stuffing in it. Well, you guessed it. I would pluck out all the stuffing. The hole got much bigger, and of course, I got into a lot of trouble, but I had my stuffing! I would suck my thumb, holding my stuffing. Oh my goodness, I thought I would be married with kids before I would stop doing it. Just for the record, I did stop before I married, thank God, quite literally. But I know many women who have been in the same circumstances that still suck their thumbs. There is absolutely *nothing* wrong with that.

You see, that's why I'm writing this because I know there are many women and men who need to hear my story. I need to tell it because I believe that, with the help of God, with God in me, I can help make a difference. The statistics say that one out of three women have been sexually abused and one out of five men. That is way too much to count. I believe that Richard, my ex-husband, was most likely sexually abused.

Okay, back to me sucking my thumb, rolling the stuffing up in a tight ball, rubbing it up against my nose. I did that for years. I really thought that I would never grow out of it. Uncle Ed, the youngest of the brothers, and I were only eleven years apart in age, so every time I stayed with Grandma, he was there. Uncle Ed had won a great big stuffed animal at Cedar Point. He was going to give it to me, but I had to promise that I would not pluck out the fur as I had on all the other stuffed animals he had given me. Boy, did I promise that I wouldn't. One time, when Uncle Ed came home to Grandma's house where I was once again living at the time, guess what I was doing. You're right. I was sitting there with a huge spot on the animal where I had plucked the fur. I was so scared I thought he would be mad at me. But he was fine; he just laughed about it. We were so close. He really cared.

Just sitting here writing this reminds me of all the fear that I lived with 24-7. It *never* went away; it was *always there*. When I was little at Grandma's, every time someone would knock on the door, I would run and hide or I would hide behind her legs. Grandma even said I did it *every time*. That is so sad to think about that someone that young could be so scared. Something had to have hap-pened.

As I grew older, in my twenties, I remember Grandma telling me that every time Uncle Don came over her house, I would cry and hide behind her. It made me wonder, and then that's when I started getting my memories and just maybe something hap-pened with him too. Just maybe.

Grandma's house was very small. It had two small bedrooms. The front bedroom was dark, small, no closet. There were no doors for the bedrooms. They had old vinyl accordion-like doors. The back bedroom was Grandma's bedroom. I remember when I was growing up, I was never allowed to go in the boys' room, that is to say my uncles' room. Then when I grew up, there seemed to be, I don't know, bad feelings, something eerie about it. This is so hard after all these years later. I still don't want to believe it hap-pened. So much happened. Just trying to remember all these old memories is still so painful.

I was at Grandma's a lot; she half raised me. From the time I came home from the hospital, just a couple of days old, I went to Grandma's house. I don't think I even made it home from the hospital. As soon as my mom and I got discarded (okay, so the word is supposed to be *discharged*, but *discarded* seems right) from the hospital, we went straight to Grandma's house where I stayed for two weeks. I guess I was too much for my mother. That's what one person said, that I was too much to handle. Another person said that she went back to the hospital because she had blood clots in her legs. Then another person said something else. At this point, I don't know what to believe, and I guess it doesn't even matter. The fact of the matter is, I was rejected basically from day one. Not only did I stay at Grandma's from day one but I also think the abuse started very early on too.

My mother and father, neither of them are very warm and fuzzy. It's amazing how warm and fuzzy I am. Actually, I am one of the warmest and fuzziest persons I know. Every time I was with Grandma, I needed to be loved and nurtured the most, but that is when I got the cold shoulder. "It's not that bad," everyone would say. It took me thirty-five years to know that *it was that bad*! Grandma, I truly believe, really tried to do her best, the best that she could understand with such a dysfunctional family as mine. I believe knowledge is power, and she did the best of what she knew. I believe the whole family lived in so much *fear*! They did their best.

As I was saying, Grandma's house was very small. Besides the two small bedrooms, the living room was small. There was enough room for a small couch. Yes, a normal front room with a couch, a TV, and Grandpa's chair, a recliner. I remember he always sat in it after he came home from work. Boy, was I his little girl; we did everything together.

One of the very few memories I have is when I was little sitting in front of the furnace, just like the one that was in my house. We used to sit there and eat neck bones and sauerkraut. The biggest joke was that Cindy could eat the neck bone better than Grandpa. The other memory that I had which included my grandfather was . . .

One morning, I was at Mom's and was supposed to get dressed to get ready for school. I think it was for school. What I most remember was that I was supposed to get dressed. I think I would have been in kindergarten. Well, I didn't get dressed. I was watching *The Beverly Hillbillies* on TV. I could see the TV from my bedroom. My mom came in, and she must have been mad. What I remember is her beating me really bad. She threw me across the room and broke my arm. After she finally stopped, I guess I was messed up pretty bad.

My mom told me to go to bed. I was shaking uncontrollably. I was lying there, unable to move, too scared to move. The *fear*, oh, the *fear*, lying there thinking she would come back again. She must have known that this time she hurt me really bad. I was lying there, not moving. She called Grandma and Grandpa. I remember leaving with my grandparents so scared that my dad would be mad. Mom hit me, hurt me, and I was scared—everyone was scared—of my dad. If he got mad, bad things would hap-pen. Mom hurt me, but I didn't want Dad to hurt my mom. I don't remember if Grandpa was carrying me or holding my hand as we went out the door; it's all so fuzzy.

We went to Grandma's, and they were talking about what to do. My grandparents didn't want Mom and Dad to get into more trouble, so they didn't want to take me to the doctors. But I was so bad that they had to. And yes, my arm and shoulder were broken.

A couple of years after that, Grandpa died. I think I was eight. I knew he was sick and in the hospital. I wanted to go with my dad to see Grandpa, but Dad wouldn't let me. I wanted to go so horribly bad. I really loved him. I think he was the only one that brought some kind of normality into the family. When we would drive by the hospital, I would wave to him even though he couldn't even get out of bed to see me, just because I wanted to be close to him.

The morning that he died, I do remember. My mom got the phone call that Grandpa had died. I just cried and cried. I was mad at my little sister because she wasn't crying; she was just bouncing up and down in her crib. She was only two or three. She didn't know any better.

The day of the funeral was very sad. They made all of us go into a special room. I wanted to cry and cry. I was so sad. I had lost my grandpa. With all the horrible, horrible things that my dad had done, one of the worst things was that he did not let me *cry*. The pain of not being able to cry on top of the pain of the loss was, indeed, horrible. When I started healing from all this, I think I made up for it.

When I start crying, and I think I might not be able to stop, it's okay. The best part about crying now is that it is *my choice*!

Fear. I lived in fear my whole life. Fear controlled my life. I was a walking, talking, breathing robot. Even in my first marriage and into my second, there was always fear.

Rich was my second husband. He was so cute and had blond hair, beautiful blue eyes, big broad shoulders—every girl's dream. It was a fairy tale at the beginning.

I was working at Holy Cross Hospital as a unit secretary and in the administrative office for the mental health unit. It was about five o'clock. I had worked all day, even stayed late. The brakes on my car were making a lot of noise, so I took my car to the only place that was close by, a Speedy Muffler King. I didn't really want to go there. I had had some bad experiences there, but again, it was the closest place. I was worried about the brakes, and I had a warranty through them. (It's amazing how God works. It's all in his plan. It's our place to follow our heart.) So it was the best choice. I remember this clearly, like from something out of the movies. I got out of my 1985 Cavalier that I loved, having opened the car door, first putting my left leg out, then the right, feeling the eyes looking at me as I walked across the parking lot, like in slow motion, all the way across the lot and into the door. I still felt the eyes on me, then I looked to my right. There he was, walking through the bays, still looking at me, not able to take his eyes off me. Then our eyes met. Love at first sight.

I look back all these years later, seventeen years ago, and so much has hap-pened. Never in my wildest dreams could I have ever imagined what would hap-pen to us.

Rich and I went out that night. Yes, that same night, just a few hours later. Rich fixed my car and gave me a great deal; he only charged me half of what the job should have been. So right from the very beginning, he was good to me, me being a single mom and all.

Well, anyway, we talked and decided to go out that very night. My dad and sister Mary came over to my house to watch PJ. Since I had only just met Rich, I wasn't sure how the night would go, so I told Rich that I had to be back home at 10:00 p.m. because my dad had to take his insulin (he was a diabetic).

Rich came over around 7:30 or 8:00 p.m. We went down to the corner restaurant and bar for a couple of drinks. We ended up having a really good time. We laughed and joked a lot; we talked about everything. I told him that I was divorced and all the craziness that came with that. Rich told me that he was also divorced. This was in April, and he said his divorce was over last November (boy, was that ever wrong). He said he had a son; his name was Jeremy and was two at the time. That seemed like a good thing that we both went through horrible divorces and were both so lonely. We were both hurt so badly and now it was time for happiness, right?

The time went by so quickly at the restaurant; before we knew, it was time to go back to my house. However, I think Rich was ready to go anyway because I only drank foo-foo drinks. Still do; strawberry daiquiris are my favorite. At $5 a drink for me and he loved his beer, but they were $2.50 when he was used to $1 for a beer and no foo-foo drinks at the bar he normally went to.

Rich told me that he lived in Hamtramck. I grew up in Detroit. Hamtramck is an old Polish community inside of Detroit, and Grandma used to pray all the time for me to meet a nice Polish boy. She got her wish—a really cute, nice Polish boy. But when she was praying for me all those years ago, she forgot one thing; she left one thing out. Grandma forgot to pray for a nondrinker. Rich said that if we went on a second date, "we are going to Hamtramck for a buck-a-beer" as he put it.

That's how Rich and I started. We met, and he was my knight in shining armor. I needed my car fixed; he fixed it, drove me home, picked me back up so that I could pay him, and drove me to my car. We went out and had a wonderful time, both divorced single parents, each with one son. How perfect. Rich was the manager, had a good job. Life was good. Did I mention that he spent the night after that first date? And did I mention that after that first night, he *never left*?

This is how it went. We pulled up in the driveway in his blue 1989 Grand Am. Oh, how I loved that car. It was my favorite make and year at the time. Rich thanked me for a wonderful time, and I think he asked me out again. (This was all so long ago.) Here we were, sitting in my driveway. Rich said it was getting late—10:00 p.m. That's a laugh. I didn't realize that was actually early for him. I invited him in; we were having such a good time. Rich said that he better go because my dad was there and had to take his insulin. Well, when I told Rich that this was my house and that my dad and sister had to go back to his house to take his medicine, that was another story. Rich said sure, he would love to come in.

Rich met my dad and sister; they both thought he was very nice. Rich made himself at home; he put his shoes on the floor under the wall phone. We laughed at that for years. That was his place for his shoes literally since day one. We sat on the couch talking. We talked about everything for hours. We must have said goodbye a hundred times; neither of us wanted him to leave. When he was finally ready to go, he put his hands on my face ever so gently, said how beautiful I was, and asked me if it was okay to kiss me because I was so beautiful. Of course I said yes! It had been so long since I had been with someone and never had anyone asked for a kiss, let alone ask because they thought I was beautiful. Rich slowly put one hand on my face, then the other hand, so gently, with so much passion and caring on his face, slowly looking so deep in my eyes as though he had known me for years. The bond in our eyes was magical; it felt like forever, and I didn't want it to end. Then he slowly came closer and closer, and ever so gently, our lips met and he kissed me. Magical. A kiss like that could last forever.

Rich spent the night. And the next night. And the next night. Since he worked not even a mile down the road, he said it was just easier to stay. Every night, we both made excuses to see each other. The next day, when I went to work, I felt like, pinch me, is this real? I had met the man of my dreams and then some. With all the crappiness in my life, I finally met the one, the one I could finally have that true family that I had so desperately been wanting my whole life. A true family, someone that loves me unconditionally, no strings attached. Just true love the way God had intended it to be. Three days after I met Rich, I knew he was the one. We were going to get married and live happily ever after, or was that just for the movies?

As I'm sitting here, I ask, what is true happiness? Talking to a friend of mine and Sheryl, my counselor, these last few days, I've learned that everyone's idea of true love is different. I never really had a family. Of course I had my mom and dad, but was that really a family or just my bio-family? One of the hardest parts of all this is that God chose my parents. At first I was so angry at God for choosing my parents, knowing that before I was ever born, the choices that my parents were going to make God knew, and he knew that I was going to be able to handle it. A lot of times I got angrier and angrier, saying to God, why? Why did you choose for me a life that was going to be that bad and then some? I could only ask why. But then I always had to remember that God is always right, and as long as we are doing his will, things will always be right even though it seems like everything is falling apart.

It took me forty-two years to figure out that every time something hap-pens, then something else hap-pens, then something else hap-pens next. I got to the point that I stopped asking God what else could hap-pen or go wrong.

Writing this is still so hard. It's probably the hardest thing that I have ever done, and I gave birth to three kids! Naturally, no drugs! But this, now, is the hardest and most painful thing I have ever done. Okay, so I am sure you are tired of hearing how hard it is to remember so many things. How could I have actually lived all this? I want you to know that I have felt the pain and hurt that you may be feeling because I have lived it and felt the same pain and tears as you did. But the only one that has felt the pain, the same fear, the only one that can really truly know what you are feeling is God.

Until I watched the movie *The Passion of the Christ* by Mel Gibson, I really believed that God was all knowing, that God knows all and feels all. I believed it, but I didn't get it. The pain was so bad for so many years. How could anyone, including God, know the pain? The saddest part is I didn't even know how much pain I was truly in. The beautiful but sad thing is that God does truly know.

I was in the middle of counseling when *The Passion of the Christ* came out. Rich and I went to see the movie with my cousin Will and his wife, Kathy. I told Mark, my counselor, that there was no way I was going to see that movie in the middle of counseling, bouncing, sometimes literally bouncing off the walls. Mark again let me know that, yes, I can do *anything*, especially with God. So I finally got my courage up to see the movie, knowing perfectly well what could happen to me.

When we got there, I made sure we sat at the end of the row so that I could leave when I had to, knowing the odds were against me that I could stay. Well, I was right. During the fights and beatings, I did have to leave. It was just too much for me to bear. Even thinking about it now, my heart pounds. After I watched the movie, or tried to, I really got that he was really feeling my pain and hurts and that he does know every tear that I have cried. The saddest part was I truly didn't even know all the pain and hurt that I went through just until last summer.

Last summer, probably my worst summer, well, at least in my adult life, I was still trying to deal with all this junk. It really is junk, like getting out all the nasty icky stuff. Stuff that has been stuffed away, like being hidden in the back of a junky closet buried under all the junk that you just didn't remember or want to remember, was there. Like a nasty sock that was wet and mildewed and got nastier and nastier and you forgot about it. As you're going through remembering things that you had, remembering the good and bad stuff, asking yourself, *why* am I keeping this? Sometimes wanting to deal with the good or bad memories. Like, why do you keep it in the first place? You just don't want to let it go, so you pile everything back in your closet, not letting anything go—the good and the bad stuff. It's easier to put it all back and not even get to that old nasty sock. And it just gets more moldy and more stinky. So by the time you finally get the courage to get to that nasty sock, it's a million times worse now than if you would have gotten it out earlier and a thousand times harder to get clean.

Last summer, I guess I was trying to clean all my nasty dirty socks. I went through all the other nasty stuff, but last summer, I was trying to make sense of all the nasty socks and what they were and trying to make them clean.

What I'm trying to say is that there are lots of different layers that you have to go through for healing. If God would have given me all my memories at once, I would have gone crazy. I believe with my whole heart that giving me different layers is what saved me from going crazy because if it were not for God, I would have been crazy, locked up somewhere (even worse than my mom), or dead. Trust me, sometimes I do wish they would have killed me, but for the *grace* of God, I survived. I am here for my children, for them to grow up and be strong, healthy men. And I am here for all of you who are reading my story—God's story. Remember, he allowed all of it and he saved me and he can save all of you.

Remember when I was talking about October, another October, always something about October? Well, here it is. I believe I was only two years old when my parents were in an occult group that practiced satanic ritual abuse (SRA). Satanic groups generally hold rituals on Halloween, making Octobers really difficult. The abuse was so bad that I became DID (dissociative identity disorder). My little mind couldn't handle the abuse, so my mind would go somewhere else, out of the situation, because I couldn't handle it, so parts of me could survive.

Imagine when everything goes wrong, you're so mad, angry, upset, you just can't take it anymore, you just want to explode, you can't take it anymore. Well, my mind couldn't take it anymore, so my mind went somewhere for one situation, then in another situation, my mind went somewhere else and so on. For every different horrible situation, my mind went somewhere else. Sounds crazy, huh? I agree that it sounds crazy. Imagine living it. I don't want to scare you off, but it's the truth because I lived it.

CHAPTER TWO

> You saw my bones being formed
> as I took shape in my Mother's body.
> When I was put together there,
> you saw my body as it was formed.
> All the days planned for me
> were written in your book
> before I was one day old.
> —Psalm 139:15–16

After I got stung by the bee years ago, I met with the counselors in the mental health unit where I worked. I didn't meet with them on a professional basis; we met as coworkers. I always knew that there was something different about me, but I didn't know what. Talking with them made me realize that my childhood was really that bad. The panic attacks were getting worse. I could hardly function through the day. I would finally get to work and try to get through the day. My heart would start pounding, and my body and mind would start to remember all different things. I could literally feel my mom beating me. There were so, so many different times.

As I lay here in my bed trying to remember those days at Holy Cross and remembering how bad it really was, I still feel sick! Just a couple of days ago, as I was writing this, I thought, *This is too crazy. Did all this really hap-pen?* Remembering about Holy Cross and those days and, again how, I'm feeling now all these years later, yeah, I guess it did really hap-pen!

Like I was saying, things got so bad when I was working at Holy Cross. Talking with the counselors, they recommended a psychiatrist for me because I was not doing well at all. I went into a deep depression. The house was a mess, not dirty but livable. I had a couch with a bed in it. I opened it up to sleep on it because I was too scared to sleep upstairs alone when PJ was with his dad. The couch would be open for days, all the curtains closed. I would lie on the bed of the couch, not wanting to die but not wanting to deal with the world, especially not wanting to deal with my feelings.

I tried to go to counselors before, but every time we would talk about my feelings, I would clam up and not say anything. My insides would say, "No, I don't think so," "I'm all right," "Things are not that bad," and on and on. Well, this time was different. I couldn't clam up and say, "Everything's all right." I finally had no control of what my body was doing. So as much as I didn't want to talk with the psychiatrist, I finally took her number and made an appointment. If I couldn't take care of myself, how could I take care of PJ?

I finally called Dr. Carol Stratman. I was living in Detroit and her office was far away. Actually, not that far, but back then it seemed far. Even now when I drive by her office, I almost always think of those days. Even after I stopped seeing her, sometimes my heart still races. Not so much now but especially in the beginning. The first time I called her, her voice was so soft and calming. It took everything I had, I guess, and then some just to make the call, so I thought. Anyway, her voice was calming, very quiet, and soft-spoken. The biggest thing I remember from our first conversation was her voice. "Go to a happy place, just think about a meadow where all you can see is tall flowers. Everywhere you can see flowers, nothing but blue skies, so blue as blue can be, no clouds in the sky, warm sunny day, the warmth of the sun on your face, not too hot, but a clean, relaxing warmth. A small breeze so the wind is in your hair, ever so slightly, just to relax you, no cares in the world, just the beautiful blue skies, the warm sun, the warm, calming breeze, and flowers as far as you can see."

It seems so long ago. I guess it was. Just thinking that I was in that much pain 24-7. Pain, pain, pain. I thank God every day. Well, I try to thank God every day, but not nearly enough, that even now on my worst days, it's nothing compared to how I felt before, 24-7.

Her office was in a professional building—a big, white building. I believe her office was on the second floor. It's funny, as many times as I went there, I can't quite remember where her office was.

Inside her office was dark. I think it was like a cherry wood color. Dark furniture. Her chair was a big tall dark leather chair with round buttons around the trim. She had bookshelves on the wall of her office. On the wall to the left of her chair was a window. On the opposite side of the room, where I sat, were two chairs. I think they were flowered chairs—big dark green with big light-colored flowers. Again, it makes me mad that as many times as I was there, I still can't quite remember some things about it and I still can't quite be sure of what I remember; it's sketchy and vague.

So much of my life I cannot remember. To think I was so messed up that I can't clearly remember such a silly thing as what the inside of her office looked like. It makes me so mad that my mom and dad messed me up so bad that I can't even remember for sure what the office looked like or, even worse, why I was there in the first place. I remember how awful, horrible I felt all the time and then the financial responsibility for the counseling for what *they did* to me. I'm still suffering for what *they did* to me and what *they* allowed everyone else to do to me. When I was going to her, I only knew or remembered what Mom did to me. The only thing that was safe to deal with was what Mom did to me. If I remembered anything else, I would have gone crazy. I was close enough to that as it was.

After the beesting, the panic attacks were getting worse. During the day, my body would start remembering. I literally felt like I was getting hit again by Mom. I couldn't stop her from hitting me. Trying to run away from her, like reliving the beatings again, feeling every punch, hearing all the yelling. Worse of all was the fear, the horrible dreadful *fear*, the fear that *controlled* my life and all my parts, my alters, whatever you want to call them. As much as I hated all my parts, never knowing who I was from day to day, when I finally, years later, got it, that without my parts, I really would have gone crazy or really would have killed myself.

At work, I lost it when I remember her hitting me. The panic attacks were worse at work. I didn't know why it was worse at work. I never really thought about that until now. Maybe it was safe for me to lose it at work. People there cared about me; my defense mechanism was down. I don't know. Maybe it was God. I know he had his hands on it all the time. If God didn't have his hands on it, you would not be reading my story now. I never could have written this book if he was not in it.

One day, I lost it so bad at work that they took me down to the ER. My aunt Dawn, married to my uncle Ed, who gave me the stuffed animals, worked there. She was always good to me. She is a short woman, about five feet, with short blond hair and with blue eyes. I was young, eleven or twelve; again, I don't remember for sure when she and Uncle Ed got married. She always took care of me, like with doctor's appointments and so on. You see, my mom never drove. Mom has epileptic seizures. So I guess that's why she never drove. My life was such a lie that I don't even know what the truth is. *My life* was a *total lie*. So much of what I was told was a lie.

I just left Sheryl's. We met shortly after I wrote that last line. She and I were talking about what I was writing, so I shared that last line with her. She asked me if *my life* was a lie. I had to think about it. She asked me who I was. I could boldly say (thanks to Mark), "I am loving, caring, understanding, very romantic." I was confused. I was mad that everything around me was a lie, but I was not a lie. I know who I am. Again, thanks to my counseling with Mark. As long as I have been dealing with all this, I'm still learning. Thank God that I know that *I am* not a lie, that God allowed all these things to hap-pen, and that one day I could share my testimony to help others. One day, someone would read my story. Oh, that may be hap-pening today! One day, a day like today, everyone can and will be set free from the demonic cycle. I thank God that he gave me the peace and courage to be set free from all this. This is God's testimony. God chose me. God believed in me to carry out his testimony. So yes, I do believe that *my life* is not a lie. All my surroundings were a lie, but not me.

Just thinking about my mother not driving makes me realize how little I truly know. Why? Talking to Sheryl about it showed how much control there was in that. The only way my mom could go somewhere, anywhere was by my dad taking her. Imagine that the only way you could go to the store, doctor, or anyplace is with your husband. What a form of bondage. Stuck in the house 24-7 is another form of control. We are so used to having our freedom to go to work or to the store without having to tell someone where we are going or for how long. Yes, that was my dad. In everything he did, he had to have control.

Thanks, Sheryl, for sharing that insight. I'm still having a hard time knowing that all my surroundings growing up were a lie. What really was the truth? Fortunately, or unfortunately, my memories are the only truth about my past—what I can remember in my head, what I am seeing even when I really don't want to see it, or, worst of all, my body memories. Even though I want to believe that I am putting these visions in my head, how in the heck could I have really made up all these body memories?

I was working at Holy Cross when all these body memories started hap-pening, my heart pounding, feeling like it would pop out of my chest. You could put your hand on my chest and actually feel how hard it was pounding. The anxiety was through the roof and climbing higher and higher. Just when I thought it couldn't get worse, it did. It got worse and worse. Little did I know that it was just the beginning.

As I was saying a page or two ago, one day at work, I was bouncing so bad that they took me down to the emergency room. I was upstairs on the floor going through a huge panic attack. The doctors and nurses on the floor didn't know what to do, so they sent me downstairs to the ER. The body memories were so bad I was literally going through a beating. I felt every punch, every hit, every smack. I was feeling everything that had hap-pened. I was that little kid again reliving a beating. They tried to restrain me, but that made matters worse. (Just now, writing this, I realize why. The leather restraints!) In the ER, they called my aunt Dawn; luckily, she was working that day. The doctors wanted to give me Haldol, an antipsychotic medicine. It made things worse. I was always told that it was the medicine that confused my mom and that made her hit me. I don't really remember what hap-pened that day in the hospital. I don't remember if they gave me the medication or if they did end up restraining me or if it even matters. All that matters is that it did hap-pen, and that was the first step toward healing from all this.

It still makes me angry that they hurt me that bad. But this was just a little bit, just the dust blown off the top, and just a nudge could throw me that much.

For weeks after that, I was pretty much in zombie mode. The joy of being dissociative is that you can make your body go numb. I remember being at Grandma's one day in zombie mode. I could make myself go totally numb. I kind of knew at times what was going on around me, but I was numb. I couldn't move my arms or legs. I just stared out into outer space. I could hear things and see things but remain numb. The crazy thing about all this was that I was at Grandma's, blaming all this on my mom, thinking that they had me at Grandma's to make sure I was safe. But I think I was there so they could keep an eye on me to make sure that I didn't remember any of this, and this probably made it worse for me. That ugly demonic cycle. Thank God that he has had his hand on this since before I was born.

Okay, so I took a break in the conversation, not that you would know this. It's been weeks since I have written. Every page seems, at times, to get harder and harder. I've lived it and, for the most part, known it, but writing it makes it seem so much more real—all the feelings and emotions that go with it. The more I write all the pieces of the puzzle are starting to fit together, the more it makes a lot more sense.

Rich wanted me to stop working at the hospital. He said that he wanted all this amazing family stuff with me at home. Exactly what I wanted too. So I stopped working at the hospital and picked up a part-time job working for Scott, who has his own company.

Scott is such a sweetheart. I know that God brought us together. Scott was always like a big brother to me. Scott basically took me under his wing—a big brother I never had. Scott is about six feet, two hundred pounds, a big man. We connected from day one. Scott has dark-brown hair, hazel eyes, and a heart of gold. I still miss him. I haven't seen him in years. He will always have a special place in my heart. I guess I forgot, well, I did forget, that Scott always believed me.

One day, I kind of freaked out and started getting memories of my dad, and I didn't call Grandma. Why is it significant that I didn't call Grandma that day? Well, you see, I needed to get ahold of Grandma every day. I called her when I first woke up and during the day at least five to six times. I didn't do anything, I mean anything, without calling Grandma. I was a grown woman with three children, thirty-something years old, and still calling Grandma. I guess it was to get approval. Or maybe she needed to know where I was 24-7. Sick, isn't it? Anyway, I didn't call Grandma for a few days. Here I was, starting to get my memories, and of course, I didn't really want to talk to my family. When I did go over to Grandma's house, I just talked very vaguely about it. Immediately, she referred it to Grandpa and said that he never abused me. Why did she even go there? When I talked to Uncle Hank, he immediately went on the offensive. I didn't want to believe any of this was true. Then here is my family acting so weird (well, weirder than normal). So if any of this is not true, and at the time I was wishing it was not true, why were they acting so weird?

So again, I was at work trying to make sense out of all this. Grandma and Dad were calling me at the house, but I wasn't picking up. If they called at work, I just let people take messages. For some reason, I knew that they might come to work, like they were going to come and get me. I had a lot of fear and anxiety about this. I was sitting at my desk at work and Scott heard a car pull in the driveway. I looked through a peephole in the outside door and saw my dad. I ran to the supply room with Scott just crying and crying, not wanting to believe that any of it was true. My dad, who had never come to my work before, came. Why on earth did he come that day? That's when I had no choice but to believe that maybe there was some truth in this because when I saw my dad, I freaked out. Ever since then, my bio-family that I loved so much and wanted to be accepted by was never the same. How could it be? Just like that, my whole family was slowly taken away from me.

As I am sitting here by the pool, trying to get some sun, I know just how important it is for me to write this. It is important for me and for you and for the family I have now—PJ, Robby, and Joey. As I'm sitting here, I am crying for the loss of my bio-family, everything that has been taken away from me and my children. I have to think of all the blessings that are going to hap-pen from all this. I was the *one* that broke the demonic cycle, the generational curse. It took only one person to make a difference in my children's lives, my grandchildren's lives, my great-grandchildren's lives. I have had every attack, anything you can think of hap-pened, but I made the difference not only to bless my true family but also to you reading this. That you may know that you can also make a difference for yourself and stop the generational curse in your family. That my story will make a difference in your life.

Yesterday, Joey turned eleven. I still deal with missing my bio-family. The enemy is trying to do anything that he can to stop me from writing. Yesterday, for Joey's birthday, I made plans for us, but Joey chose to be with his dad. I felt bad that we didn't have a party for him, but I've learned that we all have choices. Even Robby, I'm so proud of him; he really gets it about choices. It's still sad to me that I have a huge bio-family so I could have had a big party for Joey. But I know in my heart that they are just my bio-family. My true family are my boys—Robby, Joey, and PJ.

I would do anything for my boys, and I can proudly say anything and mean anything.

Rich and I did get married, and when things were good, they were great. It felt like I was the luckiest girl in the whole world. After my crazy marriage with PJ's dad, then another crazy relationship with Steve, Timothy's cousin, I met Rich. I was so happy after we met. Rich was my knight in shining armor. He was everything I ever wanted in a man. Like I was saying before, he was gorgeous—blond hair, blue eyes, big broad shoulders. Gorgeous to look at. Rich always wanted to be with me. The day we met and went out, he *never* left. Every day we were together. After work, he was always there. Finally, after all those years of being alone, I finally had someone in my life. I was still seeing Dr. Stratman since I had to go see her once a week, and Rich was there every night, and my appointment was at 6:00 or 6:30 a.m.; he had to know where I was going to so early in the morning. I was embarrassed about telling him that I was seeing a psychiatrist for what hap-pened to me when I was little. But Rich was so caring and understanding. He would always be there for me and protect me, so nothing or no one would hurt me anymore. Little did I know.

Rich and I did everything together. Well, I thought we did. Everything we did together was perfect. Well, I thought it was. A couple of days after we met, he finished working on my car and gave me a great deal. Then a couple of days later, he fixed the rest of it for free. He let me use his car to get PJ from school. He even gave me his paycheck to cash that week. We bonded that fast; everything fell into place. We were a family overnight, and family was always what I wanted. I believed God had finally blessed me with a family.

Rich told me that he was also divorced, that his divorce had been final the previous November. We met in April, and that would have made him divorced for five months. He also said that he had a son, Jeremy, that he didn't really see. Rich told me that his ex-wife didn't let him see Jeremy but that he did get to see him once a week and that he was little. I think two or three years old. Jeremy was a sweet little boy, and how he loved his dad. PJ and I fell in love with him. We were all a seemingly perfect little family overnight.

A couple of days after Rich and I met, about four days later, he figured out he better go home, at least to get a change of socks and underwear. Rich had moved back to his parents' house after his breakup. I went with Rich to his parents' house. I kind of felt funny, thinking, *What are they going to think of me?* I had just met this man and was letting him move in! They were very sweet. They opened up their home to me and made me feel like family. Rich's mom is very quiet and soft-spoken. She has salt-and-pepper short hair, actually mostly white, wore glasses and no makeup. She is a tall woman, about five feet nine inches, very sweet, kind, and loving. A real mom. Rich's dad is a really fun guy, always laughing and cracking jokes. He has dark-brown hair (he's in his late fifties and still has dark-brown hair). He styles it like back in the '50s. He is a shorter man, about five feet, six inches, small framed with dark-brown eyes. Dad, as I called him from the start, always made me laugh. From the first day we met, he knew I felt uncomfortable about meeting them, of what they would think of me, but they wanted Rich to be happy since he had been through so much with the breakup with his wife and son. They saw that their son was happy. See, every part of our relationship was perfect. Rich's parents were great, and they adored me and PJ. What more could I ask for? My family that I had so desperately wanted had finally come true. I was praying for this, and my grandma was praying for this—a cute Polish boy and hard worker that wants a family. But again, Grandma had left out one thing—to pray that he would be a nondrinker.

After meeting with Sheryl, I really realize how much family means to me, and Rich and his family were really what family means to me. My lifelong fantasy of family was really coming true. After all those years of pain and suffering, a man really wanted to be with me.

I was still seeing Dr. Stratman. I was feeling much better. I was still on medication, and therapy was slowing down; we were talking about the same things over and over again. As I look back, I can see why. Sheryl explained it so well. No offense, Sheryl, but I knew it was all coming from God that he was revealing it to the both of us. My life, up until I started passing out, was Hurricane Katrina, a massive storm that blew through New Orleans that caused massive damage. The rain, the strong winds, the flooding, such horrible damage. That was my life; it was so bad, but God gave me coping mechanisms to survive all of it. But just like in New Orleans, after all that devastation hap-pened, no one thought that things could get any worse, and that's when the levies broke and the true devastation started.

That's what hap-pened to me—all the years of abuse from my mom and dad, Grandma, my whole family, then all the years of abuse from Timothy, PJ's dad, then after the divorce and all the drama from that, then with Steve and all the confusion that came from that. My body literally could not handle anymore. From switching all the time just to survive, my body could not handle anymore. My walls could not handle anymore. The pressure was so severe that my walls—my levies—broke. So here I was at the very bottom of the dam, with all the walls piled on top of me and all those years of abuse, just like all the mud, cement, debris piled on top of me, not being able to move. So I had to go piece by piece, slowly removing each one, slowly removing each piece. Each piece being another memory that I had to deal with. Just like when the levy broke and each piece of debris, big and small pieces, came rushing out. When you're moving a big piece, sometimes it seems impossible to move. You don't know what angle, what tool to use to move it; your mind is figuring out how in the heck are you going to move it. Your mind can be on overload, trying to figure it out. But after you finally pick it up and carefully, very carefully, because you surely don't want to drop it and start all over again from the beginning, going through the process of figuring out to how to start all over again. You very slowly, carefully move, picking a piece up, making sure you don't touch any other pieces, knowing that you will deal with that piece next. You don't want to stir anything else up. One memory at a time is more than enough. After concentrating on that piece only, it slowly goes up and up and you see that you can move it off to the side, putting it safely to rest, then you can move onto the next piece.

After Sheryl put it to me that way, I could understand more clearly why the memories of being in the hospital and starting to see Dr. Stratman are so confusing but so strong. That's when I couldn't hold on to the memories anymore. I could finally start to heal and become a whole person. I thank God for giving me my walls; as much as I always hated them, they made me survive.

I saw Rich again yesterday when he picked Joey up for dinner. Writing about Rich and family still makes me mad that it was so perfect (I thought). After talking to him yesterday, though, I know that I made the right choices, as you will see.

As I was saying, I couldn't believe that here I finally got my family—a wonderful man, PJ, and Jeremy. We were making money, fixing up my house. After months of dating, Rich and I decided to go down to Florida for a vacation. I had never been to Florida, so I was excited. Going down there, the drive was wonderful. I love going on vacation, and it had been years since I had had one. When we were driving, we both wanted to get into Florida before we stopped for the night. When we got into Florida, it was about 11:00 or 11:30 p.m. It was dark out but a beautiful warm night. I got so excited just seeing my first palm tree. Rich saw how excited I was over a palm tree, so when we stopped at a rest stop to sleep, he parked right under a palm tree. Wasn't that sweet? When we woke up in the morning, we were both excited to get to Key West, so on our way, we went.

When we finally got to Key West, it was late and we were both tired. Sleeping in the car, you don't get much sleep. I wanted to get a room and settle in for the night. But Rich wanted to go to the bar, which one, I don't remember. We were kind of fighting over what we were going to do. Well, since Rich was driving, we ended up at a bar. Remember, when Grandma was praying for a nice Polish boy, she forgot to include asking for a nondrinker. After a while, I was getting really tired and I wanted to call it a night, but Rich stilled wanted to drink. Well, he can't have just one or two, and when he starts drinking, he cannot stop. Rich will be nice and sweet one minute, then boom, just like a light switch, he will explode. And that's what happened. When I finally talked him into getting a room, all the hotels were full. Everywhere we went they were full. Of course, that just made it worse. I don't remember what finally caused him to explode, but when we were driving, he hit me across the face. Then he stopped the car and threw my bags out of the car, called me terrible names, and drove off.

Boy, was I in a bad spot. Almost two thousand miles away from home, stranded in the middle of Key West—what a wonderful way to start my vacation. I was in shock from him hitting me. The last time I had been hit was when Timothy hit me. That had been at least three years earlier. I was seeing Dr. Stratman, my levies were broken, I was trying to process my past, and now here I am, hit, triggered through the roof, and then some. And I'm stranded. Not in a good situation. So imagine, here I am under a palm tree again, with my bags on the side of the road, one open from when it hit the road. Just thinking about it now, I don't know whether to laugh or cry. Anyway, here I am, walking with my stuff, trying to find a hotel. There's no way of anyone finding me. This was before everyone carried cell phones. I could have been anywhere. When I did find a room and got settled in, thinking of the long walk I just had, I was in shock. After everything I had been through (although I didn't know much of it at the time), here I am stranded in Key West supposedly with the man who loves me, the perfect family I thought I had finally gotten. How could this be love?

I called my girlfriend Gloria, whom I had met in a support group for women that had been sexually abused. Gloria was the leader of the group. My memories had been buried so deep that I didn't remember hardly anything during that time, just Mom hitting me and I thought sexually abusing me. I knew that things were crazy at the house, but nothing else. Well, Gloria had also been involved in satanic ritual abuse (SRA). It still amazes me all these years later how God truly had his hands on everything. My stuff was buried so deeply that when Gloria was sharing at the support group of acts of the SRA, I experienced no triggers at all. After we became really good friends, I used to go over to her house, talking in depth about the SRA, still no triggers. It's amazing, no triggers, my walls were that thick. When I started getting my memories of the SRA, I thought back about Gloria and how I blocked everything out. She had also blocked everything out. So every time I question memories of this, that, and whatever, I always think of Gloria and how she blocked everything out too.

When I called her from my hotel room, she couldn't believe what hap-pened either. That everything that was going on in my life right now while I was just starting to make sense of things. That in all the times that something like this could hap-pen, this was the worst possible time. When we were talking, I was so confused. How in earth could he have done this to me? Here we were, young and in love, our first vacation together. How could this be hap-pening? It just didn't make sense. No sense at all. Now I was really confused! Gloria didn't know what I should do either. Stranded in Key West, well, I guess it could have been worse. Key West, not so bad. What should I do? Try to get a plane ticket back home? Call Rich's parents to come pick me up since they were living in Florida for a few months? Did I really want to call his parents and tell them what he did to me? Would they care or even believe me? I was so confused. I didn't have much money for a plane ticket. I had all kinds of emotions toward my own family, so I didn't really want to call them. I felt like a lost puppy dog.

A part of me, of course, wanted Rich to find me, be the knight in shining armor again, and rescue me. I knew it sounds crazy. I knew he would be rescuing me away from himself. I even knew it was crazy, but that was my mind-set, my way to survive. Gloria did talk me into calling his parents. That was kind of my only way back home since Rich had no clue of where I was. As a matter of fact, I had no way of knowing where he was. When I called Rich's mom, I thought she would be in shock, but she wasn't. She was sorry it happened, but not too terribly surprised. That should have been a red flag. It was, but I chose not to see it; it just hurt too much. A little bit of love, even though it was destructive, was far better than no love at all. When I called her, she said, "Stay put and I will come and get you." What a mom. It was at least a three-hour drive to Key West, and I had absolutely no idea where in Key West I was. Mom told me to stay put, we would talk in the morning, and then she would come and get me.

It was a long night. I talked to Gloria almost half of the night. I hardly slept. I was hungry; really hadn't had anything to eat all day, just snack food. I remember leaving my hotel room alone and afraid. The only thing in the area was a 7-Eleven or something like that. I got a sub and something to drink. Here I am, traveled almost two thousand miles, alone in Key West, all this for a sub?

When morning came, I still didn't hear from Mom. I was just lying there in bed, thinking, what should I do? Then the phone rang. It was the front desk. They told me that I had a visitor and was it okay to tell him what room I was in. At first I was so surprised. "Oh my god, he loves me and cares about me and he came to rescue me." Again, I forgot that he was rescuing me from himself. Messed up, isn't it? I was confused. I didn't really know what to do. I guessed the best choice was to let him in. I told the gentleman at the front desk that it was okay, so against his better judgment, he told Rich my room number. Little did I know what was yet to come.

Rich knocked on my door, seemed so sad and sorry. He couldn't believe he could have done something like that to me. Rich blamed it on his being tired, having no food in his stomach, the whole nine yards, and I believed every word of it. Rich told me everything I wanted to hear and then some. Looking back, it was at that point in our relationship that he had total control over me. It is so hard for me to admit that, but it is the truth. Rich had total control, and I let it hap-pen.

As I am lying here in bed, remembering all this, it's sad but it also reminds me of how real all this is. Rich and I had a wonderful time. We made up, and of course, he made me believe that this would never hap-pen again. Rich did and said everything right, and I wanted to believe him. Why wouldn't I? Remember the family thing? Some love is better than no love at all.

Rich called his mom to let her know that everything was okay. We went to a bed-and-breakfast. It was truly beautiful—palm trees, gardens, hot tub and pool area, water gardens with tropical fish, an outside kitchen area. Just beautiful. Every time we went back to Key West, that's where we stayed and that's where we went for our honeymoon. That's right, our honeymoon too. Our first vacation in Key West was really the start of the abuse, and we kept going back.

Not only is Rich an alcoholic, but he was also using crack cocaine. The crack should have made me run, but I was trapped in the situation. Rich and I would go out to the bar quite a lot. When we didn't have PJ, all we did was party. I have always been a Goody-Two-Shoes. With my dad, I really had no choice. I got beaten one way or another. So I chose to be good so there would be no reason to get yelled at. Unfortunately, I always got yelled at anyway. I did love to drink at one point. Luckily my girlfriend Sandy helped me with that. I never ever did drugs. I was always too scared to. I'm not quite sure if there was drug use in the occult and whether they made me take drugs to make me forget. I think they did, but it's okay until God makes it clear. I believe I really don't need to know.

As I was saying, in the beginning with Rich, we used to go to the bars when we didn't have PJ. I had PJ so young. I really hadn't done much except for being a mom, and I love being a mom. Literally, my whole world was PJ. Well, Rich introduced me to the world of drinking at bars. I was twenty-seven and at bars for the first time in my life. Blue Jays was a small bar in Hamtramck. Everyone there was nice; it was mostly an older crowd—retired men. It was family owned and operated. It was funny that the first time we went there, I asked for a strawberry daiquiri and they all looked at me funny. A what? A strawberry daiquiri. They were like, sorry, but we don't have anything for a strawberry daiquiri here. I asked for a couple other foo-foo drinks, and all they could say was sorry. I ended up with a wine cooler. Rich and I used to go there a lot. I forgot that we were only dating for three days, sitting in a booth at Blue Jays, when he told me that he loved me. Wow, only three days. How could he have loved me? The funny thing is that two days after we met, I knew I was going to marry him; the day before, he told me that he loved me and would always take care of me and would always make sure that nothing would hurt me. Come to find out *he* would hurt me most of all. Nothing, I mean nothing, could ever have prepared me for what was to come. Nothing.

Rich and I were young, in love, partying at Blue Jays, having fun. Well, Rich wanted me to have more fun. He desperately wanted me to try smoking crack. Luckily, God was with me. As much as Rich wanted to me smoke it, I always said no. Rich was starting to drink more; the crack problem was definitely getting worse. My walls were getting thicker and thicker when it came to Rich. By that time, I was giving him more and more control because I wanted a family so much. After that first trip to Key West, when he basically got away with hitting me, Rich thought it was okay, so he started hitting me more and more. We would be out drinking in Hamtramck and he would get drunk. He didn't care what would hap-pen and would take me to the crack house with him. The drinking and drugs got so bad that he would go to the ATM and take all the money out for crack. By that time, we did open a checking account together. He would take out all the money, knowing that checks had to clear and there was no more money. He didn't care; all that mattered was his crack. A couple of times he would pretend that he was putting money into the ATM envelope so he could get money out, saying that he deposited a $300 check so he could take that money out.

You would think after that I would have kicked him out of the house, but no, I loved him and he was family. Well, I thought. It took me years later to learn what family truly is. So here I was, in another messed-up relationship.

Timothy was definitely my mom and Rich. Well, he was my dad. I just found out or realized that my dad is a hundred times worse than my mom. Mom did try to get out of the relationship just like me. But the biggest difference was that I wanted to make a difference and did not want to be the victim. But Mom did; she wanted to be the victim. It was always "poor Sandra" and she liked it. Unlike me, I didn't want to be the victim. I just didn't know how to get out. I was way too trapped.

Well, I had my really good days with Rich, and I had my really bad days with Rich. After a long time being with Rich, we were at his mom's house one day and she wanted to know if I had a chance to get ahold of an attorney yet for Rich's divorce. Can you imagine the look on my face? I remember sinking further down into the couch, thinking to myself that I had to have heard it wrong. I remember saying, "His what?" Remember all this time I thought he was already divorced. Mom didn't know that I didn't know he wasn't divorced.

Can you imagine how I was feeling? Boy, a lie from day one. Rich's mom was thinking that we were getting closer together and that we should start thinking about getting married, but we couldn't because Rich was already married. I didn't know to laugh or cry. Just something else I would have to deal with. All that time I was living with a married man and I didn't even know it. Everyone had lied. I didn't know about any of the occult stuff yet. Good thing I didn't.

Shortly after I found out that Rich was still married, I realized I was pregnant. I found out early. I must have been six weeks along. I was still seeing Dr. Stratman, and Rich was very supportive of that. I was still on medication—Prozac and Valium. My OB was the same doctor that delivered my sister Mary and tied my mom's fallopian tubes. I was always told that the courts made her do that because they didn't want my mom to have any more kids because things were so very bad at my house. So my doctor knew a lot about my past. At that time, he may have known more than I knew or remembered. So my OB agreed with Dr. Stratman, knowing all the circumstances that the best thing for me to do was abort my baby. That was the second time in a row I would have an abortion. The first was with Timothy.

This time it was done at the hospital. I was put to sleep and a dilation and curettage was performed, calling it a missed abortion. The second time, I had to have an abortion. And you know how much I wanted a family. I had all kinds of complications after my dilation and curettage, but God did bless me with two more children. I gave two of my children to God, and God is a good God. What the enemy has taken away from me God will restore. God is true to his word and blessed me with Robby and Joey. At times when they were driving me nuts, like they have been all day today as I am writing this, I have to remind myself that God blessed me with my boys, all three of them. The best part is that God chose me to be their mom. Pretty lucky, huh!

After my second abortion, I was pretty done. For months after that, I was in robot mode. Wow, I just thought that when I had it done, it was late September. So many things throughout my life bunched into that time of year. Talk about a trigger. That seems so long ago. I've always had a hard time with that, but Mark would always remind me that one day I will meet my children in heaven.

Rich didn't have that hard of a time with it. He always assured me that we would have another child together. That was always in my head, and that was another form of control. Rich knew that I wanted another child. Well, after I got over the shock of Rich being married, I asked him why he lied to me. Rich had so much control. I believed everything he told me. Rich said, "If I would have told you the truth, would you really have gone out with me?" He had me so hooked. I use to get mad that he had that much control. With everything that has hap-pened to me, it could have been much worse. He could have killed me. It's amazing that he didn't.

My girlfriend Gloria, the one who had been an SRA survivor, worked for an attorney. When I called her and told her that Rich needed a divorce attorney, I thought she was going to fall over. After all the stuff that hap-pened in Key West, well, of course I should have dumped him. But of course, I didn't. Gloria did talk to her boss and set up an appointment for Rich to start his divorce. We were still seeing Jeremy at this point. Rich's wife at the time, Wendy, was pregnant from her boyfriend, so she also wanted a divorce so she could marry her baby's daddy. Wendy and I became good friends. We would talk on the phone for hours, talking about Rich and making fun of him. Talking to Wendy, I found out even more lies; at that point, I guess it didn't matter. Rich started drinking more and started seeing Jeremy less and less. The divorce was pretty simple. Rich was living with me, and Wendy was living with her boyfriend. The house that they had been living in was Wendy's. Her grandfather bought it for her as a wedding present, I think. Things seemed to be going smoothly with us and Wendy until PJ's birthday party.

We always had really big parties for PJ's birthday, around thirty to forty people. It was one time of the year that the whole family would get together—Mom, Dad, Grandma, all my aunts and uncles and their kids, lots of family. At this time, we had a huge party with Rich's parents, PJ, and Jeremy. We had tons of food and one-fourth barrel of beer. Rich, his family, my uncles, they sure did like to drink. Anyway, we had a blast. Everybody got along so well. Nobody wanted the day to end. We had people come and go all day. To me, life was perfect until the boys both had to go back to their other parents. I always hated PJ going back to his dad. Just hated it.

I think I took the boys back by myself that night. I dropped Jeremy at Wendy's first. I talked to Wendy, and everything was fine. The boys even played together outside before we left. Then I took PJ back to his father's. Well, a couple of days later, I had protective services at my door, stating that, at the party, Rich hit Jeremy over his head with a beer bottle. Can you imagine how upset I was? Here I was, thinking everything was fine just a couple of days ago, and now protective services are at my door. I freaked out. Freaked out. Full-blown panic attack.

I remember when I was young, maybe two or three, my mom ran away with me to get away from my dad. I think we were living in an apartment in downtown Detroit. Gosh, I really don't know for sure. Anyway, I was with my mom somewhere, and there was a knock on the door. It was a man and a woman in the background, along with two big police officers at the door. They seemed ten feet tall. I was so little.

I remember being so scared. All I wanted was my mom. They were there for me to take me away from my mom. I remember their dark blue shirts, their shiny badges, and their dark hats. I don't remember their faces or what they looked like, but I sure remember their hats. Isn't it funny what you remember? The next thing I know, I was holding my mom's leg, screaming "Don't take away my mommy," then being in my mom's arms, screaming, "Don't take me away." My mom was begging them to please let her change me out of my pajamas, please let her get me dressed, but the police wouldn't listen. They took me from her arms. I remember yelling and screaming, "I want my mommy! I want my mommy!" but they didn't listen to me either.

They took me in my pajamas and gave me to that man and woman. I was so scared. I wanted my mom, and they took me from her. The man and woman put me in this big black car. Back in the '60s, the cars were big. I was still fighting and screaming when they put me in the back seat. I remember crying, kneeling on the back seat, looking out the back window. They didn't use seat belts back then either. The police were still with my mom, holding her. I was watching out the back window, watching as she got farther and farther away. I was scared and alone again. I believe they took me to a foster home. I don't know for sure because my family never talked about it.

The next memory I have is standing in a long line with other boys and girls. I think we were in line to take showers; again, I'm not sure. I just remember being so scared and wanting my mom. The lady at the head of the line gave me a stuffed animal. Then I remember being in a huge room with beds on each side of the room. It had white walls. The beds were small with gray blankets and white pillowcases, just like you see in the military, boot camp, something like that. On the very back wall, there were no beds but a huge door wall, so I could see right through to the outside.

Outside the door wall was the playground. I don't remember playing out there, but I do remember the pony. It was brown with small white stripes and a big smile. (It's funny what you remember as a child about things.) It was a bouncing pony, hung from metal springs. You could sit and bounce on it or go back and forth. Oh, how I loved that pony. I don't think I even sat on it, but I would stare at it all the time.

The other side of the room, across from the door wall, was my crib. The only other thing on that wall was the doorway into the room. I used to stand in my crib, holding on to the rails and rocking back and forth from side to side, crying, "I want my mommy" while staring out at that pony. I kept everyone up at night with my crying. There were kids there of all ages. I look back and feel sorry for all those kids that I kept awake at night. Even the staff there. There were two or three different people at night that would come over to my crib and try to comfort me, but nothing worked. All I wanted was my mom.

I wanted my mom, which is crazy because she had been hitting me so bad and so often that she had to take me to the hospital. The hospital staff contacted the police, protective services. Heck, I don't know who all they told. Someone called someone, and that was why the police came and got me from my mom. The very worst part was that when my dad and grandma came to get me to save me and keep me safe from my mom since she was the one who was hurting me so badly to land me in the hospital, I freaked out. I didn't want to go with my dad or my grandma. I guess I knew that they were the ones who were hurting me even more than my mom. Imagine that. And imagine what the people at that home thought. And that was only the beginning.

So when protective services came to my door regarding Jeremy and Rich, I freaked out. I was literally back to that two or three-year old little girl, reliving that experience all over again. Somehow, the woman at the door knew exactly what to do. That was the first time Rich saw me like that. I remember sitting on my front porch, having a full-blown panic attack. I'm so thankful that she knew what was going on and not to take me away. The woman was so nice. She was an older woman, like a grandma. Her voice was soft-spoken. Rich didn't know how to act or what to do. She told him to go back in the house and she would talk to him. She and I talked for a long time. I explained to her my past (what I knew) and how I was in therapy with Dr. Stratman. The woman was able to get me calmed down, then she spoke with Rich about what I was going through. After I got myself together, Rich and I explained everything that hap-pened at the party. It seems that she believed us because nothing ever came of it. I probably don't need to say that after that incident, Wendy and I didn't talk much anymore.

When Rich's divorce was final, things were a lot better between him and me. At times, things would be perfect, I mean perfect. I was the luckiest girl in the whole wide world. But when things were bad, they were terrible. As much as it was good, it was that bad, really bad. After all these years later and everything that has hap-pened, I'm still mad at him because as crazy as it was, it was still the most normal thing to family that I have ever had. My mom and dad were (are) crazy. My first husband, Timothy, was crazy. Steve couldn't love me or commit, and then there was Rich.

We were in Hamtramck at a family restaurant and bar. We were sitting at the bar drinking, having a good time. Then out of the blue, Rich looked at me and said, "We've been together for a long time, so I think the next thing to do is get married. Will you marry me?" I just about fell off my chair. I couldn't believe that he asked me to marry him. *Pinch me, I'm dreaming*, I thought. *Is this really hap-pening to me after all these years of being alone? I'm getting married again. I must be dreaming.* Marriage, family, and everything I ever wanted was coming true. Or so I thought.

CHAPTER THREE

> Lord, you have examined me
> And know all about me.
> You know when I sit down and when I get up.
> You know my thoughts before I think them.
> You know where I go and where I lie down.
> You know thoroughly everything I do.
> Lord, even before I say a word,
> You already know it.
> You are all around me—in front and in back—
> And have put your hand on me.
> Your knowledge is amazing to me;
> It is more than I can understand.
> —Psalm 139:1–6

WHEN I MARRIED PJ'S DAD, Timothy, we got married in a hallway with people coming in and out of the door and people going up and down the stairs. Not the most romantic experience. As a matter of fact, the morning of the wedding, I woke up not knowing if I was getting married that day or not. If Timothy came over Grandma's, I was getting married. If Timothy didn't come over, then I wasn't. Just thinking about it, it sounds so crazy. That was how messed up I was.

Then Steve, we never fought or argued, but he couldn't and wouldn't commit. Steve was Timothy's first cousin. We ended up together, just another dysfunctional relationship. Steve would never tell me that he loved me or that he was committed to me. Our relationship was a closet relationship, and behind closed doors, we were perfect. Out in the real world we were just friends. We presented that to everyone, other friends, and family alike.

Then here is Rich, asking me to marry him. I got all excited about it when, really, at the time, he was worse than Steve and almost as bad as Timothy. Boy, was I messed up. So of course, I said yes. I wanted a family and I thought if we got married, things would be all better. Unfortunately, many women that I have met have felt the same way.

I was so unsure about what Rich asked me. The very next day, I went up to his work and asked him if he really meant what he said when he asked me to marry him. He said, "Of course. If I really didn't want to marry you, why would I ask?" Well, Steve said all the time, "Let's get married," and there was no ring or anything. It was just talk. So when Rich was actually serious about talking about getting married, I was thrilled. Remember, no matter how bad it was, it was still family. Even if we had one good day a month, one day is a million times better than no days at all.

We were engaged for a few months, and we didn't tell anybody. So I thought maybe it was just like Steve—all talk. Then we started talking again about getting married. We had been living together a couple of years, I guess. So we thought it was time to start making wedding plans. We decided that we wanted to announce our engagement in a special way. So we decided to have everybody over for Christmas Eve. All the family. We had done it for the last couple of years, so it was no surprise to anyone for us to invite everyone over for Christmas Eve dinner. Here I am with family again. Just can't get enough.

Anyway, everything was perfect. I cooked for two days, had lots of food, appetizers, and dessert, but one thing was missing—the future groom. I was so excited for days that this was real and all this was finally hap-pening, and when that night came, no Rich. He had to work a half day on Christmas Eve, and he had to stay and drink with the guys. I had everybody at the house and no Rich. I didn't want to start dinner without him, especially on such a special day. Did Rich care? I called him at work to see where he was, and we got into it over the phone. Everybody was ready to leave; they didn't want to be around fighting. That would have been the worst thing to happen!

Rich finally did come home. Everybody ate. We all had a really good time. I was just able to switch and pretend everything was okay. My wonderful Rich was home. The mean one stayed at work. This was how my brain was thinking. I was able to switch and everything could be just fine. The sad story of my life. The whole family was thrilled we were getting married. That Christmas went okay.

The previous two years, I had Christmas lights torn off the walls and the Christmas tree destroyed, which was not fun. Rich had come home drunk and beat up the Christmas tree. That's right, beat up the Christmas tree. I forget what he was mad about. He started hitting the tree, knocked the bulbs off the tree, threw them on the floor, then picked the tree up, threw it on the ground, and broke more bulbs. I had a lot of bulbs that had meaning from when PJ was little, and many of them got broken.

That was the start of Rich breaking things of mine that meant something to me. What made matters worse was that when I was little, my mom would never let me play with my toys. For whatever reason, I think it was because it was supposed to be dirty. If the toys had anything to do with my dad or grandparents, I wasn't allowed to play with them. Have I told you yet that my mom would throw my brand-new toys away outside in the backyard? It was so hard to look outside and see my toys in garbage bags Mom was so mentally ill.

Every time Rich would destroy something of mine, it was to hurt me. My cousin Kathy and I were talking one day about Rich destroying my stuff. She would always wonder why every time she came over—well, almost every time she came over—things that she had bought me were not in the same place anymore. She wouldn't see them again. Then she figured out what hap-pened to them, that they were gone, destroyed. Kathy couldn't figure out why Rich would do such a thing. Most of the time, Rich was drunk or he was plain old mean.

So here I was, happier than ever, going to marry the wonderful man who loves me so much that he chose me over everyone else in this whole wide world. Boy, was I lucky. I look back and think, what was I thinking? All my dreams were coming true. I never would have guessed what was to come.

After the holidays, I started thinking of us as officially engaged. Finally, after all these years, my fairy tale was coming true. Rich and I still didn't pick out a ring. Rich was in no hurry; he had everything just how he wanted it—total control over me and everything around us. One day, when I was out shopping, I looked at rings. I thought it was about time. When I was there, I fell in love with a ring. It was gorgeous! The center stone was a marquise diamond. There was a row of baguettes on both sides and smaller round diamonds around the rest of the center stone. It was beautiful. Of course, we couldn't afford it, but the lady at the jewelry store was so nice and she encouraged me to go get my fiancé and we could work something out.

When Rich got home, I talked him into looking for rings. We still didn't make any wedding plans, and in the back of my head, I was still thinking about the Steve situation and being led on, all just talk. When Rich said, "Sure, we'll start looking," I was thrilled. I was excited just like a little kid. All my dreams were coming true. When we got to the jewelry store, that lady I had spoken with wasn't there, but her associate was. He was just as nice. Of course, we couldn't afford the ring that I picked out. There was a similar ring— just a ring with baguettes, no center stone—but we got to pick out one separately, and we finally found a small marquise diamond. The diamond was perfect; the cut and clarity was amazing. Rich had no credit, so we put the ring on layaway. It was funny, every time we went in to make a payment, I got to visit my ring.

I had bad credit from my divorce with Timothy and the wedding was still pretty far in the future, so I didn't put money down on a ring for Rich right away. When the jewelry store moved locations, they lost the ring that I had picked for Rich, even the item number. I finally did get his ring. We ordered a couple of rings, hoping that one of them was the right one. It had three diamonds across the top and a brush cut on the sides. I really felt bad that he didn't get the ring he wanted, especially since he would barely wear it. Boy, was I wrong. Rich wore his ring 24-7 because that ring meant everything to him.

My ring always had special meaning because my ring was made just for me. Nothing was ever just for me.

All this writing about Rich and how we got engaged started stirring up a lot of emotions, good and bad. So yesterday, when I was having a jammy day, just me and the boys, I watched a wedding show marathon. Guess what wedding video I watched next? Yeah, you're right, mine with Rich. I almost cried through the whole video to see my dad, sister, grandma, my whole family. And of course, Rich. The love on his face all day when he looked at me. For one day, real or not, I did have my fairy tale.

When Rich and I started making wedding plans, some things started settling down between Rich and me. And some things did not. Rich and I still went to Hamtramck a lot. We would go to the bar, and when he started to get drunk, I would think it was time to go. He would keep drinking, of course, and would start a fight. After we would finally leave the bar, he would be on a crack binge and he would take me with him to the crack house. I would always be so scared when we went. I was scared about going to jail. I was scared about a lot of things.

The crack house was a horrible place, as you can imagine. It was in a bad area in Detroit. Worn-down houses, no real working streetlights. It was dark. Imagine how my heart would pound as this brought back so many other scary memories. That's when he would hit me the most in the car. I was tired and scared and wanted to go home. A lot of nights he would finally take me home, then leave drunk and go back to the crack house.

After he would take off, I would be so scared, waiting for him to come home, not knowing how he's going to act when he gets home. I used to pray that when he did get home, he would go straight to bed or go play video games. The worst part was, if we had been fighting earlier, then he would want to have sex. If I was sleeping, he would wake me up and that would be really bad. Rich would start touching me between my legs when I was sleeping. Boy, what a trigger. I would go through the roof. All the times he would touch me, I would freak.

I still had no idea what my dad did or any other abuse, but I was responding to those events anyway. And when you don't want to be touched, you don't want to be touched. All I thought was that whether he was drunk or high or both, if he wanted to have sex, I wasn't allowed to say no. It was a lot worse after we got married because then I was his wife and that was my duty. What a wife has to do for her husband. I have learned a woman's body is her own. Nobody, I mean nobody, has the right to touch her. No means no! I know how many of my girlfriends just hate having a drunk come home wanting sex. They too pray that when their man comes home that he would finally, even if for just one night, not touch them.

I don't know if you've ever been there—being scared for him to come home, pretending to be asleep, your insides shaking, praying some more that he would just go to sleep. I thank God now every time I hear about this from one of my girlfriends. I am sad for them, but it's not me anymore. I lost everything and then some. Stuff I would never think I would lose, I lost everything. But it's not me anymore. My heart goes out to them because I lived it for way too many years. Sometimes the fear is worse than the act itself.

The benefits, I guess if you want to say that some good had to come out of all the past abuse in my life, was being dissociative. When Rich was having sex with me, when that was the last thing I wanted to do—him being drunk and all and just the smell of this breath, of course, was a turn off—I could go numb. I just gained this little recognition over a year ago. When my dad or anybody else in the occult was raping me, I would say my ABCs. I was so little that all I knew was literally ABC. I would stare at the wall and repeat it over and over again.

I was dressed in a white gown, lying on a table. There was a long line of men standing at the bottom of the table where my feet were. One right after another would rape me. I would turn my head to the right, pick out a spot on the wall, and repeatedly say, "ABC, ABC, ABC." I don't think I said it out loud. But in my head, "ABC, ABC, ABC." I only have a few memories. I thank God that I don't have more than what I do. At one point, I wanted to know everything. I thought I needed to know everything. I thank God that he didn't listen to me and only gave me the memories that I needed in order to accept that what hap-pened hap-pened.

The nights that Rich would wake me up, if I wasn't just pretending to be asleep, I would just give in so he could hurry up and get things over with so I would be able to go to sleep when he would pass out. I would do the same thing as when I was a little girl. I would pick out a place on the wall and just concentrate on that. Being dissociative, I could just be there and make my body go numb. I learned that when I was little. It was a way to survive. I could live and not go crazy. Rich would wake up in the morning like everything was just fine. That was normal for him.

When we started to really seriously make wedding plans, things started getting really good between us. We, for the most part, stopped going to the bars. We needed to start saving money for our future (remember, I wanted family).

Rich really didn't have that good of a childhood either. His dad was an alcoholic as well as his mother's father. As time went on, I could see the pattern. One day, even Rich's brother said that the reason that both he and Rich are dysfunctional came from their mom and dad. Rich's dad always worked. He left the house around three thirty or four thirty in the morning, something like that, to be at work at five. It was very early. He went to bed around seven in the evening, so the house had to be quiet. All the curtains would be closed to block out the sunlight so he could sleep. Also, the kids couldn't be home because they would be too loud and would wake him up. So they roamed the streets. Rich and his brother were rejected early in life. Rich's mother worked full-time, so she wasn't there for the boys during the day. They were alone to do what they would. Rich was in baseball for years. Not once in all the years did his dad go. Rich was in Little League and in the minors, then the majors too. It had to be at least seven or eight years and never did his dad show up. He was always too busy or too tired.

It had been the same way with Timothy, PJ's dad. Timothy was in karate for years. His dad worked for Ford on the afternoon shift so he could make a little more money since every little bit counts. Timothy's mom worked at Hudson's, so her kids were alone running the streets. Timothy's dad never went to any of his karate tournaments even when they were local or on the weekends. He would never go. All of Timothy's life, he was repeatedly told that he wasn't wanted and that he was a mistake. Timothy's older brother and Timothy were only eleven months apart. It was like having twins. Timothy's mom would say all the time, or at least as long as I knew her, how hard it was with two babies and that Timothy was not wanted. I remember one day when we were living in Kansas that he was crying and crying just like a baby because his mom and dad, especially his mom, did not want him. It was so many years ago. But that moment with Timothy was the first time my heart really went out to him. To live with the fact that your own mother that gave birth to you didn't want you and, even worse, was always throwing that up in your face, who could be that mean? I guess she could.

Did I tell you that Timothy was my uncles' paperboy? Both of my uncles, Uncle Don and Aunt Carol and my other uncle, Uncle Ed and Aunt Dawn. You remember her. Anyway, they only lived a half block, maybe fifteen houses or so away from each other, and Timothy was their paperboy for years. It was funny, Timothy told them both that there was this nice, pretty girl that he wanted to get to know better. Timothy was talking to the both of them, trying to get advice, since they were both happily married (well, everyone thought so anyway). Well, little did they know that the nice, sweet girl that

Timothy was talking about was, well, who do you think she was? It was me. Little did I know that I would still deal with the wrath of Timothy and his family for over twenty-five years. Timothy's sister is around twenty-three months younger than Timothy. We always heard about how Timothy's mom had three kids all under the age of four.

However, Timothy's mom also always talked about how everything was so perfect. The house was always perfect; she scrubbed her kitchen floor on her hands and knees. The clothes were always clean and ironed. Always the best clothes for her kids, always the best furniture for the house. Everything was always perfect. I've learned there is no such thing as perfect. Timothy's mom, like Rich's mom, was abused. Timothy's mom grew up in an orphanage in Greece. I know they were little too, she and her sister Effie. It is truly amazing how much your childhood affects your adulthood. Of course, if that wasn't true, I wouldn't be writing this.

My nights are getting worse. I don't know what to do anymore. I'm so, so tired of feeling this way. A few hours after I'm awake and at work, I'm okay. It's just the nights. The horrible, horrible nights. Last night, I slept on the floor in the boys' room. I took my pillows and blanket off my bed, laid the blanket on the floor, and wrapped up like a cocoon. I just kept telling Robby that Mommy will protect you, that Mommy will protect you, and nothing will ever hurt you. I kept saying it over and over again. Robby must have thought that I was crazy. The night was horrible. I was not able to get comfortable. I slept under Robby's bed. Just trying to get safe. There is never a time where I feel safe. Never. I just want to go home, go under the covers, forget about everything and everyone. Nobody, nobody will ever make me safe. Well, actually I do feel safe with Mark, Sheryl, and PJ.

Well, after that last paragraph, it's been weeks since I've written. It was just that bad again. I couldn't even write. My nights were running into my mornings, my days were running into my nights. I *felt like* they had complete control of me again. Sheryl helped me figure out that it only felt like they had control of my nights. For the very first time in my life, I really thought that I was crazy, that there must have been something really wrong with me. After all these years, I never thought that I was crazy. I always thought that all this was crazy, but never did I think that I was crazy. Well, fortunately, or unfortunately, I am not. I've been talking with Sheryl, trying to figure out what was going on next. What am I trying to heal from now? Well, we figured out that some of my little parts, some of my dissociative parts that haven't healed yet, the little ones that protected me so much during all the occult stuff, they were still being raped and beaten every night. More of my parts were being healed and becoming integrated, but my little ones had to be healed too. Everything in my life is coming together and being healed. Well, the little ones were still getting hurt at night. They still thought they had to offer themselves up for abuse and torment. They didn't know that it had truly stopped.

Talking to Sheryl, this still seems crazy. Listening to all this sounds crazy. As much as I knew that what I have been feeling sounds crazy, at night it feels real. My feelings are real. What I was reliving every night was real. The times I was woken up at night was real. If I ever want to sleep through the night, I have to accept that it's real. Again, as much as I have wanted to believe that this wasn't real, there was nothing else to explain what was going on. There was nothing else to believe but that it was real. All this is real. For weeks I was not sleeping or barely sleeping. I just kept saying I'm so, so tired. Not only was I so tired of not sleeping but my parts were also so tired of being raped and beaten every night. So Sheryl said that when nighttime came again, I was to help the little ones go on vacation. They have lived this for so, so long that, of course, they are extremely tired.

I picked Florida. I love Florida—the water and palm trees. So at night when I woke up, I was to hold them and rock them, physically hold them in my arms and rock them and tell them they are safe. Thank them for doing such a wonderful job of protecting me from all this. Honor them for all of the abuse that they had taken for me to protect me. For loving and caring about me so much to go through this every night to protect me. And I want to thank you from the bottom of my heart for reading this. You, reading this, have given me the strength and courage to write this. You have given me the God-given strength to tell my story, not only to give me total healing from this but, most of all, to tell my story to help others who have encountered this. If I can help one other person to try to sleep through the night, to help unanswered questions that you might be going through too . . . So again, I thank you for giving me the strength and courage to go through this.

Another night came, and just like clockwork I woke up again at 2:30 or 3:30 depending on the time change. It was better, I kept telling myself. I am safe and nobody can hurt us anymore. Just like Sheryl said, I sat there, rocking back and forth, holding my little parts in my arms, like holding a little baby. I told them, "It's okay, you're safe." I said that it's okay, they can go to Florida to retire because I know how tired that they are. For forty years, they were being raped and beaten to protect me from knowing all this. Their job was to protect me. You see, if I didn't have parts, I would have gone crazy. So my parts protected me from going crazy. Now they have to know that I am safe and that they did protect me, but now they can retire because I know I am safe and the others can't hurt me anymore. So they can heal, and I can become more integrated. The next couple of nights were better. I still wake up, but I am able to go right back to sleep. I'm still having weird dreams, but at least I am sleeping. Thank you, God!

I needed a break from everything. I'm still working, but I took a break from everything else, writing, friends, everyday stuff. Just trying to go through the motions.

It's an early September morning, sitting outside, writing again, with the warm sun beating down on me, feeling total peace, wrapped up in a blanket. Total peace, only the peace that God can give you. Just looking at the green grass, the beautiful trees, blue skies, and peace. A true peace. A peace that I thought I would never feel.

There was so much darkness for so many years. So much confusion, unanswered questions. Just going through life like a robot. My life with Rich was robot mode. So much confusion and pain with Rich. It's almost our wedding anniversary and the anniversary of our divorce. For one day, I almost got my fairy tale. I still miss my family life. The good days with Rich were really good. I felt like I was the luckiest girl in the whole world. But then there were the bad days, and they were really bad. As I think back, the bad days were *really* bad. It's sad to think about what could have been or what I thought could have been. It's still hard to believe that on our wedding day, he could love me so much and yell at me, hit me, and even rape me. How can that be love? Well, that's not love. But he's the closest thing to love that I have ever had. It's been almost five years that I've been alone. That's a good thing because I know I couldn't completely heal with Rich in my life.

After Rich and I got married, things got worse. I was his property. The fighting got worse. It got to the point that PJ didn't even want to be around us anymore. Do you really blame him? I was mad at Rich for that, but I was even more mad at myself for not being strong enough to leave Rich. I didn't know how to get out. Rich was so controlling. I didn't even realize how much. As much as I don't want to admit it, maybe PJ was better off with Timothy. Maybe not. Timothy still tries to control PJ and PJ's life.

The fighting got worse, and Rich was hitting me more. One time, when we had the boys, it was October no less, we were painting the kitchen cabinets. We were having a bad argument right after he spoke with his parents. Rich came into the house and started hitting me and kicked me in the nose. When I saw the blood, I called the police on Rich for the very first time. I had the boys go to the neighbors. I always did my best to protect them from the police. When the police came, they did arrest Rich and took him to jail.

The township where we lived didn't have a local lockup, so Rich went straight to the county jail. After everything that he did to me, I should have not cared, but I did. I was sorry for what I did. Rich kept calling collect from jail. I didn't want to answer, but I was too scared not to. So I left and went down to the neighbors to check on the boys. They were okay and too little to know what was going on. Talking to Shelly, my neighbor, she said, "Enough is enough. You have to get out of this relationship. Rich, one day, is really going to hurt you bad." As much as I wanted to get out, I didn't know how! I cried for hours over what had hap-pened. I was really scared of Rich, thinking, *What is he going to do to me now?*

The next day when he called, I was so scared. He sounded madder and madder at me, so I thought that I better answer the phone. When I finally did, instead of feeling sorry for what he did, just like I thought, he was extremely mad at me. Enraged. A couple of days later, he was arraigned. Rich's bond was set at $5,000, which would mean he would have to pay $500, which was 10 percent. Since I was the victim, I couldn't bail him out. Someone else had to do it. I was too scared not to bail him out. Go figure, he hurt me, he did wrong, and I felt guilty. (What control he had!)

I called my other girlfriend Michelle and asked her to go down to the jail and please bail him out. We didn't have the extra $500. I figured something out since you could only bring cash. What I should have done was let him sit there. Okay, now I have figured this out. I was too scared to let him sit in jail. I was scared, but I was *safe*. He couldn't hurt me, right? Wrong. Not knowing what he was going to do was even worse than having him hit me. Not knowing is the *fear*! Just like when I was little, the fear of not knowing was much worse than the abuse itself. It's that sad. (Thanks, Mom and Dad.)

My girlfriend took the money and bailed him out. Well, that was just weird. When he got home, he felt like he was the victim, that I was the one that did something horrible to him. Rich was enraged and then some. When he got bonded out, he was not to go around me or the house. If he did, I was supposed to call the police. Did I? Of course not. I was way too scared. That fear is bad. Rich walked in yelling at me and told me that he was going to take a shower and then go out for a good dinner, a very expensive dinner at that, to reward himself for everything that he went through. And he did just that. Made a big deal of leaving to go for dinner, even bragged over the leftovers when he got home.

Luckily, Michelle was able to stay with me until he got home and things settled down. I think he was half embarrassed at that point since Michelle was still there, and he went to bed and went to sleep. I got the boys to bed. Michelle helped me calm down, then she left. That whole ordeal cost us thousands of dollars. Between his lawyer, which I helped him get—I still can't believe I did that, but I know it was the control and the fear, again, that horrible *fear*, and again, thanks, Mom and Dad—court costs, fees, and fines, it was a lot of money.

The worse thing is that I'm extremely embarrassed about it. Well, not really embarrassed. Okay, yes, I am. As a rule of thumb through the court system since he pleaded guilty and stated that he was truly sorry, they ordered Rich to go to anger management classes once a week for so many weeks. Gosh, I forgot how many weeks, maybe twenty or so? It was for a while. Anyway, he hated the classes. It was all my fault that he had to go there. Also, he had homework to do. Guess who did his homework for him? That's right, it was me. I was doing his homework. Rich hit me, I got hurt, I didn't do anything to get hurt, yet it was my fault, so I'm doing his homework. Makes plenty of sense, right? Right? And what makes even more sense is that I would call and try to get him out of it. One time, I remember talking to the lady that answered the phone. I don't remember why I called that time. Anyway, I was telling her that Rich is different from everyone else, that he is a good guy, and Rich was abused as a kid and that's why he did that. She told me once an abuser always an abuser and that I was a typical abused wife.

Well, I did have my facts right. Rich was doing all these things because he was abused. But the biggest part that I was missing was Rich had a choice to get better or stay in the victim role. I had to learn that God gave us our own free will, that we *all* have choices. I have to choose to get better and heal from all this, just like Rich had plenty of choices to heal from all his pain. I said it before, and I'll say it again. The very hardest part of all this is that my mom and dad both had choices, and the choices that they made will affect me for the rest of my life. The best part of all this is, I also have a choice. My choices will not only make a difference in my life but in my children's lives and my grandchildren's lives and so on. I can also try to make a difference in your life. I can help encourage you and give you the strength so you can make the choice to be truly happy and make a difference in your children's and grandchildren's lives.

God has always given me the strength and courage to go on. Even on my darkest days, somehow, someway God has always given me the strength to go on. Even when I don't think I have the strength, God is such a loving, caring God. He always, always comes through.

I am sitting here thinking about all this, feeling the warm sun beating down on me. I have always felt like the sun was God, giving the beauty of God in that great big light, the warmth of the sun that only God can give you. Way too many times I've looked up to the sun thanking God, cursing God, yelling at God. Anything you can think of, I have done, but you know one thing? He's always, always there. You can never run away from the sun, like you can never run away from God. He's always there.

Things got crazier with Rich and me while he was going to his classes. Oh, of course, this was not his fault. He did nothing wrong. But going to these classes stirred stuff up inside of him. He couldn't hit me to get the anger out. This was a different time for him, but not a better time.

It's been weeks again since I have written. It's the middle of September. *October* is just around the corner. Another October. In these past few weeks, I kept thinking about when I was on the floor in the kitchen, talking to Mark on the phone in complete denial. That was seven years ago. Seven years, that's a long time. My life has never been the same since I started seeing Mark. The choice to see Mark, I think, was the hardest one at that time. Seven years later and still going to counseling and still not knowing how much longer. Granted, I'm a million times better. I'm leading a normal life about 95 percent of the time. But when things are bad, boy, are they bad, and I used to live that 24-7. I thank God for giving me all the resources that he did.

Every time I questioned if seeing Mark was the right thing to do, that I was making all the occult stuff up, I could never question it for long. I know beyond belief that Mark was sent by God.

One time, when Rich was in jail for hitting me, I woke up on a Sunday morning to get ready to go to church. A strong feeling came over me to go to PJ's church. PJ was very involved in the youth there. I remember like it was yesterday. It was 10:25 a.m. Both of our churches started at 11:00 a.m. My church was only five minutes away. PJ's church was at least forty minutes away. The boys and I were almost ready, but as usual, PJ was not even awake yet. The desire to go to PJ's church was getting so strong that I knew that's where all four of us needed to be that day. I told PJ again that we needed to go to his church and that it was 10:25 a.m. and he better get going. PJ said, "Ma, we only have thirty-five minutes to get to church and it's forty minutes away." But I said again, "We needed to go to your church even though it means that we will be a little late." PJ still didn't want to get up, but he did, so off to PJ's church we went.

All the way there, PJ and the boys couldn't believe that we were going to PJ's church when we only lived five minutes from our church. But I knew with my whole heart that I needed to be at the other church. When we got there, PJ's friends were glad to see him and glad he was at church. My other boys were little—Robby was five and Joey just turned four.

I had to have Joey's fourth birthday party all alone, well, not all alone. I had two black eyes and a broken nose for company. It's funny, but then again not. Every time that Rich was being Mr. Nice Guy and I truly wanted to believe that he wanted a family, I had to keep reminding myself by kinda singing it, "Two black eyes and a broken nose" over and over again until I finally got it. It took me a very long time, but again, I have to thank Sheryl for that one.

When we were sitting in church, I kept asking God why I was there. It didn't make any sense. After praise and worship, they had a guest speaker there. And guess what? The woman was telling her testimony of how she was in abusive relationships and how her childhood was abusive. She spoke about how your childhood affects your adult life and the choices that you make. Her message was wonderful; she touched me in so many ways. I said, "Okay, God, I get it. This is why you wanted me here. I get it." But there was more. They had an altar call, and my spirit kept leading me to go up. I had the two little boys, and I didn't want to leave them alone. But the urge was so strong that the people sitting next to me could tell I wanted to go forward. They said, "Go ahead. We will watch the boys." Thinking back about this, I didn't really realize how God had his hands on all this. Even to where I sat, for these perfect strangers to watch the boys and me to be okay with that. When I went up for the altar call, I was kneeling there crying and crying. Here I was again, Rich was in jail for hitting me; every time Rich went back to jail, he hurt me worse than the time before. Crying there, I felt so helpless. I didn't know a way out. The cycle kept repeating itself over and over again. Just like me, Mom, and Dad. Now I'm living it, just like my mom.

Crying and praying about this, two ladies came up to the altar to pray with me. Still to this day, I'm really not quite sure what they said, but I know that they both prophesied over me that, basically, the abuse will finally stop and everything will be okay. They were saying things to me, things that there was no way for them to know about. I had never met them before. So I knew that everything was from God. I have wished so many times to remember what they said; I guess it was for my spirit to know.

After the service was over, God told me to talk to the guest speaker. He didn't ask me; he told me. I'm arguing back and forth with God. I kept telling him in my head that there's no way, no how that I'm going to talk to her. First of all, I was too scared and embarrassed to go up there. Second, she was talking to so many people. Why on earth would she to talk to me? I'm nobody (or so I thought). We are all children of God, and he loves us all the same. So here I am, arguing with God. Guess who won? You're right, it was God. I'm so stubborn. I am so thankful that God always wins.

The woman started the conversation like God put it on her heart to talk to me. The conversation went great. She knew that I was abused; she must have known through her spirit. There was no doubt in my mind that it was all God. She gave me hope that things would work out. Telling her my story, I guess, sounded so typical. We all have our own story and God always has his hands on every single one of us.

I thanked her for taking so much time with me and sharing her story with me and listening to me. She could tell how much I loved my husband and how I wanted things to work out. She gave me a number to a pastor that could counsel us as a marriage counselor. Little did I know what would come from that phone call. The pastor couldn't help me but gave me another number to call. Three people later from that first phone call was, well, you guess. Yes, it was Mark from Hope Counseling Service.

So after that Sunday at PJ's church, how could I question Mark? I was so impressed with Mark at our first meeting. Mark wanted to meet with both Rich and me for our first meeting. Even though Rich was going to court-ordered counseling, it was our life that Rich and I were having problems with. Mark has always reminded me that there are always two people in a relationship.

Mark was not so sweet like Anna and Sheryl. He was kinda cold, very professional. Unlike Dr. Stratman, Mark was more laid-back but still professional.

When we met with Mark, he needed to know our background as a couple, how we met, our kids, how we handle things. But he dug a little deeper and wanted to know about our childhoods and upbringing. I remember like it was yesterday, telling Mark about my childhood, how I was the ward of the court, the abuse from Mom, and seeing Dr. Stratman. I look back at how I just rattled everything off like I was reading a book—no thoughts, no emotions, just reading facts. Now that I have feelings (thanks Mark), it's still painful to just think about what a mom would do to her child.

Obviously Mark saw right through me; he must have seen some of my parts. Mark asked if I was seeing a counselor. I told him that I was okay. I just needed to work on my marriage. But Mark saw so much more.

Mark agreed to meet with Rich once a week, then meet with us once a month. This was September, and I still didn't understand about the significance of October. I was seeing visions of my dad and was also seeing burning crosses and just weird stuff. Mark explained that this was typical for people who were SRA survivors for the last week in September that your anxiety goes through the roof this time of year, especially with headaches (which is common with dissociation). I had all the typical signs. I was still spending time with my family.

One day, my sister was over with my dad and my niece. My sister and I went to get pizza. We were just casually talking and she asked how Rich and I were doing. I was still very careful what I told my family. At this point, I was really trying to protect myself.

I was telling her how bad my headaches were getting again, how high my anxiety was. For the first time, some of this made sense. She also had the bad headaches, anxiety, and every other thing that I was feeling. If none of this was real, how can she be feeling the same things at the same time that I was?

After all that, how could I question Mark? That I was making this up in my head, which he said I would be the first person that could do that or that Mark was trying to put things in my head. And why couldn't I stop shaking from the body memories if they weren't true? Mark may be putting these things in my head, but there was no way he could have made me shake. But why on earth would he do that? He was here to help people. If it wasn't true, then why would my body be shaking? If I couldn't stop it, then it must be true.

Every time after that when I questioned Mark, how could I? God just put too much into place. That God loves me that much, that he would put so many things into place for me to heal and write this book. For me and for yourself.

When Mark said make a choice, feel like this forever, or chose to go to counseling or choose not to go to counseling and feel like this forever, it was my choice to get better. It is also your choice to make the right choice for yourself because you are a child of God, who loves you so much that he wanted you to be healthy and whole from the choices others make that affect all of us so much. It is always our choice.

So here is it just a few more days until October. Knowing everything I know and how very, very hard I have worked, hopefully this will be a beautiful month of October. Just celebrating the month of my favorite season. When Sheryl and I talked, it was empowering to know how much I have grown and healed. True healing to the point that I don't have to think about it at all. It's just coming naturally for the kids, to my friends, to work. Finally, it's all coming naturally. I honestly don't know if I will ever be truly healed from all this, but I believe I will be as much as anyone can be healed from a horrible past.

On my really bad days, I keep telling myself God doesn't start something that he never finishes. I am so proud of myself for everything that I have accomplished. My boys are doing great, all three of them. I still miss my family, yes, my bio-family. It was so hard to make the choice not to talk to any of them. Not one family member. I do miss the family. The family that I never had, the one I thought I had.

This October has been different. It has been such a beautiful month. For the most part, it has been warm and sunny. I'm finally sleeping through the night even a couple of times the alarm clock has woken me up. I've always been awake at 5:30 a.m., the time my dad went to work. It was somewhat safe when he was gone. So then I could finally go into a deep sleep, except I couldn't because the alarm clock goes off at 6:00 a.m. Go figure, even little things were taken away, like sleep. Thanks to Sheryl for helping me on this. I do believe that so, so much was taken away from me. Just about a month ago, I did believe that everything was taken away from me: my childhood, my children, my husband, and even my parents. But all those things were not my choice; it was the choice of everyone around me.

I just got back from Sheryl's and we were talking about how the writing was going. I let her know it was really, really slow. Sheryl gave me suggestions for when the writing gets slow. There is so much more to tell you. The surface hasn't really even been touched. I'm dealing with emotions of my own motherhood toward my children. The choices my mom made years ago, I'm still dealing with now. It's making me question my own choices with my boys. My emotions are so stirred up. Thanks, Sheryl. The standing joke is, every time she stirs something up and makes me feel poopy and I say thanks a lot, Sheryl, without missing a beat, just keeps talking. Oh, she says thank you but never gets offtrack. I just thank God that I did make the choice to heal from all this. A choice I thought I didn't want to make way too many times. It is hard it to keep up with counseling when I just wanted to run out of the door and never come back. But where would I be now? Now when I get the pot stirred, I'm still fine. Only about 1 percent ick still remains. I don't know what other way to describe it, a really grown-up way to describe how I was feeling.

For your information, feeling is a good thing. Like I think I said before, for years I was able to totally shut off my feelings. I could actually numb myself. I could literally slap my face and not feel a thing. Totally numb. Not the smartest thing I've done, slap myself. The first time I slapped myself in the face and I did feel it, boy, did that hurt. Can you imagine having the ability to numb yourself? Just like when you are drunk, you can't feel the pain, you are numb. You can hit yourself or hit your head on the wall and not feel anything. Well, I taught myself not to feel any more pain. So some part of myself learned how to numb to the pain. But when you're numb, you're numb to pain and pleasure.

I haven't written in a week. I just left Sheryl's, and she stirred up more stuff. (Thanks, Sheryl.) I told her that my writing was going really, really slow. There's a hundred different reasons why I haven't been writing. It's November now. October was wonderful. The month itself was gorgeous. The trees this year were more beautiful than ever. Orange and red leaves. Just embracing the warmth in the air, mid-'60s all month, you can't ask for more than that. You can smell the autumn in the air, the smell of leaves in the morning, the crispness in the air. Just a beautiful month. After the last seven years especially, I have hated October. October makes all that junk more real. I had a harder time in September. Pre-October jitters, I guess. What a beautiful experience that was.

Before, I had to make October okay. I would always talk to myself, talk through the anxiety attacks, saying, "*We* got through one week, now *we* have to go through three more weeks, and so on." This time, it was a piece of cake. Actually I think that this was my best month this year. Normally, for me (what my normal was), the last week of October was, by far, the worst week of all. There were no memories or any particular memory that presented. It was always that last week. Even this year when the last Sunday of the month came, the edge was on, but nothing bad, absolutely nothing. I still can't believe it. For almost twenty years, starting with those days at Holy Cross, I was passing out and going through all these horrible body memories and all the horrible panic attacks, anxiety attacks, and everything else linked to this. It is amazing that this October I can actually embrace this month and, in a strange way, honor this month because, after all those years of mastering bottling up all those emotions, I can feel now. I finally did that. Hurray!

The emotions that had been bottled up for so many years, I had to let them out. Took almost twenty years to do that. Very slowly and very carefully dealing with one thing (memory) at a time. Trying to process it, then letting it go. Heal from it. Now does that make any sense? Any sense at all? No, it doesn't. The fact of the matter is it doesn't at all. But as crazy as it seems, it is the only way (trust me, I wish it could be different) and it is the only way to be set free from all this bondage. Now here comes November. Sheryl thought that November would be worse than previous Novembers. Boy, I really hate it when Sheryl is right. I still keep saying it's been five years. I can't believe that it's been five long years, the symbolism of five years. In one afternoon, my life changed forever. Forever. The life that I knew—good, bad, or indifferent, my life that I knew, the life that I fought so, so hard for, the life that I so longed to have—was gone, gone forever.

CHAPTER FOUR

> You made my whole being;
> You formed me in my Mother's body.
> I praise you because you made me in
> an amazing and wonderful way.
> What you have done is wonderful.
> I know this very well.
> —Psalm 139:13–14

That one day in November, that day I will never ever forget, it was the end of the life that I fought so desperately hard for. I remember that day like it was yesterday.

I woke up that day just like any other day. Woke up and had breakfast and coffee with my husband. It's funny, no matter how mad Rich and I were, Rich always got up and made us coffee. He would get up, start the coffee, and jump in bed and cuddle until the coffee was ready. Then he would get back up and bring the coffee to bed for both of us. We would drink a couple of cups, watching the news.

So that day, like all the previous days, after having coffee together, Rich got up and started getting ready for work. I got the boys ready for school. Robby was seven, almost eight, and in the third grade. His birthday was in a couple of days on Thanksgiving Day. Joey was six and in first grade. Just another morning in the Purser household. I got the boys ready, made their lunches, gave them hugs and kisses, and sent them on the bus. The bus used to pick them up right in front of the house.

Then Rich got ready for work. We owned our own business, so he really didn't have any set hours. I made his lunch, gave him hugs and kisses, and prayed with him. Every day before Rich left for work, we would hold hands at our side door and I would pray. I would pray for our family, business, and our everyday life. Even though our life had its real crazy ups and downs, it was our life. After he walked out the door, I waited by the side window to wave goodbye as he drove down the street and around the corner. Just like any other morning.

Kinda sounds funny, two grown adults wanting to say goodbye one last time before going to work and starting our day. After everything that has hap-pened these last five years, thinking about the good times (the normal times) is what makes all this so hard. Meeting with Sheryl last night made me realize that—for the last seven or eight years of going to see Mark, Anna, and Sheryl, trying my hardest to be normal, putting everything I had into working so hard to be normal—in a sad, confusing way, I will never be normal. But it is a blessing that I will never be normal or have a normal life. That's a very hard thought to handle. Sheryl made me, *us*, realize that I have defeated all the odds. Everything that I have gone through is not normal. If I was normal, I would have died or ended up locked up in a mental ward. So thank God that I'm not normal, that something inside of me made me fight and never ever give up. Something so strong that I can't explain it; only God knows.

Most of the time, I am thankful that I don't know the future and only God knows. Sometimes when life gets so confusing and you don't know the future, you get excited to think about what is about to hap-pen, like a fortune-teller. Well, if I had to know what the future held for me, that everything that had hap-pened would hap-pen, would I have made all those choices in these last five years?

I'm lying here in bed getting ready to write again, just rereading the last couple of pages of this book. Again, I have to thank God for all the blessings, blessings that only God can give me. Here I am, five years later from that fateful day that I'm having trouble writing about. My life is totally different than my life was five years ago. On that one November day, when I prayed with my husband, hugged and kissed him goodbye, watched him go around the corner, I was thinking what I was going to do. I was so very confused, not ever thinking in my wildest dreams that that would be the very last time that I would hug and kiss him and say goodbye and watch him go around the corner.

After he left, I never felt so empty, alone, and confused. Things had been so bad that I was going to see an attorney to help me get a personal protection order (PPO) on Rich. Things got that crazy and out of hand. I had nobody at that point in my life. I was really in robot mode. And remember, I had already been in counseling with Mark for three years.

I didn't have to go into work that day so I could go to the attorney. Getting ready to go, I felt sicker and sicker. I just really didn't know what to do anymore. Things at home were not going to change. They were actually getting worse. And the more I healed, the stronger I got and the less abuse I would take.

As I left the house, I felt like a zombie. Here I am, going to an attorney to get a PPO on my husband so that he couldn't hurt me or the boys anymore. On the outside, we were the perfect family. Our business was doing great, making money. We had more money than ever, starting to really not worry about money. We had a beautiful home, vehicles were paid off, no debt, except in the business itself. The boys were in school full-time. Life was good, except when we closed the door at night. Then it was a very different world. It seems so unfair. If a man has a beautiful wife, good kids, a home with lots of equity, money in the bank, and investments and owns his own business that's doing really good—as hard as we worked for all this to finally get to this point in life—what more could he want? I guess I will never know.

As I was driving to the attorney's office, all these things kept going through my mind. What more could I do for him to love me more, to try to save our marriage? We even saw Mark together, but that just made matters worse. I got strong, and he got more defensive. I was really trying to be the perfect housewife. The house was always clean, dinner on the table every night, laundry done. The kids were always clean and dressed nice. They were little but did well in school. I helped out at the school a lot, was there at least once or twice a week, very involved at school. The moms even wanted me to be in the parent-teacher club, PTC, as one of the officers. I was also very involved at church. I taught catechism for first and second grades. That year, I was doing second grade for the first communion. I was on the decorating committee. I was a Eucharist minister. I taught vacation Bible school (VBS) in the summer. Rich was a knight for the Knights of Columbus through the church, and we were very involved. There were always events, charity work, picnics, you name it. Fish fries, something. I was always involved. We even got family of the month award. Go figure, we had the perfect life, the family I always wanted, and it wasn't real. How was that fair? Trust me, it wasn't.

I felt like I was driving forever and forever, but before I got to the attorney's office, I had to stop at one of our customers to collect money that he owed us. Jerry had moved off the route, so I had been seeing this customer once a week to collect money. Over the months, we became really close. The first day, I went to see him to collect the money he was the meanest, crankiest man there was. I was thinking, *Oh great, I have to see this man every week and deal with him every week to collect money. What am I thinking?* I wasn't sure if the money was worth all the trouble and heartache. But as mean and nasty as he was week after week, we formed this wonderful bond.

Jerry was older, around mid to late fifties, salt-and-pepper hair, and a white mustache. Just thinking about him now makes me feel warm and fuzzy. He is a lot like Mark, honest and to the point, even if it wouldn't make me feel good. We would talk week after week. It got to the point that I was looking forward to seeing him for moral support. I guess, at the time, he was my only friend that would listen and support me. I remember one day we were talking and he was being his old grouchy self. He said to me, "How can you be so darn bubbly and upbeat? Look at everything that's going on in your life. What's up with that and the glow around you? Why? How?"

I told him that it's not me, but it's the man upstairs. Even through everything that was going on in my life, the love that I had was from God! God is in me and is seen through me for me to show other people. I was so, so surprised when I said, "It's not me. It's the man upstairs," and he knew and understood. So somehow, someway, God used me to make a difference in someone's life. And in return, he has blessed me more than he can ever know. As hard as everything was, through counseling, it was really working. I was working on me, and that shone through me to help other people.

That Monday morning when I went to see him, Jerry was grouchy. "Where was I on Friday?" He wanted to know. Friday was my normal day to see him. He told me he had no money today; he only had money on Fridays. But that didn't matter to me that day. I needed him for moral support more than anything. After months, the money was only an excuse to see him. He could tell I had been crying. He already knew almost everything that was going on with Rich. He sat me down in the front office and told me straight up, "Look what a strong person you are. You can do this. You can do anything that you put your mind to." He said that he saw God in me and through me, so how could I not do this? How could I not make a difference in my life and in my children's lives? He always helped me have more confidence in myself than anybody. He had been just a stranger, but he made such a great difference in my life. A perfect stranger that had more confidence in me than my own family and friends did. I will never forget him. After I left that day, I only saw him maybe just a couple of times more. And when I saw him, he never said anything, but I knew in my whole heart how proud he was of me. Jerry, thank you for making such a big difference in my life. I look at my children today, at how healthy they are. Their lives are totally different. They can go to bed at night and not live in fear. For that I am truly grateful.

After I left Jerry, in a strange way, I was more confused than ever. In one way, I *thought* I was doing the right thing; in another way, I *knew* I was doing the right thing, that there was *only* one choice to make. But knowing that didn't help. It still amazes me how God works. God always has his hands on everything, especially when you give it to him. As I was driving to the attorney's office, I felt even more empty. I knew that I really had only one choice here. As much as I didn't want to do this, Rich gave me no choice. When I parked in front of the attorney's office, I didn't want to go in. The anxiety was through the roof. If I wanted this to stop, change, I had no choice.

I got out of the van, walked up to the door, feeling sicker than ever. I opened the door. It's funny, my memory is so clear—the dark long hallway, the dark wanes coating paneling on the walls, the stillness in the office. I walked in and waited to sign in. I sat down in the hallway waiting for someone to wait on me.

The attorney that I was supposed to see that day was not in. I'm thinking to myself, *Oh great, here I finally get up enough courage to get a PPO to protect myself and the boys so that hopefully all this craziness will stop and the attorney's not here today.* The attorney was busy. Doing what, I don't know. It's been so long that I've forgotten. Anyway, she wasn't coming. There was a young girl in the office. She gave me the PPO paperwork to fill out, but at that point, why even bother? Everything that I ever tried to do always fell apart.

I prayed to God for three years to try to save my marriage, but God kept telling me that Rich had choices. I can pray for him with my whole heart and soul, but it is *his choice*. The hardest thing I've learned is choices. My mom had choices. My dad had choices. God gave us our own free will. The hardest lesson was choices. But by God, all three of my boys have learned that they have choices. Whatever choice they make, good or bad, it's their choice. I believe the greatest gift, besides love, is teaching my boys about choices.

I left the attorney's office. Didn't fill out paper work to start a divorce, not even for the PPO. I felt like, "Why bother? No one cares, no one understands." It took everything I had to go to the attorney and she wasn't even there. Boy, did I feel really alone. I took the long way home. I took Jefferson home. It's the main road that is right next to Lake St. Clair.

When I was little, well, younger, in my teens, the water always relaxed me. My mom and dad's house was like a ten-to-fifteen-minute drive down to the water. When Mom was really crazy, when I felt like I was going to lose it, I would walk down to the water. It was a long walk, but being DID, the long walk gave me what I needed. The water has always calmed me down. It was the only thing that would give me some kind of release. As I was driving down Jefferson along the water, I was so empty inside. It reminded me of an earlier time that I was driving down Jefferson.

It was almost two years earlier. It was in December, almost a week before Christmas. Of course, Rich and I were having problems. I believe Rich and I were still seeing Mark, for sure I was. Over and over again, I've said how God was his hands on everything. Well, Robby was in Cub Scouts and in catechism. The mom of the one of the kids Robby was friends with and I were hanging out a lot since the boys were doing so many activities together. We, the boys and I, were over their house a lot. The other mom and I both had dysfunctional relationships in the past, very similar. We both got out of dysfunctional relationships and right into other dysfunctional relationships. Anyway, we spent a lot of time together.

So this particular morning was just like any other day. I got the boys ready for school. Robby was in first grade, Joey was in morning preschool. That morning, Robby had a bad stomachache, but he still wanted to go to school. They never missed. I told Robby that when I pick Joey up from preschool I would check up on him to see how he was feeling. I took the boys to school and ran errands. I went to the UPS store to get something shipped out for our business.

The strangest thing was hap-pening all morning. I kept having the thought to call PJ. Sometimes the thought was overwhelming. At first it was call PJ. But that didn't make sense since PJ was in school. The feeling got stronger and stronger. Call PJ. Call PJ. It was a feeling I had never experienced before. I kept ignoring the feeling, thinking, *This is crazy. He's in school.* But the feeling got stronger and stronger. Then it got to the point that it was go see PJ. It kept getting stronger and stronger to the point where I started to think maybe there's something to this. Maybe I need to get ahold of him. But I was in line at the UPS store, and it being right before Christmas, the lines were horrible. When I finally got out of the store, I had to get Joey from school; it was too late to go to PJ's school to see him. So I jumped in the van to go get Joey, still very confused about the feelings I was having about PJ. Then it got stranger. I was halfway out the parking lot when this big gust of anger went through me. It's so hard to explain, but it was like this huge gust of wind that felt like anger. It startled me. The force that went through me made my whole body move to the point that I had to slam on the brakes of the van. It was the weirdest feeling ever. I still can't really explain it.

It took me a few minutes to get myself together. I first sat there in the parking lot, trying to make sense of what had just hap-pened. The desire to call PJ was gone and the desire to see him was gone. And by that time it was too late to drive to PJ's school, I had to go get Joey. Shaken up, I drove to the boys' school to get Joey and check up on Robby. When I got to the school, I went to get Joey. After I got Joey, we were leaving and I realized that I forgot to check on Robby. As I was heading back into the school, I heard my name. "Cindy, Cindy." I didn't see anyone but my name got louder and louder. Then I turned around and I saw Sally, the lady I had been hanging out with lately.

Sally was on crutches; she was having surgery in a couple of days on her knee. She said, "I don't know why the school asked me to help out on popcorn day for the kids. I never help out. When they asked me, my head was saying no, but my mouth was saying yes. Very weird. Well, there must have been a reason why I said yes."

I checked up on Robby and he still didn't feel very good, so I said he could come home, which was odd because he's never come home sick. When I was in the office signing Robby out of school, I got a phone call from Timothy, PJ's dad. I will remember that phone call forever. Timothy told me that PJ was in a major car accident and I needed to get to the hospital now. When I asked what happened, all he said was that it was bad and I needed to get to the hospital now. By the time I hung up the phone, I was shaking, in shock. I ran down the hall to tell Sally, but the time I told her what happened, I wasn't able to drive. The ladies in the office also said that I was in no shape to drive. I think they were right. Sally said that she would drive us to the hospital.

God is such a good God. God took care of everything. I had both boys and someone to drive me to the hospital. It's all in God's timing. God took care of everything. On the way to the hospital, I couldn't stop shaking. I kept having visions of PJ's face all bloody, especially of his one eye bleeding. Every minute took longer and longer to get there. It felt like an eternity, especially with the visions in my head of his face. Sally and I just kept praying that he was all right. I still didn't know what happened. All I knew was that I had to get there. When we were driving, Sally said, "Well, I guess that's why I said yes to help out with the popcorn sale." By the time we got there, I was a mess, but I had to hold it together for my little boys.

When we walked in the hospital, I saw Timothy next to PJ on a gurney. PJ still had the neck brace on and was strapped to the board that the EMT brought him in on. His face looked just like the visions in my head, all bloody, especially one of his eyes. At this point, I still didn't know what happened, but all that mattered was that PJ was alive. I couldn't believe it. My PJ. The one precious thing in the world to me. Don't get me wrong. I love all my children, love them more than life itself. But this is my PJ. I know it sounds a little odd, but PJ I fought for more than anything. I had to fight for him from the very beginning.

I had just graduated high school. Things at Mom and Dad's were crazier than ever. Mom was getting more out of control. And the older I got, the more I could finally stand up to her. School was good. My ninth grade I did okay; my tenth grade, well, something horrible must have hap-pended. I went from As and Bs with one C to all Ds and Es. Something was going on. To this day, I still can't remember what hap-pened. The joys of being dissociative, I guess. In a way, I'm glad I don't know. I think I know enough. Anyway, in eleventh grade, I did better, and in twelfth grade, I got all As and one B. So I was back on track.

I was dating Timothy when I graduated. Boy, that was a different relationship. When I met him, Timothy was always trying to be something that he wasn't. Very different. Well, different was all I was used to. Things were going quite normal for me. I had a boyfriend, graduated high school, had some friends. Seemed normal. I turned eighteen a couple of months after I graduated. I started working in a nursing home. I had a car. My uncle Hank had given me his old Gremlin, a 1972 or 1977. Boy, did I have a lot of fun in that car. Again, things seemed to be normal.

Mom was getting worse and worse. She was still hitting me and yelling. She was seeing things like snakes and demons outside of the house. Mom was really sick.

As I'm lying here writing, thinking about Mom, sadness, an overwhelming sadness, just came over me. I can't even remember if Mom came to my graduation. I know my dad and sister were there, but I can't remember who else. Just so sad. Wow, I can't remember if I even wanted her there. She could be so embarrassing, always acting crazy. The strangest past of it all was that I dearly loved my mom. I still do. She's my mom.

The day before my eighteenth birthday, Mom kicked me out of the house. That I remember like it was yesterday. There was a big fight at home. I don't remember what it was about. I dissociated some of it out, but I can see me standing next to Dad in his chair. I see me, Mom, and Dad, all yelling horribly. Yelling, fighting, hitting, and screaming was normal, so I guess there might not be a reason to remember exactly what it was about. Anyway, Mom said, "Tomorrow you will be eighteen" and that she wanted me gone and to never come back home.

I was surprised beyond belief. My mom, the one that I loved so dearly, the mom that I always made excuses for, the mom that I always wanted to have there for me, the mom I dreamed of going shopping with, the mom I wanted to tell my secrets to, the mom that I wanted so desperately to have love me unconditionally, a mom that was just mom. All the things I so desperately needed and wanted—a mom, my mom. All these years of crazy, everything I had done for her. My whole life revolved around her. She just told me to move out and never come back. So that night, I packed my things, went to Grandma's, and never went back home again.

Within the next couple of days, I got pregnant with PJ. Timothy had already added a bombshell when he told me that he was going to enlist in the air force. Of course, I had no say in the matter. Timothy always did what Timothy wanted to do. He had enlisted before we found out I was pregnant. He talked to his recruiter about the pregnancy. Timothy had three choices: one, that I keep the baby and the air force will not take him; two, I get an abortion and he can still enlist; or three, we can get married and he can still enlist. So we decided to get married, well, kinda.

When I found out I was pregnant, I was thrilled. I wanted this baby more than I ever wanted anything. This was my baby. Everything, I mean everything, had been taken away from me and no way, no how was anyone or anything going to take this baby, my baby, from me.

Timothy didn't know what to think. Timothy's parents, especially his sister, did not want me to have this baby. His sister told her family that if I came over to their house, she would push me down the basement stairs. She was actually mean enough to do it. Timothy's parents had mixed emotions, like any other parent. Timothy and I were so young. I just turned eighteen, and Timothy was not yet nineteen. So they had reasons for their reservations. Timothy's family had been hoping that Timothy's going into the air force would get him away from me. Needless to say, it was quite the opposite. Timothy and I decided to get married. Well, kinda.

We were planning to go to Ohio to get married because there was no waiting time. In Michigan, there was a three-day wait, I think for blood work and other stuff. It was a lot easier and a lot simpler to go to Ohio. Timothy's parents were totally against it. They would have done anything for us not to get married.

Timothy and I got our wedding rings. Grandma and I got my dress. It was pretty. It was a short white dress that came down to my knees, long pooffy sleeves, V-neck with silver patterns running through it. It was really pretty. I also had a little hat with a small veil. My aunt Dawn got me a bouquet. It had at least two dozen red sweetheart roses, baby's breath, and green holly in it. Just beautiful.

Timothy and I were fighting about his parents. Timothy's parents said they would disown him if we got married. I know that Timothy loved me somewhat, but since he was never loved himself, how could he really give love to me? It took me a very long time to be at peace with that. Well, the night before we were supposed to get married, he called the wedding off. As you can imagine, I was devastated. Here he is, the man I loved, or thought I loved, whose child I was carrying and who would be going into the air force in a few days for who knew how long.

I told Timothy that if he didn't come back in the morning to take me to get married, he would never see me or his baby again. Timothy left and I didn't know what to do. That night went on forever with me not knowing what was going to hap-pen in the morning. Whether Timothy showed up in the morning or not was going to determine what my future entailed.

A part of me wanted Timothy to show up, and another part was saying, "What the heck are you doing?" I knew deep down Timothy was dysfunctional, and I guess I really didn't truly love him. First, I didn't really know what love was. Mom and Dad showed me that love was fighting, screaming, hitting, all kinds of abuse. That's what love was in their household. And Grandma, she taught me that not saying anything was for the best. Boy, was that wrong. Again, thanks to God that the only thing that I truly loved unconditionally, besides my little sister, was this little baby growing inside of me. The love only a mother can have for her child, a true mom with unconditional love. A love that was new to me, an experience I could never explain. The first thing that was mine that I could protect and keep anyone or anything from hurting. I wasn't able to protect myself, my sister Mary, or any of the other children in the occult. But this baby, my baby, I could protect.

Be careful what you wish for, especially when you don't know what to wish for. Here I had mixed emotions about whether Timothy did or didn't show up and we did or didn't get married. The only person I couldn't protect PJ from was his dad.

December 7, Pearl Harbor Day, a day that will live on in infamy for me as well as the country. That morning, December 7, Timothy did show up, so I was getting married. We took pictures at Grandma's house. Timothy brought his suit with him. At this point, I don't think Timothy's parents knew where he was or what he was doing. My dad and sister Mary showed up and drove us to Ohio to get married. It was only an hour drive, but it seemed like it took forever. When we finally got there and filled out the paperwork, the judge took us in the corner of the building. We were right next to a revolving door and right behind us were people going up and down a flight of stairs. How romantic.

When the judge said we were husband and wife and that we were officially married, anger went right through me. I couldn't believe what I had just done. I regretted it right from the beginning. What did I do? The roller-coaster ride began from there. Timothy and I went back to Grandma's. We didn't have a cake or anything. Dad stopped for lunch afterward, I think. It's crazy. You would think I would remember my wedding day.

That night, we tried to get a hotel room, but when we got there, we found out we were too young to get a room. Go figure, we were just married with a baby on the way. Timothy was leaving for the military in a few days, but we were not old enough to get a hotel room. Too funny. We called Grandma's house, and my uncle Don was there. He was kind enough to come to the hotel and paid for the night for us as a wedding present.

Our wedding night. A young, beautiful bride. Timothy to leave in a few days. What does Timothy do? He watched a special about Pearl Harbor Day on TV. Talk about rejection.

The next morning, I woke up sick as a dog. Morning sickness, gotta love it. Timothy dropped me off at Grandma's, went back to his mom and dad's house, and went to work. What a honeymoon! I didn't even see Timothy again until two or three days before he left for boot camp. Timothy's parents threw him a going-away party and did not invite me, his wife. Be careful what you wish for.

PJ and I were alone before he was even born. Timothy was gone for months. Christmas was strange without him. I felt really bad that he was in boot camp on our first Christmas married; he was all alone for Christmas. At least I had our unborn child living and growing inside of me. When I was so, so lonely that I couldn't stand it, I would rub my stomach and think of this baby. This baby was the only thing I had.

When Timothy got home from basic training, we actually stayed together at my grandma's next-door neighbor's house. She was staying with her daughter, so she said it was okay. Actually, she insisted.

Timothy was home for about a week and a half. By the time Timothy got home, I had a little belly. I was six months along. It was April, and I was due in July. My family gave us a baby shower at my aunt Carol's house. We did have a lot of fun there. It was one of the few times when we really had fun together.

Timothy was stationed at Kansas. The night before we left for Kansas, Timothy stayed at his parents' house, and believe it or not, I stayed my parents'. I remember my dad saying, "Are you sure this is what you want? It's not too late to stay here and not go to Kansas with Timothy."

For the most part, my mom and dad were very supportive. When I told my mom I was pregnant, the first thing she said was, "I'm too young to be a grandma." My dad was okay. What could he do at that point? That's why he drove me and Timothy to Ohio to get married. I had forgotten, but my dad was the one who drove me to the airport to pick Timothy up from boot camp. All my family was at the baby shower. Timothy's family was not. They were invited, but they chose not to come.

The night before we left for Kansas, we loaded up all the baby stuff in Timothy's van. Timothy had an old brown van. It had rust spots that Timothy painted green. It looked like an army van. He used it for work, so the only seats in it were the driver's and passenger's seats. The inside was full of the baby stuff, my clothes, some personal stuff, Timothy's clothes and stuff. No furniture at all. Timothy's mom gave us a window air-conditioning unit and a box fan since we were going to the hot temperature of Kansas. That was it.

It had been months since I slept in my bed at my parents'. As I lay there, I thought about how my life can change overnight. I thought about my childhood, all the bad memories in that house (the ones I had at the time), and I thought about what my future held. The only thing that was for sure was my baby; the only thing that was sure and certain was this baby, my baby.

Leaving for Kansas in the morning was bittersweet. Here I was leaving all the old junk in my life, all the craziness I was leaving behind. Here I was with my new life, my husband going into the military, a new experience, starting over as a young woman, a wife and a mother-to-be. What I always wanted and dreamed about. My life was just beginning. Or so I thought.

Driving to Kansas took forever. I think it took us three days. When we got there, we had no place to live. Timothy checked in at the base, and we lived in a hotel until we found a place to live. I remember sitting in this hotel room all alone. I missed my family, especially Grandma. I missed her dearly. When we lived together, she and I talked and laughed all the time. Grandma was the closest thing to a normal relationship, to having a mom. Grandma was good to me in all of the everyday life. Always cooked and cleaned, made sure I was always taken care of, but never told me that she loved me, never gave me hugs and kisses, and when she did, they were very cold. As I sat there in this hotel room, the four walls, they were dark-brown, one small window, with dark-colored curtains and a dark-colored carpet, the room smelled and all I kept thinking was, *What did I do?* Alone, no friends, no family, just me alone in this dark dingy hotel room. All I had to hold on to was this unborn baby that I was carrying.

It took me and Timothy awhile to find a place to live, but when we did, it was really nice. Rose Hill, Kansas, a very small town. It was one mile long by three miles wide. Not very big at all. The apartment was in a fourplex unit. It had four apartments right next to each other like a duplex. There was about four buildings in the complex. A lot of the people that lived there were also in the military.

The apartment was really nice. We lived upstairs. We had our own entry to the apartment, a big stairway going upstairs. You walk into the living room, a big room with a fireplace. How funny, a room with a fireplace in Kansas where it's never cold. Then you walk straight to a big kitchen, one wall with a sink, stove, dishwasher, and all the cabinets. There was a huge place for a kitchen table. On one wall was a door wall with a small deck. Directly on the other wall was the refrigerator. Nice and big. Down the hallway to the right was a nice-size bathroom. Then down a little farther was a bedroom to the right. We used that as the nursery. To the left was our bedroom. It was really nice and a hundred times better than the hotel room.

Since Timothy and I didn't have much, it didn't take us long to set things up. For the living room, we had a black-and-white nineteen-inch TV and the window air-conditioning unit we used as an end table. No couch, chair, table, bed, dresser, nothing. Grandma bought us a crib. With no dresser, I stacked up boxes on top of one another next to the crib with all the baby stuff on top—diapers, powder, destin, etc. Like a changing table. I cleaned out boxes and put the baby clothes in there on the floor. I hung up what I could in the closet. I put a rocking chair in the corner. Boy, did I spend a lot of time in that chair.

We got money from Timothy's parents, and we bought ourselves a king-size waterbed with dresser drawers on the bottom. Timothy went to garage sales, and we got a couch and chair. We were in heaven with that. Finally, a place to sit down. The chair was holey and torn, but we were so glad to have it. We just took an old sheet that Grandma gave us and covered it up. Life was good.

Friends of ours, Lou and Fran, treated us like family. They were an older couple that went to the same church as Timothy and me, a Greek Orthodox church. Even way back then, God was always taking care of me. They gave us an old table and chairs for the kitchen. We were so blessed to be in that church. We were young, and they took us under their wing. What better people to have do this than these two Christians. We never missed church. That was one good thing about Timothy. For years he always pushed us to go to church every Sunday.

Things were okay between me and Timothy. He worked three afternoons, three midnights, then had three days off. As you can imagine, with his work schedule, when he was home, he was sleeping. I was lonelier than ever. We only had one vehicle, and it made no sense for me to work. There really wasn't much to clean in the house. Timothy wasn't even really home for dinners; he was always gone or sleeping. With no car, I couldn't go anywhere. I didn't have many friends, and the ones that I had were not home during the day. The only thing I really looked forward to was this baby. I couldn't wait. The bigger I got, the longer the days were. My excitement was found in going to church and to the doctor for my checkups. I had a pretty good pregnancy. I had morning sickness for the first three months. I did have horrible leg cramps, but besides that, it was a good pregnancy. My doctor was wonderful. He was the nicest, kindest doctor. I was so young, and he took extra care of me. Timothy even liked him.

I was four days past my due date when I gave birth to PJ by natural childbirth. I didn't want to have needles in my back. I was terrified of needles. I think that fear may be about something that they did to me in the occult. I was able to control the pain and gave birth to my baby.

However, something was wrong with my insides. After PJ was born, my insides were really messed up. I'm not sure what hap-pened, but right after PJ was born, the doctors took about fifty minutes to an hour trying to put me back together. They kept working and working on me; one doctor had his hands inside of me, trying to fix things. The doctors talked back and forth until they were able to start stitching my episiotomy. I felt every needle, every poke. The doctors were amazed that I was feeling them stitching me up instead of me not feeling anything at all. Then they tried to freeze me, but I felt every shot that they were giving me. It also made no sense to the doctors that I was having so many problems down there. Thinking back, the pieces of the puzzle start to make more and more sense. There would have been a lot of scar tissue from what they did to me all those years ago in my childhood.

It took a long, long time to heal. But I didn't care. I finally had my baby, and my baby would keep me going for a long time. This baby would keep me alive for many years. All the times that were to come when I would want to die, I wouldn't because who would take care of this precious angel if something hap-pened to me? The angel that God sent to me when there was no hope of living. All the days when I wanted to die from the pain of what Mom and Dad did to me. The pain that no one can understand. A pain that feels like it would last forever. A pain that only death could take away. A pain that God can only take away in heaven. But I couldn't go yet because God chose me to take care of his angel, and I couldn't let anyone hurt him. This angel that only I could take care of. Mine.

Now this angel was lying on a stretcher, not knowing what was going to happen to him or what happened at all. When Timothy told me what hap-pened, I couldn't believe what he said.

PJ was staying with his dad that morning when he went to school. For whatever reason, Timothy grounded him from his pickup truck. It was a black Ford Ranger with some rust spots on it. Unlike his dad, PJ painted them black instead of green. Boy, how he loved his truck.

I still don't know why he was grounded, but at this point, it doesn't matter. For a very long time, I was mad at his dad for grounding him. If PJ would have taken his pickup truck, this would never have happened. Well, PJ went to the high school for half a day and then went to the career building for his business and computer classes, which was a couple of miles away. Since PJ didn't have his truck, one of the kids gave him a ride. When they were driving on a two-lane road, they followed another car of kids going to the career center.

Being kids and being careless, they were passing one another on the left side of the road. One would get up to the bumper of the other car, then pass on the left side, then the other would do the same thing. Every time they did this, they were more and more careless. After several passes, the driver in PJ's car decided, "Okay, I'll show you" and gunned the car. They hit a patch of ice, started sliding sideways, and the driver lost control of the car. They were going so fast that PJ's door hit a telephone pole, went right through it, and sheered it in two. Then his door hit and went through brick pillars in front of a house. The car finally stopped when they hit the house. Then telephone pole they had hit fell on top of the car. What a mess. PJ was knocked out, and when he came too, he had a car door on his lap. Somehow he was able to get out of the car through the sunroof, working his way around the telephone pole.

While Timothy was telling me this, I couldn't believe that PJ survived. Just the impact of his door slicing through the telephone pole could have killed him. Then going through the brick pillar and hitting the house could have killed him. Then the telephone pole coming down on the roof, breaking the sunroof, could have killed him. PJ not only could have been killed but probably should have been killed with the amount of damage on his side of the car. I believe only an act of God could have saved his life, did save his life.

In the ER they kept PJ on the gurney because they still didn't know the extent of his injuries. He was pretty out of it and was in a lot of pain. We were all just waiting to see what they were going to do. A police officer walked through the emergency room doors. You could tell that he was very upset. Then I heard yelling and turned around to see what was going on. The police officer was yelling at the mother of the kid that was driving the car PJ was in, yelling at the top of his voice. The whole ER could hear him. "Do you see that mother? Do you see that mother down there?" he yelled over and over again. Then he said that that mother (me) should not be with her son right now, that he should be at my front door, telling me that my son had died in a severe car accident. That there was no way that PJ should have survived, no way except that it was a miracle. That PJ would and should have been the third child whose mother he would have had to tell that her child died in the last week. At that point, I knew that there were angels, yes angels, around that car, taking the impact of every hit. Some way, somehow my child was alive and it was a true miracle.

Thinking about it still, God amazes me. How God sent angels to surround the car. How God sent Sally into my life. I had both boys with me. Robby was fine. I didn't have to worry about getting Robby. Sally was a moral support to me besides taking care of the boys. If it wasn't for her, I would have had no one to get Robby from school. I wouldn't have had someone to watch the boys when I was in the hospital with PJ. Since the boys were so little, they wouldn't stay with anyone, but since we had just spent so much time at her house, they were fine there. I didn't have to worry about anything. God took care of it all.

Sally told me that after the police officer left I must have gone into shock because, for the next two or three hours, all I said was "He's alive, he's alive. He should have been dead but he's alive." I didn't even call my family until hours after the accident. I still don't know why I didn't think of calling them. At that time, I was still calling Grandma for everything.

Last night, I saw Sheryl. I was excited to let her know how much writing that I've been doing. Still just trying to get everything out of the pot. We have done so much work to get to this point, Sheryl and I. I can't stop now. Since I've been writing about PJ lately, of course, things are getting stirred up in the pot.

Sheryl and I were talking about how good I was doing, actually better than we thought. Christmas and New Year's come and left. I did really good. I didn't miss my bio-family. Really not at all. Working with Sheryl, I really get it on the one hand. I have this large circle of my bio-family, a great big family, tons of people, and I crave family. Then on the other hand, I have this very small circle of my family, my true family. Family doesn't matter how big or small, it's what family means. It doesn't matter if it's just your husband or wife, a single mom or dad with a child or children, or, sadly, if you're by yourself on Christmas. As long as you're in your normal, that's all that matters. I never thought in my wildest dreams that family could be big or little. It's really not the size; it's all about the quality of life.

This Christmas, I was definitely the most healed. Since Robby and Joey are getting older, it's harder to buy presents for them. I took them both out one at a time. I had a lot of fun with each of them. I'm still amazed that they both have learned the whole choices thing. Even in everyday life, these boys are applying choices. It's funny, when we went shopping, Joey was looking at stuff, taking too long, wanting everything but knowing he had a limit. I only have to say, one time, make a choice and they listen. Amazing. I never thought my children would even listen to me, let alone the first time I say something. Thanks again to Sheryl. My best Christmas present was having all three of my boys on Christmas morning together.

Joey was going crazy, opening up all his presents. Robby was taking his time, one at a time, looking at each present, enjoying each one. PJ was also there on Christmas morning with his new girlfriend, Heather. She is so sweet, nothing at all like his last two girlfriends, totally different. Heather is definitely someone you can bring home to Mom. Heather's around twenty-two or twenty-three, very soft-spoken. She has a small frame, around five feet, four inches, blond hair, and green eyes and is very athletic, mostly soccer, which is a good thing. The boys have played soccer for years, six or seven, since they were little. Anyway, she is so very nice.

PJ, Heather, and I even went Christmas shopping together, just the three of us. Oh my gosh, we had so much fun together. I haven't been out shopping with PJ in years. Wow. I think the last time we went shopping together was right after his accident. That time, we were shopping for black boots.

PJ had wanted a pair of black boots for such a long time, but we never found a pair he liked, or when he did find a pair he liked, they didn't feel right. So we tried again. He still wasn't feeling good from the accident, but he had to get out of the house, so it was a late

Christmas gift. We had so much fun, just the two of us, laughing and kidding around, one of the moments you want to keep forever. Just when he was getting tired again, as we were walking out, he found a pair he liked. Since they were a lot of money, he didn't even want to try them on, but I insisted. We got a salesperson. They did have the boots in his size. PJ's funny; he's like, "Oh darn, they have my size." Still reluctant, he did try them on, and he fell in love with them. PJ still didn't want me to buy them because of the price, but that didn't matter. PJ had gone through so much for such a long time; for once, price didn't matter. PJ's such a good person, always worried about me since he knew money was tight for Rich and me. PJ was so happy. God blessed us both. For me to see my child so happy and for him to know that Mom didn't care about anything else other than making him happy, wow. It's sad that it's been eight years since we went shopping together.

So while Heather, PJ, and I were Christmas shopping this time, we looked for a kitchen table for me. We all went shopping together. We looked for stuff for the boys. Heather and I took PJ over to the clothes section to have him try on pants. PJ didn't want to at first. PJ told Heather that it had been years since he went shopping for clothes. PJ lost weight and goes to the gym on a regular basis. He looks really good, but he needed more pants. We finally talked him into trying on pants.

He was so funny, each time he tried on a pair of jeans, Heather and I made him model them for us. Too funny. PJ was amazed to see how good he looks. We were both teasing him about what a cute butt he has. I think he loved every bit of it. We must have had him try on at least twenty pairs of jeans. It was so much fun to see him model them and see that he knew how good he looked. He was so amazed about what pant size he was in. He had never been that size before.

It reminded me of how, when I had been heavy and then got really thin, I always still felt fat. I could be a size 18 or 5 and I would still feel fat. It amazes me when someone calls you fat. You always get that image in your head. You'll always feel fat.

I felt bad for PJ. I was just telling Heather that he felt uncomfortable about his weight and pant size and had different emotions about what size he was. Then PJ got out of the dressing room and began to tell us what he was feeling, the way that I was just describing to Heather. Heather and I just looked at each other with amazement and kinda laughed. We both began to tell him how good he looked and that he should get what he felt comfortable in. PJ went back in the dressing room to try on another pair of jeans.

Heather told me what an influence I had on PJ. When I asked why, she told me that she asked him lots of times to try on jeans, pants, or any clothes. But since I asked him, he actually did try something on, and then I even knew how he was feeling. She just laughed. I reminded myself about what Sheryl said that I'm getting everything back that I lost with PJ one piece at a time.

Heather and I were still laughing and joking together, looking for different jean sizes and styles. She sat on the floor looking at jeans and told me about the fun she was having because she didn't like to go shopping, and we were there for hours. That was just the topping to a perfect day with the kids. It was one of those times that I could put in a box and keep it and open it up to enjoy a wonderful memory. Something that *no one* could ever take from us.

On Christmas morning, when PJ was done opening up all his presents, with such sincerity in his eyes, he looked up at me and said, "Mom, thank you." That thank you was the greatest gift that I can get.

I never understood why I had such an emotional attachment to PJ. I know he's my firstborn and I've explained how much I went through and why he meant so much to me. After talking to Sheryl the other day, I saw that there was so much more. I'm so embarrassed to share this with you, but I believe it will be helpful, so here I go.

When I was with Sheryl, I was explaining how Christmas was. Just like I got done writing about. But Sheryl believed that there was more to it than needing PJ more than life itself. Believe me, it's so hard to tell you. Sheryl was reading this book, what I have been writing, and God led her to help me figure out what I was holding on to.

Like I was explaining before, there was this big pot and there were lots of parts in the pot. My parts that had to heal. Stuff in the pot represented them. This one, a great big soaked white sweat sock. I told you this is embarrassing. Anyway, Sheryl knew there was something else, and there was. We were talking about PJ's car accident because I had just written about it. Sheryl kept asking me how I was feeling when I was next to him on the stretcher. I kept telling her that there was no feeling. I didn't know what I was feeling; there was just emptiness. I could see myself dissociate out. I could see myself looking at myself next to the stretcher, like looking at a movie. I can still see myself next to PJ down the hall. I know it seems odd, but it's true.

When I was telling Sheryl about this, I believed that I did something right in my life for once because PJ was alive. Everything in my life that could go wrong went wrong. If anything bad could happen, it happened to me. That's all I never knew. But Sheryl knew there was something else, and I've learned not to disagree with her. There's no way I would be where I am now without listening to her. I know that she will never ever hurt me. She would do nothing at all to ever hurt me or my children. I believe Sheryl cares about my boys, all three of them, more than anything. Sheryl knows I want them to grow up and be strong, healthy men. So when Sheryl was telling me there was more, as much as I didn't want to believe her, God was telling her, "Go ahead, keep asking, keep trying to find out." As much as I didn't like it, I also told her to go ahead, keep asking. Well, Sheryl asked about Helen, one of my alters, the one that knows everything and that always protected me. Sheryl asked my parts what was going on.

I kept seeing me in PJ's room in Kansas. I was sitting in the dark, rocking PJ. I can still see the vision now. Still in my head as I am writing this. I'm about a quarter to half of the way in the bedroom. I'm looking at myself, rocking PJ. It is so dark that I can't tell what I was wearing or what PJ was wearing, like a dark silhouette. PJ was around two or three months old. I was holding him on my left side over my heart. I was telling him how much I loved him and that I would always protect him and keep him safe, that I would never leave him. I was feeling emptiness and loneliness but also all the love that I could have for someone, the love you just can't explain. Unconditional love. I guess it's a love only a mother could have for her child. I remember I just cried and rocked him for hours. I don't know how long. Well, Sheryl kept asking me how I felt when I was with PJ at the hospital, and I kept seeing me watching me in the room in Kansas. I told you it sounds strange.

Well, Sheryl suggested that when I was rocking him twenty-five years ago, I was in so much pain that I dissociated out to take the pain away. That part of me got buried away so I wouldn't have to deal with the pain of being so lonely, and that part just stayed there, rocking PJ. And then she suggested that when I went to work the next day, where PJ and I both worked, that that part of me needed to meet PJ. That she got left behind and still is rocking her baby for the last twenty-five years. Sounds normal, right? Sounds perfectly normal. But I know to get healed that I needed to do this. You ask how? I don't know how, except to pray and ask God to help.

Well, as Sheryl was explaining all this to me, boy, did I *feel* the pain, the loneliness, the feeling of "Oh god, what did I do?" Here I am, twelve hundred miles away from all my family and friends. All alone. Timothy and I were doing horrible, worse than ever. I didn't even have him. I was totally alone, with just PJ, this little bitty baby. In Sheryl's office, I was feeling all the pain from twenty-five years ago. I was crying uncontrollably. That way down deep in your belly cry. I cried for a long time. Sheryl hugged me and comforted me, what I desperately needed so many years ago. I would have cut off my arms and legs for a hug, anything, just to be held. That was the worst sense of torture, not being held.

When I started to calm down in her office, Sheryl kept suggesting that I, she, needed to meet PJ. I asked, "How? Why? What do I do?" She just said over and over, "Remember to meet PJ at work tomorrow. You'll know when it's the right time." How can I not agree with Sheryl? This was not the first time she suggested such a thing like this. Well, I guess I have to correct that. It's my choice to listen to her.

When I got home that night, I was so tired. I felt like I got run over by a Mack Truck five or six times. But I was feeling blessed that I could feel. I was so sad thinking about what we had talked about. A part of me was still sitting in that rocking chair, rocking PJ. A part of me got left behind. A part of me didn't get to see PJ grow up. Here PJ is a grown twenty-four-year-old man. And she missed out on everything.

The next morning, I woke up knowing that she, me, would get to meet PJ. To see what a handsome man that he grew up to be. That she would get to see that the other parts of me did a great job raising him. Just thinking about it sounds so different. Okay, so what I wanted to write was *crazy*. But I don't like writing *crazy* because I'm not honoring my parts that worked so very hard to keep me not crazy. So all this sounds different.

I dropped the boys off at school, then drove to work, thinking about everything. Now I thought, *How am I going to do this?* The part of me that never met PJ was nervous about meeting him. She didn't know what to think or how PJ was going to act. Of course, PJ will not know the difference, but my part sure will. When I got to work, my boss could tell there was something wrong, but he didn't ask. Thank goodness. That morning I kept thinking, *How am I going to do this?* It's not like I have control of my parts. They have worked so very hard together for all these years to keep me safe and to protect me. I really don't have control. It just works! I called Sheryl to ask her and tell her that she didn't know what PJ would think of her and left a message. As soon as I hung up, I looked across the shop and saw the boys—the shopworkers. I thought I saw PJ, but it wasn't him. Then I saw his shoes, and I knew it was him. And then she knew he was there, and for the first time in all these years, she saw him. I began to tell her about how good PJ was doing and how proud all of us are. That all of our parts were proud of him. As I stood there, I could just see his boots. I could just see him from the chest down. I still couldn't see his face.

I turned around and walked back in the office, thinking about how different this was (again, not crazy). Way different. So I tried to shake this off and started my day. As soon as I walked back through the door, back toward the shop, back to the boys, she saw PJ. It was such a shock, like a wave went through me. There he was, all grown up. My baby that I rocked for so, so many years all grown up. I felt like a mother who gave up her son for adoption because it was the best thing for her son and, years later, meets him out of the blue. What a shock. I felt like I got hit by a bolt of lightning. I (she) looked at his face, his dark-brown hair, his pretty brown eyes. So handsome. My baby, my baby, the one I would protect in my arms forever was all grown up. PJ walked past me. What a shock. There he was, and now she gets to meet him.

 I lived it, and it still sounds different, even to me. Well, she did stay out and started crying. I hugged him like I was doing it for the very first time. As I was holding him and hugging him, I whispered as quietly as I could. I wanted him to hear me, but at the same time, I didn't want him to hear me. She needed to tell him, but I didn't want him to hear her. PJ is so wonderful, and he didn't know what was going on. He probably was thinking, *Why is my ma crying and holding me like she's never seen me before?* I told him that I was dealing with a great big soaking wet sweat sock from my past. This seemed like enough explanation to him, and he just held me tighter. Someway, somehow, I did something right.

 Yesterday, when I met with Sheryl, the most amazing thing happened. As soon as Sheryl saw me, she hugged me and held me for the longest time. I love hugs and believe being held is the most amazing thing to experience. You see, last week during the PJ moment at work, I kept calling Sheryl and leaving her messages. I wanted her to know everything that was happening, everything that was going on. So she got a play-by-play account of everything as it was happening at the moment. No one else knows about this. Well, now that you're reading this, you know about it and I am embarrassed. But I should shout to the world that, after twenty-five years, I have seen my son! Sheryl was so happy and excited over what had happened and that was why she held me for so long. Sheryl is such a blessing. Then we got to her office, and we went through the current events of the week, especially what had happened with PJ.

After last week, I am even more driven to finish this book and get the rest of the pieces out of the pot. When we talk about the SRA stuff, that's the hardest part of all to deal with. I'm still not wanting all my parts to know. I believe 80 to 85 percent of them know; it's just a handful that need to be caught up to speed. As Sheryl and I were talking, I saw in a vision in my head, a little girl outside. I know she's only four years old. She was in so much pain. She would do anything for the pain to go away. Anything. So I created a part, and she took the pain so that I didn't have to feel the pain. Makes perfect sense, right? Sheryl was asking me and my parts if we wanted to bring her up to speed, integrate her into the adult Cindy, or if we wanted to leave her behind in the front yard, singing "This Little Light of Mine." I guess I would sing it for a very long time. It was one of the things that I did to not go crazy. This is how I calmed myself.

I loved Jesus when I was little. I loved him more than anything. Jesus was all I had. It's funny talking about the song. See, I'm here in my bathtub writing and singing "This Little Light of Mine" for the last twenty minutes. (Yes, much of this book has been written while I'm in my bathtub.) I know that it's a way of healing. That little girl on the front lawn was me. I can see myself looking at her. Beautiful blue sky, dark pine trees, green grass. A perfect sunny day. Singing a song with no cares in the world. I see myself turning away. And I see myself with PJ, sitting in that rocking chair in Kansas. I can see myself get up out of the rocking chair and walk away with PJ.

But then I see the little girl. I don't know what's memory and what's the enemy messing with me, but I see her, me, go into the house with Mom. I'm standing in the kitchen next to Mom, and then I see me on the kitchen table. I'm lying down on the table, and I'm not sure if I have clothes on or not. There is a red hot water bottle hanging, and it is hooked up between my legs, filling my bladder. I had to go from a precious moment singing a song to Jesus to something like this. My mother was sick, just sick. Both of my parents were sick. When I think of everything, I can't not believe that all this was true. But I don't want to believe it. Your parents are supposed to love you and protect you. How can parents be capable of doing something like this? It's unthinkable. And thinking about it makes me sick.

I thank God that he made me so different from them. Or like Sheryl says, I have choices and I made the right ones. That four-year-old little girl in the front yard singing, "This Little Light of Mine," her little spirit, her love for God that she held on to for so many years, it kept her going. It kept me going. She always prayed, "Please, God, help me one day to help other people so that they will never ever go through all this pain, not even a little bit of pain that we, all my parts, went through." The more I prayed to God to make the pain go away, the more I thought that he didn't answer me. In fact, God did make the pain go away by giving me my parts. The parts that he gave me took some of the pain away from me. There was still plenty of pain, but I thank God that I can't even imagine in my wildest dreams what the pain would have felt like if God didn't give me parts to take some of the pain away—24-7 pain, belly-aching pain. Unbearable. I don't even want to know how bad it would have been without my parts.

I'm thinking about my sister and the last memory I got. It included what my dad made my sister do to me. How on earth or why would I ever put this vision in my own head? If I would make up this vision and stick it in my head, I would be the one that was sick. I worked way, way too hard to be sick or crazy. If I didn't believe all this, I would be dishonoring me, my parts, my children, this book, and all of you reading this. It would be a dishonor to everyone who has experienced SRA to not believe that this could be true. I have met three other people that were abused in occult groups, and they did want to believe it was true. If this wasn't true, they would be crazy and crazy is not a good, healthy thing to be. But in my case, crazy was normal. Crazy made sense. It was as safe as you could be. Mom was crazy. That was the excuse that everyone used. Somehow, if Mom was crazy, it made everything okay. In our house, crazy was accepted as normal, so what I think of as crazy (different than the life I lived) was actually normal. I hope you're making sense of this. Mom was crazy and did horrible things to me. But in truth, she was the normal one compared to Dad.

CHAPTER FIVE

> Where can I go to get away from your spirit?
> Where can I run from you?
> If I go up to the heavens, you are there.
> If I lie down in the grave, you are there.
> If I rise with the sun in the east
> And settle in the west beyond the sea,
> Even there you would guide me.
> With your right hand you would hold me.
> —Psalm 139:7–10

I'M BACK IN THE BATHTUB, writing. For the first time, I have to believe all this hap-pened. Nothing else makes sense, and I love myself and want to get better. I love my children. I love you. Every single one of you reading this. The love that I have, the passion and desire for you not to hurt, that if you can use even one part of this book to make a difference. That little girl almost forty years ago standing in the front yard, singing, desiring for people not to hurt anymore, her desire was so strong back then. Praying to God that one day I would be able to make a difference, that people wouldn't hurt anymore. It would be a great dishonor to that little girl singing with all the desire in her heart for me to stop now. Every word I write is to honor her and God. That little girl who has fought with her whole heart and soul. Writing this makes all those promises come true. I believe I know that God will always give you the desires of your heart. It's taken almost forty years, but it's happening right now.

So much healing has happened writing this. But writing this sometimes has been even harder than counseling with Mark. I'm actually writing this all out by hand, you know. Of course it would've been so much easier to type it on the computer, but there is no emotion for me typing on a computer. There are no tears on a computer. I have all the tears on this paper, and I am honoring all the tears. In handwriting, I am honoring all my parts and emotions. When my hand hurts so much from writing and I'm thinking that I can't write one more word, I pray to God. This is his book and testimony. God chose me to write this, and God has given me the strength to keep writing. God was on the cross, and I will never know the pain that he went through there, but he knows all the pain that I went through. It took me a long time to realize that. He did this to give me the strength to keep writing no matter how painful it is—emotionally, mentally, and even physically. This is in God's hands. I asked him for this over forty years ago.

These last couple of weeks have been so healing. Thank you for giving me the encouragement to write. You are helping me when I don't feel like writing anymore. Sometimes I still don't want to deal with this anymore. So what? It hap-pened. There are days I don't feel like doing this anymore. That's when I have to dig deep, refocus, and write. When I don't feel like praying, I will pray in the Spirit. It helps me to start writing again. Sometimes when I am hoping that this book will be written, that it will get done, and the only way to get it done is to do this. So again, you are helping me along this journey. When you feel like giving up and have no hope, remember that I've been there, I've done that. We are all in this together.

After these last couple of weeks of writing, I need to get back to writing about PJ again. I bet you're wondering what happened to him.

It was just a miracle what happened. I was I standing next to PJ in the hospital, holding his hand, looking at his face with all the cuts and scrapes, one eye bleeding. They didn't know what happened to his face. It felt like it took forever for them to look at him. PJ was in one hallway, then another. He was in the main hall, then they took him back down another hall. That really was the first time that Timothy and I were together in a long time. Just thinking about it, I think that was one of the few times that Timothy and I weren't fighting; we were just being PJ's parents. For the first time, Timothy just let me be PJ's mom. For years, Timothy tried to keep PJ away from me. There were so many times that he tried to keep him away from me.

When Timothy and I were in Kansas, things got much worse between us. Even after PJ was born, I just got more and more lonely. When PJ was a week old, my dad, grandma, and sister Mary came to Kansas.

It wasn't until just now, while I'm writing this, that I realized that was the worst thing that could hap-pen. When Timothy and I were in Kansas, we were all safe. PJ and all my parts were safe; my dad or anyone or anything couldn't hurt us. Even Timothy's parents. No one could hurt us; no one knew where we were. That would explain so many things. More pieces of the puzzle. When we were in Kansas, no one knew where we lived, so my parts were safe because my dad couldn't come and hurt me, especially PJ.

It was just a few years ago that I remembered about my dad and the occult stuff. Because of all the craziness of the occult, my dad would drug me and threaten me not to tell anyone about what they would do to me during the sacrifices or rituals. My dad kept me quiet from telling anybody about the occult stuff by not only beating me with leather belts, on my knees, kneeling down with my hands tied up behind my back, telling me not to tell or the big people, as I called them, would threaten to kill my babies and cut them up in little pieces. But my dad was the meanest of them all. Dad would tell me that if I told anyone about the abuse that he would cut out my children's tongues before he cut them up into little pieces so he wouldn't hear them scream when he cut them up.

Nice, huh! Just what every little girl wants to hear from her father. And he was the one to protect me from my crazy mother. Again, how did I live through all this? Yeah, my parts. As much as I'm embarrassed about my parts, they all need to be honored. I believe they protected me more than I will ever know.

So here I have this baby and I have to protect him. Now that Dad was at my house, he knows where I live. Now Kansas wasn't safe. Nowhere was safe. After they left, things got even worse. I remember, one day, Timothy and I were both crying about our pasts. Timothy had so much pain in his heart over his mom and dad. I was losing it more and more. The pain and hurt were getting worse. I had no idea why!

As much of a hard time as I have been having with the occult stuff, it's becoming so real. That it actually hap-pened. Nothing else makes sense. Nothing. God put it on my heart to read my old journals from when I was seeing Mark. The hardest thing that Mark had me do was write. I had every excuse in the world not to write.

But Mark kept telling me, "Go ahead, don't write, feel like this forever. It's your choice. It doesn't matter to me one way or another." Again, it was my choice. So as much as I didn't want to write because the pain was so bad and the anger was off the charts, it was my choice to write and get better and to feel the pain instead of not feeling the pain, anxiety, triggers, depression, and everything else that goes along with it. I'm sure you know where I'm coming from. Maybe you have felt one or many of them feelings. You know that the feelings are *real*. And that they don't truly go away.

When I was seeing Dr. Stratman, she also suggested for me to write. That was also hard. The anger and pain were so deep back then. Remember, I was passing out because my body was remembering all this. It's like my body was waking up very slowly after sleeping for over twenty years. So everything hurt to the point that I couldn't take the pain and I would pass out. Well, writing kinda was the same way. It's like smashing your finger in the door and not being able to scream out, "Oh, does that hurt!" Imagine not being able to scream out hundreds of times over. There's a lot of screaming that needs to be released. So if something triggers you, you slightly remember the pain and want to explode. My body went, "Oh, I remember that," and I still couldn't take the pain, so I would pass out. Now imagine writing, your mind and body remembering stuff, trying to write out the emotions on paper. Your mind trying to process what you're feeling and then trying to write out what your mind's confused about. Wow! Not easy at all. So now, you have to write what your mind and body are trying to process.

Anyway, I did make the choice to write with Mark. Like I was saying with Dr. Stratman, when I was writing with her, the pain and anger were so bad that the parts that remembered about the occult were writing about killing her babies. When I was writing, the rage was so bad that I tore the pages writing with my ink pen. I would tear through five or six pages at a time. The rage was always over killing her babies. I remember that each page would just have a letter on it; each letter would take up a whole page, eventually spelling out *kill her babies*. It never made sense to me. At that point, I didn't care or want to care. I just wanted to survive. And that's all I was doing—just surviving each day, sometimes each moment at a time. Thanks to God, his angels, my little spirit, my parts, and that little four-year-old girl that I didn't lose my mind.

I remember how bad writing had been before and now Mark wanted me to write again. Was he nuts? Mark laughed, and the session was over because he had another client waiting. Ha, ha, ha. I thought to myself, *Okay, Mark's gotten me this far. I know that Mark was sent to me from God. I can't question that. So God knows what he's doing.* I didn't want to feel like this anymore. So did I really have a choice? Again, the choice was all mine. Try to heal and maybe be healthy and whole or feel like this forever. What a choice. Go through the pain again and heal. Or go through the pain and not heal. It was a lose-lose situation. But still my choice. None of this should have ever hap-pened, but it did. And as much as I and all my parts wanted to keep stuffing this, it did hap-pen. So I did make the choice to write again. And just like I thought, it was *horrible*!

Now I had flashbacks of my dad molesting me, but I also had flashbacks of the occult. Yeah, for me, woo-hoo! Let's go through this again. Well, that's how I felt. Mark kept telling me that feelings are a good thing. I was so good at switching my parts that I could actually slap myself in the face and not feel anything. Then one day at Mark's, when I slapped myself, it actually hurt! I felt the pain, and it really hurt! Mark was as surprised as I was, and he said, "Good, you felt that." That was the beginning. My feelings were healing. Mark reminded me all the time that to feel is a good, healthy thing because before I had so many parts, I could switch and not feel the pain.

There I go again, going on and on. Like I was saying, Sheryl said that all parts of me have to know that all this is real. After the experience with PJ and the four-year-old little girl, it makes all this more real than ever. All this has to be real for there to be this much pain. So as I was writing, God led me to look at my old journals from Mark. They were in the very back of my closet. And again, I've been so embarrassed by them instead of honoring them.

Well, it took a lot of courage to bring them down, open them up, then actually read them again. I could see the change in handwriting. Sometimes there was a small difference, but a couple of times, there was such a huge difference. Some of the handwriting looked like a very small child, maybe five- or six-year-old's writing. Looking at it makes me so sad that I was in so much pain and that it must have been that bad. What else could make sense? If it didn't hap-pen, what else can explain all this? Nothing, so it must have hap-pened, reading the journals, remembering how I felt and what was going on with me at that very moment. Why was my heart racing? Why was my anxiety through the roof? Why was I seeing things in my head? Why? Why? Why? Nothing could explain all this if it didn't hap-pen, and I want to help you so you can also heal from this. It's been seven years of healing, so it was that bad.

When PJ was in the hospital, they let me stay with him throughout the whole hospital, actually going with him when he went through all the testing because they didn't know the extent of his injuries. They even let me go into the CAT scan room and hold his hand until they took the pictures. They let me do the same thing throughout his testing.

The doctors were asking who PJ's doctor was. I told them one doctor and Timothy told them another. Well, Timothy and I started arguing over who his doctor was. The doctor that was taking care of PJ told me about the extent of his injuries and that his eye was bleeding and that they had to rush him to another hospital. An eye specialist was going to see PJ at the other hospital because it was that serious. Since Timothy had the insurance and PJ was living with Timothy through the week, they listened to Timothy even though I was PJ's mom.

By the time we found out that he had head trauma and an eye bleed, both my family and Timothy's family were at the hospital. I waited about three hours before I called my family. I guess parts of me wanted to protect PJ from my family. I was seeing Mark when PJ was in the accident, so I was already seeing things about my dad.

My dad and PJ were best buddies. Oh, how PJ loved my dad. They were always building models together and doing stuff. I forgot how my dad did act like a real grandpa to PJ. I don't know, maybe he was trying to make up for what he did to me. My dad did go to counseling for years. Every week. I don't know. Maybe a part of him feels bad for what he did. I know that my dad really loves PJ. I can't take that away from him. I can't believe that I forgot about my dad and PJ's relationship. And at the hospital, my parts were protecting PJ from my dad. So confusing. PJ and my dad still talk today.

PJ knows some stuff. PJ has seen a lot. How much he knows or believes is PJ's choice. Obviously, one day PJ will know the whole truth when he reads this book. I have always been overprotective of PJ. Of course, now we all know why. But I know that all this is in God's hands, and God will not let any harm come from this to hurt PJ.

I'm not so worried about my younger boys because they were never close to my mom and dad or even the rest of my family. The boys today know about the book, and they know that Grandma and Grandpa hurt Mom very bad. Both of the boys have seen and lived the aftermath of what they did to me, how it not only affects my life but the boys' lives too. They got to see their grown mother sleep in their room under their bed. They've seen me crying and a mess too many times. Sheryl and I were talking about this the other day. The boys saw me go through flashbacks of memories. If I was going through a memory of the snakes crawling on me or my dad raping me, Robby and Joey saw me crying on the floor. The second they saw me, I was able to turn it off, switch, and be okay. Well, I thought that they thought I was okay. But Sheryl believes that they knew, as young as they were, that Mom wasn't really okay. But now they know that Mom is okay. PJ has stayed away sometimes because it's easier on him to stay away than to see his mom in pain.

So at the hospital, when both families were in the waiting room, it was a form of healing for me to see the families talking, everyone getting along, with the same goal for PJ to be okay. Everyone loves PJ. He is the most special, kind, caring, loving person. Everyone who meets PJ just loves him. That warm, kind, loving heart. Kinda reminds me of someone I know—me. With all the craziness, I created someone that special, and through all my abuse, I kept it together enough to have such an amazing child. With all the threats of the occult, I protected my son as best as I was capable of. Just like today, PJ left with his buddies to Las Vegas for a week. They got a condo, rented a Lincoln, and are going to have a wonderful, healthy time. God so did bless me with all my children.

Everything that the enemy took or tried to take away, God was always in control, taking care of everything, *Everything!*

My girlfriend Sally took Robby and Joey home to her house from the hospital. The boys were taken care of. My van wasn't at the hospital, so we didn't have to worry about that. That was taken care of. Healing between both sets of parents, God took care of. As much as the doctors listened to Timothy, I was the one that never left PJ's side. I was the one that got to go through the hospital, and I was the one that was with him in the ambulance ride to the other hospital. They normally didn't let parents ride in the ambulance with their children; they have to meet them at the hospital. But since I didn't have a car, and with the extent of his injuries, they let me go with him. God took care of everything. When we got to the other hospital, they let me stay with PJ all the way up to his room. I still didn't leave his side.

PJ was very involved at his church, so his two best friends from church came to visit him. That was such a blessing. They prayed with him. It was so awesome to see his Christian friends up at the hospital. Again, God had his hands on it. When everyone left, the only person he wanted was Mom, even to the point that he wanted me to sleep right next to him. I was in the recliner at his feet next to his bed, but PJ wanted me right next to him. There was an empty bed next to him, so they let me move the empty bed and move the recliner right next to him, holding his hand all the time.

It reminded me of my best friend, Sandy. Well, we used to be best friends. We were thirteen when we met. I think I told you about her. Sitting there in the hospital, I remembered when I first heard from her that her son had lung cancer and I remembered what happened just the night before she called.

It was on a Saturday night in March of that same year. Rich and I were sleeping, and I woke up to an orange glow in our bedroom. When I looked out of the bedroom window, I saw that our garage was on fire. I tried to wake up Rich, but he wouldn't wake up. I kept pushing and shoving him to try to wake him up, but he wouldn't. You see, Rich had been drinking that Saturday night. I ran to the wall phone. No dial tone. I grabbed the other phone. No dial tone. Then I grabbed my cell phone, and I finally got through to tell the police about the fire. I ran back to the bedroom to try to wake Rich up. He finally woke up. When he realized what was going on, we both ran outside.

The fire was too bad to do anything about it. Since Rich was a mechanic, we had a lot of things that can explode—different chemicals, heater, torches, you name it, it was in the garage. The fire was so bad that it started the neighbor's house on fire and almost reached the other neighbor's garage. The garage was separate from our house and the fire did not reach it, but the trees in front of the garage did catch on fire. You could see the fire for blocks. We had a huge garage—twenty-four feet by twenty-four feet with lots of storage upstairs. There was a lot of stuff in the garage to burn.

Rich and I stood there, just watching. At this point, there was nothing we could do but watch all our stuff burn. Everything that we worked so hard for. It was cold out that night. Gosh, I don't even remember what time it was. Sometime in the middle of the night. I was outside in just my pj's, no shoes or socks, standing on the grass, well, snow. But I didn't feel cold at all, not my feet or nothing.

I started staring at the fire, the orange red glow. It reminded me of the occult burning crosses outside. A trigger. I wasn't seeing Mark yet, but I had started seeing images of memories. Things were popping up into my head. I didn't really know yet about the occult. Anyway, just standing there in the snow barefoot and staring at the fire, I just passed out. Boom. Right on the ground. Luckily, there were at least five or six fire trucks, two or three police cars; it was a bad fire. Lots of emergency personnel. They picked me up. When I came to, they wanted to take me to the hospital to make sure that I was okay. I told them that I was okay and tried to assure them that I would be okay. I think that I even told them in a roundabout way that there had been a trigger. My vitals and everything were good, so they told me that if I got a coat on and something on my feet that they would let me stay home. I agreed.

Rich was in shock more than I was, I think. We were watching our neighbor's house and dog because they were away. The fire department was ready to break down the front door to their house when Rich got the keys and rescued their dog. Rich ran across the front of the garage with all the explosions, trying to get the dog. He came running back with the dog. Everyone worried about Rich; he was just too close to the fire, and anything could happen. The fire department was there for hours, trying to contain the fire. After they left, there was nothing left of the garage. No walls were left, just a couple of two-by-fours all burnt up. It if wasn't metal, there was nothing left of it. Both of our cars had been in the garage. I had a minivan. It was fiberglass, and nothing was left of it at all. The worst part was that that was my second minivan I lost to a fire.

The first one was when I was driving to the doctor's office after a dentist's appointment. When I pulled up into the driveway, I saw smoke and thought it was the car that was parked nearby. I parked the van in front of a wooden fence. Then I thought maybe someone was having a barbeque. I got out of my van and looked underneath, and I saw a puddle and a reflection of fire. I ran in the doctor's office and called the police. I wanted to do something to save my van, but there was nothing that I could do.

I was so scared that Rich would be mad. When I had to call him at work, Rich was fine. He was just worried if the boys and I were okay. I didn't have the boys; they were at Grandma's because I had the dentist's appointment. You should have seen me. My mouth was still half numb, so I could hardly talk. Rich came to get me from the doctor's office since now I didn't have a car. Then we went to get the boys.

Luckily, the van only burnt the front end and we were able to grab the car seats for the boys. The police took a report and said they would get in touch with us after they did their investigation. Of course I didn't do anything wrong, but I so wanted to do something. I had no idea how the fire must have triggered me.

The worst thing about the second van catching on fire was that I just got the van back from the collision shop with about five thousand or six thousand dollars' worth of damage. I still had the bottle of touch-up paint in the van. And Rich just did the front brakes on the van that evening.

We had lost power that evening before the fire. We had a generator, so Rich hooked it up in the garage and back-fed the power so we had full power to the house. I fell asleep early because Rich was drinking. Well, in the middle of the night, when we got power back on, Rich forgot to unplug the generator, which back-fed to the breaker box. The breaker failed, then back-fed to the house, where the breaker did work. If that had failed as well, with the breaker box in the basement directly under PJ's bed . . . Well, the fire marshal said that if the breaker didn't break in the house, we would have all died. After the fire, I remember Rich and I sitting in the middle of our bed. Rich had his arm around me and kept thanking God that he had his family.

That next Monday morning, my girlfriend Sandy called and said her son had lung cancer, and they didn't know if he was going to make it. We had just found out from Michelle, my best friend at the time, that her husband was molesting his two stepdaughters. That was a very bad day. What else could have gone wrong? Don't ask because I learned to quit asking.

When I was in the hospital with PJ, I just kept thinking of my girlfriend Sandy. All the days she was in the hospital with her son. Thinking about how she just used me and how jealous she was of me for all those years, I had so many mixed emotions when it came to her. Why couldn't she ever be happy for me? Why did she always have to have everything bigger and better than me? All I ever did was love her and her family. We were together every day for years. Sandy had been there for me when I was going through bad times. But when things were going good for me, she was never happy for me. It was after Rich and I met and she moved away. After our wedding, she really pushed away. Here Sandy was my best friend for years, and she even hurt me beyond belief.

When I was in the hospital, I kept thinking of Sandy and all the days she spent in the hospital, thinking that I should have been at the hospital with her. Sandy didn't want me up at the hospital. She said it was because I had two little kids at home, and she didn't want me to bring the kids' germs up to the hospital. My kids weren't sick. They were never sick when I wanted to see Sandy and her son. I know she was in so much pain. I couldn't imagine the thought that my child may die, especially after everything that I went through. It just hurt to not be allowed to be there for her. Sandy didn't even want me to come around when her son was doing good. Sandy just didn't want anything to do with me anymore.

That first night at the hospital, I was all alone. Timothy and everyone left. Just thinking about everything that happened that day, I was still amazed that my son was alive. I don't think I will ever forgive Rich because he never showed up at either hospital to be with me, his wife.

There I was, at the hospital, not knowing the extent of PJ's injuries. I just knew that this was really bad. We owned the tool truck at this point, similar to Snap-on tools, so Rich had the freedom to drive to the hospital. Oh my gosh, I will never forget what Rich said, "If he's alive, there's nothing that I can do at the hospital" so he could just stay at work. Rich did have a representative on the truck, but he could have figured it out easily enough. I almost lost my son. I didn't have any idea how bad his injuries were. I just needed my husband. My husband to hug and hold me and try to tell me that everything's going to be all right. To hold my hand when the doctors were telling me how bad PJ was. My husband's shoulders to cry on and to comfort me. I needed my best friend, and where was my husband? God took care of the kids; Sally had the boys. The neighbors all got together and cried and prayed and had a candlelight vigil at Shelley's house. She was my closest friend at the time. The principal, teachers, friends, and their families were all at the hospital, supporting me and Timothy and our families. Everyone was there. People I didn't know were there. Everyone was there except for my husband. The one that was supposed to be there for everything. *Everything!* Where was my husband? Rich chose not to be there. There was no reason except that he chose not to be there. The day that I needed him the most. The thing that surprised me the most was that you would think that Rich would want to be there for PJ, if not for me but for PJ. Rich had known PJ for ten years. PJ was only seven when we met. I didn't understand it. I guess I never will. It's a good thing that I will never understand that kind of lack of love or care.

Just thinking about how Rich wasn't there for me reminds me of when Timothy and I got home from the military. I had really bad headaches and my heart was acting up. When I was going to the doctor for the headaches, they were extremely bad to the point that the doctors thought that I had a brain aneurism. The doctor's office called me at home. Timothy was actually home. The doctor's office told me to go straight to the hospital where they were waiting to give me a CAT scan stat. I called Grandma and she said of course, that she would watch PJ. He must have been three.

When I told Timothy what the doctor said, Timothy said good luck and that he didn't know if he would be at home when PJ and I got home from the hospital. Wow, what a shock. My husband didn't want to come with me to the hospital for support to hold my hand or to find out what was wrong with his wife. I could have died from an aneurism and Timothy's like, "No big deal. Go ahead and take care of business. I'll see you later." Like I was going to the grocery store, not going to the hospital to find out what was going on with his wife. I was devastated. Can you imagine? Your kind, loving, compassionate husband. Well, should have been. He was not going with me, not caring, not wanting to know if I was going to live or die. Not fine. Can you imagine the abandonment issues that I was going through? Off the charts. Shortly after that, I knew things would not work out between me and Timothy, so I finally had the strength and courage to go through a divorce.

One morning, Timothy and I were having an argument. I don't remember what it was about, but he was so mad. We ended up in the bedroom fighting. Timothy threw me down on the bed and raped me. That was horrible. I just started a divorce and he was mad at me. He said I was his wife and that's what I was supposed to do: have sex with him.

The doctors were going to give me medicine for my headaches. The CAT scan showed that I had a brain cyst, and they didn't know if they would operate or not. They said the cyst was caused by a strong blunt force trauma to my head. At the time, I thought it was from my mom, but after learning about all the stuff from my dad and the occult, who knows.

I did tell the doctors that my husband raped me, so before they put me on the medication for my headaches, they had to do a pregnancy test. The medication could cause problems for a developing baby. I went in for blood work, including the pregnancy test.

I remember that day so well. It still amazes me that some things I have no memory of at all and other things are so clear to me. It was in the afternoon when I got the call. They asked for Mrs. Petroulias. I still laugh. I'm just Cindy. Anyways, the lady on the phone said, "Please do not fill the prescription" and that I was pregnant. I was shocked. I told her that I wouldn't fill the prescription.

Here I was, pregnant again, lonelier than ever, with this little baby inside of me. Boy, was I confused. Timothy and I were doing horrible. I had finally got enough strength and courage to get out of this relationship. I wasn't working. How was I going to take care of me and PJ and now a little baby? This is so hard to say, but another baby in this crazy dysfunctional family? What was going to hap-pen to this baby? This baby would have to go back and forth between me and Timothy. Timothy's family and my family would have to help watch this baby when we worked. How would that be fair to this baby?

After I hung up the phone with the doctor's office, I was in shock. Before the pregnancy, I didn't know what to do, but I knew I couldn't stay in this relationship, for me or PJ. Now another baby? This was just a mess. I called Grandma. When I told her, she was excited. She was going to have another great-grandchild. She thought everything would be fine with another baby. But I knew better. When Grandma knew how upset I was, she called my dad to come over and comfort me. I didn't know anything about the abuse with my dad yet, so I can only imagine what my insides were going through. When Dad got there, I was so upset, just crying and crying. My dad tried to console me, but I was just too far gone.

This is so hard for me to write, but PJ was home when all this was going on. The only memory he has of me and Timothy together is this memory when he was only three years old. Over the years, he has always asked me, "Ma, what hap-pened that day?" I was always too embarrassed to tell him, but writing this and telling you makes me feel sad, not embarrassed. I've been keeping this bottled up for so many years, the guilt and shame, of all this; it's just so sad.

My dad was still over when Timothy got home with his brother. Dad went outside and asked them both to please leave because I didn't want to see Timothy and that I was very upset. Of course, Timothy didn't listen and he insisted he come into the house. When I saw Timothy, I told him to please leave me alone and leave, that he was the last person on earth that I wanted to see. Timothy wouldn't leave, and we started fighting to the point that my grandma and uncle Hank came over, and Timothy's aunt from across the street was called. What a mess. So now I have a whole house full of people yelling in front of poor PJ. I think Grandma and Timothy's aunt came for PJ.

Timothy and I were fighting horribly. I told him why I was so upset. I can't remember if he was happy or upset. I just remember the fighting and arguing. I must have reached my boiling point because I pushed Timothy, the only time I have ever done something like that. When I pushed him, he fell back over the arm of the La-Z-Boy recliner; his head was on the bottom of the chair with his neck bent, and his feet were in the air. Then I started choking him. I had so much anger and rage toward Timothy for everything that he had done to me and PJ; the anger was through the roof. Looking back, it was kind of funny. My uncle Hank grabbed me from behind, trying to get me off Timothy. Timothy's arms and legs were going in all directions, then my uncle got me airborne; now my arms and legs were going all over. I had to promise not to hurt Timothy before he would let me go. Just writing this, I can't believe I lived and survived all this. I believe the police were called. The police were called many times for Timothy hitting me. The police wouldn't make Timothy leave; they said it would be safer for me and PJ to go to Grandma's house for all of us to calm down. Of course, I didn't want to leave, but everyone said it was for the best for me and PJ to leave.

The next morning when I went back home, Timothy changed the door locks on me. Here I didn't do anything wrong, well, maybe trying to strangle Timothy. Well, you know what I mean. So here I am, breaking into my house after everything that hap-pened the previous day.

After I got back in the house, I thought, *Now what?* Here I am, starting the divorce. I may just have met with the attorney, I'm not sure. But the fact is, here I am, pregnant, really not knowing what to do. I tried talking to Timothy after things calmed down, but I got nowhere. I still get frustrated that I can't remember some things. I can't remember for sure, but I think that Timothy thought everything was fine between us; he was working and now we have another baby on the way. But that was far from the truth. Things were getting worse. I felt so trapped.

Here I love the idea of family so much I felt things should be great. Boy, I only wish.

My headaches were getting worse. I couldn't take the medicine, so now what? I started thinking about an abortion. But how could I do that? But on the other hand, how could I bring another precious baby into all this craziness? My poor PJ was dealing with all this. How could I honestly, in good faith, bring another child into this?

Again, I tried to talk to Timothy, asking to please go to counseling and try to make things work out, but he would have no part of that.

It was early in my pregnancy that I decided to have an abortion. I talked to my aunt, who was a nurse, to at least find a nice clean place. She took me there. I couldn't believe what I was doing. As hard as I had worked for family, now it's come to this? Everyone there was nice. There were a lot of young girls. It was sad to see so many. I believe with all of us, there were only a couple of married women. The worst part was that they had to do an ultrasound to make sure the baby was in the uterus and that everything was fine. So to make matters worse, I got to see my baby.

When I was on the table waiting, a Greek doctor came in. He said, "Mrs. Petroulias, that sounds Greek. Mrs. Petroulias, you're married and so young. Why are you here?" I explained everything to him. We just started talking and talking to the point that I changed my mind and would try to talk to Timothy one more time.

I was excited that I didn't have the abortion. I would talk to my husband and try to work this out if, for nothing else, for this precious unborn baby. When I got home (remember we still didn't have cell phones), I called Timothy at work to let him know that I didn't do it and I wanted to try one more time to work things out. To my surprise, Timothy actually said yes, that we could meet at a restaurant to talk. On my way to the restaurant, for the first time, I was excited that I was going to have another baby, that the four of us would be a family, the family I always wanted.

When I met Timothy, he was so sweet and nice, and for the first time, he was excited that we were going to have a baby too. We talked and laughed and tried to figure out how things were going to work out. But before we left the restaurant, we started fighting again. Timothy said that things were all my fault, that I had to do all the changing, and that I was crazy like my mom and he was fine.

I left the restaurant crying, so helpless and distraught, knowing down deep in my belly that things would never change. A baby or not, things would never change.

For the next few days, I hardly talked at all, and for anybody who knows me, that doesn't hap-pen much. Ha ha. I didn't want to talk to anybody. Again, I felt so alone. I have PJ and this precious baby growing inside of me and I was so alone. I just kept going over things in my head over and over again. Nothing was the right choice—keeping this baby and having this baby, being brought up with divorced parents from the start before he or she was born. How was that fair for the baby? How was I going to support me and PJ? And day care for two babies? How was I going to do this? I had to get out of this relationship for me and PJ. And I just couldn't bring another life into this mess knowing how bad it was.

So as hard as it would be for me to go through an abortion, at the time I knew with my whole heart that I did the right thing. One morning, I woke up and called Grandma to ask her to please watch PJ and that I decided to go through with it. I was going by myself, but Grandma strongly advised against it that I needed someone to drive me home.

I agreed, so my uncle Hank went with me. It was so different this time. There was no feeling, no emotion. I was just dead inside. Here I had to get rid of the most precious gift that God can give me. I had to give it up. When I got there, I had to go through the same thing—more tests, an ultrasound; this time I couldn't even look. I just turned my head and looked the other way. This time, when I was on the table, the doctor was cold. I was just another patient, unlike the first time. The procedure was horrible. I had the vacuum method. It was so painful. They have to dilate you, then use a machine that literally vacuums your insides. I was in so much pain; the machine was loud, and I watched the canister fill up with *stuff*, knowing that's my baby. Just awful.

Afterward, they put me in a room with La-Z-Boy recliners. They all have heating pads on the chairs to help with the pain. But nothing compares to your heart knowing that you just lost your baby. And the only choice was mine. An ache that will never go away. I just remember the look on all the women that were with me that day—something that I will never forget. That day, I didn't talk to anyone. The very last person I wanted to see was Timothy.

A couple of days later, when I felt better, I took PJ and went to my uncle's cabin up north. The only ones who knew where we went were Grandma and Uncle Hank. I begged Grandma to please not tell Timothy because I just needed to be alone. She agreed.

When PJ and I got there, it was so beautiful. It was January, and everything was covered in snow. It was so calm and peaceful up there, nice, and no phones. After we got settled in, we just played and watched TV. Up there, we only had a couple of channels, but it didn't matter. I was alone with PJ again, the only thing I had left.

I believe it was our second night there, I can't remember, when I heard a car in the middle of the street, which didn't add up because no one lived up north. There were only three houses on the block, and I was the only one there.

I was scared at first. I didn't know who it was. Then I couldn't believe who it was. It was Timothy in his mom's car in the middle of the night. He went looking for me and PJ. I just couldn't believe it. He drove in the snow. It must have taken him forever to get there; without snow, it takes two and a half hours. Let alone he didn't know the way to my uncle's cabin; he had only been there once before. I just couldn't believe he was there.

I didn't know whether to be happy, sad, or mad. My emotions must have been everywhere. When Timothy got in and settled, we started talking. He told me everything I wanted to hear, but it was too late. If he would have told me that he loved me and wanted a family and for things to work out, I would not have had the abortion. But I did. Our child, the one that I would never hold or cuddle, never have a first birthday party for, the child that was not made out of love but conceived from a rape, would never be born. When they sucked my unborn child out of me, they took all my feelings too. As much as he sat there and cried and told me how much he loved me and wanted things to work out and that we could have another baby, my heart was cold. I had no feelings. I just went into robot mode to survive.

When we got back home, I went through with the divorce, and that's when hell really started with Timothy. Not only did I lose our unborn child but Timothy also did everything he could to take PJ away from me. Timothy told me that if I ever divorced him that I would get nothing and that he would take PJ. As much as Timothy tried taking PJ away from me, I have a wonderful relationship with PJ now. Timothy could never really take the love and the bond that we share.

Just thinking about it still amazes me. Boy, was my picker broke, meaning I didn't have a very good choice in men. When picking men, I made bad choices, the only choice that I knew. Timothy was so much like my mother. He understood her. Timothy liked my mom more than anyone. When everyone thought that my mom was crazy, Timothy always felt sorry for her. Had compassion for her. Go figure. Going through counseling with Dr. Stratman one day, I figured it out—what made me so drawn to Timothy and why I stayed for such a long time. I guess that parts of me—how silly it sounds—still wanted to be with my mom. And later on, I realized that Rich was just like my dad. Good choices, huh? I made the best choices of my God-given ability.

Mark was always so good about teaching me not to beat myself up over my choices. I was always mad at Timothy and the choices that were made. But Mark always strongly reminded me that no matter what (*a*) never beat myself up because (*b*) the choice was made, (*c*) it hap-pened and (*d*) try to figure out why I made the choice, and (*e*) you did the best of what you knew how.

I could beat myself up forever for the choices that I have made. But what good would that do? Leave me miserable! Or I can look back and say, "Look where I was, and thank God, look where I am now." The choices that I made ten years ago, or even twenty years ago, it does matter because my picker was broken. A lot was broken. Most of my parts were in so much pain. I look back and see how much pain I was in. I thank God that I made the choices that I have made. Someway, somehow, my choices could have been so much worse. Much worse.

Today I don't feel like writing. Not at all. My insides have been so stirred up that I feel like I need a break from writing. But as much as I don't feel like writing anymore, the desire to write gets stronger and stronger. As I look back at the writing and everything that I've been through, you give me the desire to write, to keep going. When that's the very last thing that I want to do, I continue to do it.

At the hospital with PJ, the doctors told us that he had a concussion. PJ also had a lot of eye problems. The pediatric eye specialist was wonderful. He stayed with PJ for such a long time, making sure he was okay. The doctor actually went downstairs to the pharmacy to get the eye drops that he needed. The doctor stayed with me and PJ in PJ's room until PJ got stable enough for him to leave. That was just the beginning of our relationship with the doctor.

PJ had a couple of things hap-pen to his eye. PJ had a hyphema; his eyes was bleeding. If we didn't get it under control, he could have lost his eyesight. PJ was in so much pain in his head from the accident. He was discharged from the hospital on a Saturday. When I called Rich to come and get us, he gave me a hard time. Rich wanted to make sure that we were ready when he got there so that he wouldn't have to wait for us. Rich wanted to make sure PJ was all discharged so that when Rich got to the hospital, we could leave. Rich didn't even want to come up to PJ's room to wait with us. Rich just wanted to pull up with us waiting outside. Not to inconvenience Rich. As I said, Rich didn't even come to visit PJ in the hospital.

When PJ and I were waiting for his discharge papers, Timothy showed up. It was Timothy's weekend with PJ, but PJ was set to go home with me. PJ wanted to go home with me; he just wanted his mom. If the hospital didn't take so long with the paperwork, we would have already left the hospital before Timothy got there. Well, Timothy was insistent that PJ go with him. PJ was seventeen years old. I thought that it was PJ's choice. PJ had been through enough, just let him get out of the hospital. Timothy didn't care about how PJ felt. Timothy just wanted to be in control and have PJ on his time. PJ told his dad that he was leaving with me. Timothy didn't care; he called security, showed them the papers, and made a huge scene. PJ wanted to be with me as much as I wanted to be with him. Timothy, what a kind, loving father. PJ's been through so much, and Timothy didn't even care how it affected PJ. Timothy just cared about Timothy.

Just like the time when PJ was little, after the divorce and before Rich, PJ and I were at a birthday party for a friend of our cousin. I was playing with a baby, and the baby poked me in the eye. My eye was getting bad, tearing and really red. It was starting to hurt really bad to the point that my cousin had to take me to the hospital to get checked out. We were at the hospital for hours, waiting to be seen and checked out. The doctors told me that I had a torn cornea and that I needed to see the eye doctor in the morning. They patched up my eye and sent me home with Tylenol three. I was in a lot of pain.

When my cousin took me home, it was around two thirty in the morning. That was Timothy's night to have PJ. My cousin called

Timothy. Well, actually it was Timothy's cousin Monica. She called Timothy and told him what happened and that Timothy could get PJ in the morning. But that didn't work for Timothy. It was about an hour after Monica left, having gotten me settled on the couch. I finally got to sleep, and there was a knock on the door. They said they were the police. I couldn't tell; my eyes were so bad. One eye was covered and the other one, the good one, was almost closed. I answered the door. I just couldn't believe it. It was the police, and they were here for PJ. Do you believe that? Why on earth would Timothy call the police to get PJ in the middle of the night? Only Timothy knows. And why would the police do that to a child?

When I answered the door, they told me that Timothy called and that he demanded for PJ to leave with the police. PJ was only five or six years old. That poor baby was woken up by a police officer. Thinking about it, it must have scared PJ half to death. The police picked PJ out of bed and carried him out to his dad. That just makes me so sick, thinking about what Timothy did to PJ that night. My job was to protect PJ, even if it was from his dad. I still, to this day, can't believe that the police actually did that. What did the police think, that I was lying about having been at the hospital? After they saw me and the hospital papers on the coffee table in plain sight? They took PJ out of my arms, just like they took me out of my mom's arms.

That's not the first time that Timothy called the police on me. PJ was the one that really got hurt. Every time I tried to drop PJ off at his dad's, PJ never wanted to go. PJ would be in my arms, crying and screaming that he wanted his mommy and he didn't want to go to his dad's. How could a father call the police like that, not caring about his son or what would happen to him? Timothy only cared about himself. Always had to be in control. Through PJ's whole life, Timothy always had to have the control. PJ's a grown man now, and Timothy still wants to have the control.

Right now as I'm writing this, my anger is through the roof. It's a 12. Do you believe that? I don't, and I'm living it. My anger is through the roof, and it's only a 12. God is so amazing. I've worked so, so hard for this. A day that my anger is through the roof, and it's not 437,787. It's climbing and only to a healthy 12. Amazing. Just amazing.

Just thinking about all this stuff about Timothy and PJ still makes my stomach turn. I always tried everything that I was capable of doing. At the time, I never thought it was enough. I should be doing something more. But through the help of Mark and Sheryl, they both helped me realize that I did an amazing work and that I did the very best of what I was capable of doing. There has just been so much—so much that has been forgotten, so many things that have been lost. But I'm slowly reclaiming every day what was taken from me. All the days that PJ was with his dad, I'm getting them back, just like Christmas. I'm so proud of him. I'm thankful that PJ is living a normal life. Sheryl keeps reminding me how my actions as a mom and my daily choices have made a difference. PJ sees and he's making his own choices in his life.

After all the horrible things that Timothy has done over the years, I shouldn't be surprised by what Timothy did at the hospital. Timothy called security and showed them our court papers, showing who got PJ on what days. They had to laugh. PJ was seventeen years old, almost an adult. His father pulls out court papers like PJ was still two years old. Of course I started arguing with Timothy over all this. PJ's my baby and he has gone through hell and back again; he just wants to go home with his mom. I told Timothy that PJ's been through enough, to leave him alone, and that PJ will call him later when he gets situated at my house. But Timothy would have no part of that, almost yelling at PJ about all this. Timothy just wouldn't drop it. And now since we took so long, I have Rich and the boys in PJ's room. Rich's all upset that he had to come upstairs; the little boys are bouncing around, and Timothy is talking to security who are trying to figure this all out.

PJ said, "Mom, I'm going back with Dad just to keep the peace." I agreed with PJ. What else could I do? My son had gone through enough, and this was just the very beginning of all the troubles with his eye. As hard as it was to leave PJ, I had to do what was best for my son—not to argue with his dad and let him go. We all did leave together—Rich, Timothy with all the discharge papers explaining everything. It was on a Saturday; the next day was Sunday, and we had to go to the doctor at his office that day. Saying goodbye to PJ was the hardest thing. I hadn't left his side since the accident happened, and now because of his dad, I had to leave my baby. The pain was out of the box. Just thinking about it now, my stomach is doing flip-flops. It makes sense now why I was overprotective of PJ. My dad told me he would kill my baby if I told anyone about the abuse. And since I started to get my memories back, well, what a mess.

We left PJ, and all day I just couldn't stop thinking about him. How was he doing? What was going on with him? It drove me nuts. I still had to be there for Robby and Joey; they needed their mom too. Rich was still upset. Not only did I have to deal with Timothy, but I also had to deal with Rich too. Rich was upset all the way home. Christmas was only a week away. I still didn't have the Christmas tree up or any of the decorations. That was one of the few Christmases ever that I didn't worry about how the tree looked. I didn't worry if the decorations on the tree were all in the right place or if the house was perfect with all the Christmas decorations up. It didn't matter, any of that. The only thing that mattered was that we still had PJ.

The next day was Sunday and PJ had a doctor's appointment. The office was closed of course; it was Sunday. But the doctor wanted to see PJ at least once a day to check his eye. I met Timothy and PJ at the doctor's office. I was so glad to see PJ. It was like I hadn't seen him for months. The doctor looked at PJ for a long time. Come to find out that PJ's eye was worse than they originally thought. That was bad enough, but we also found out the second injury was worse than the first injury. They couldn't do surgery on the second injury until the front of the eye was much better. If they did the surgery, there was a good chance he could lose his vision. If they didn't do the surgery, then he could lose his vision. Not a good situation.

We met with the doctor every day. At the hospital, when the doctor was doing his rounds, we would just meet somewhere and go off into a room and check his eye. Sometimes we had to see the doctor twice a day. For weeks we had to do that. Grandma would watch the boys for me when I took PJ to all the doctor visits. I was thankful Grandma was watching the boys for me, but at the same time, it was just a little while after I started getting my memories.

Christmas was hard, not really wanting to see my family. I was trying not to talk to them, trying to figure this all out. Now they were calling all the time, asking how PJ was doing. Then Grandma and my family kept asking how Sandy and her son were doing. I just couldn't get away from everything that was going on.

I remember driving down Jefferson that day after I left PJ's doctor. Everything had gotten worse—from really bad to really, really bad. I felt so helpless. As much as I loved and prayed for my son, it was all in God's hands. There was nothing left I could do except to pray. It was at least a forty five minute drive, so I had a lot of time to think about everything that had happened in the last couple of weeks. Thankfully, I was still seeing Mark and he was able to help me deal with all this. I was trying to help my girlfriend Sandy, but she still didn't want my help. She didn't even want me to call her. Sandy said it was just too painful. I never felt so empty; my insides were so stirred up. I felt so helpless, so alone, didn't know what to do or where to go, just alone. That was the earlier drive down Jefferson.

CHAPTER SIX

> I could say, "The darkness will hide me.
> Let the light around me turn into night."
> But even the darkness is not dark to you.
> The night is as light as the day;
> Darkness and light are the same to you.
> —Psalm 139:11

So back to driving down Jefferson after going to the attorneys, again feeling so helpless, so alone, so empty, no one cares, just complete emptiness. Little did I know that my life would change forever. This is the hardest part of writing, the part that I have dreaded more than everything. Writing about Mom, Dad, Mary, Grandma, Timothy, PJ, even the occult stuff, with all the body memories, all the anxiety, flashbacks, everything combined together, this is still the hardest part. I believe this is the heart and soul of this book. This is the reason for this book, everything that I believe in, the part that makes a difference. The part that takes courage, the part that believes in God more than I would ever know. The part that is for every single one of you reading this that my story will give you the courage to press forward when there seems nowhere to go, to give you the courage to love yourself when it seems like no one cares. The courage and strength to make a difference, to say no when no means no. The courage that you are your own person, that you can make a difference, that you have your own story to tell. But most of all, to see the courage and strength of that four-year-old little girl with so much pain back so long ago that her heart's desire was to, one day, make a difference so no one will be in so much pain like she was, like I was.

Here we go.

As I'm driving down Jefferson after leaving the attorneys that day, feeling like, "Okay, now what am I going to do? Everything's really crazy now. No one cares, no one's listening. What am I going to do?" When I pulled up in my driveway and got out of the van, I looked around at my house and yard. I felt so empty and helpless, not knowing what to do. I got in the house, looked around, and the next thing I know, my next-door neighbor came running over crying, saying, "I didn't know that it was that bad" over and over again. Saying, "I didn't know it was that bad. Why didn't you tell me?" I told her that yes, I did, plenty of times, but no one listened. Or no one cared. Or no one was strong enough to do or say something. Really what could they have done? It was my choice.

I'm sitting here at work, and now two days after I last wrote. I'm sitting here in bed still trying to write. Giving myself every excuse not to write. I see Sheryl today, so I really need to write. My heart's racing. I feel like I'm going to be sick. Here we, my parts, go again. I don't know who needs to come out or who's hurting. Or it's just me not wanting to write. Not writing is not helping me or you at this point.

It's like a bad tooth. You know it has to come out and most of the time it feels okay. You know it's there, so you're careful with it—not to eat or drink on that side of your mouth. And every time you eat or drink something and it hits that tooth, you go through the roof because it hurts so bad. You don't get it pulled because it doesn't hurt most of the time. You know it's there, but you don't do anything about it until, one day, when you just can't take the pain anymore. No matter how bad the pain is, when you get the tooth pulled, it's worse right now. You pull it and the next couple of days, the pain's bad, but it gets better and better. Now the tooth is finally out forever. The tooth will never hurt again. There will be an open spot in your mouth, a hole there so that you will remember what hap-pened, but there is never that horrible pain again. Sometimes if you hit the hole once in a while, you will remember how painful it was, but the pain you're feeling now is nowhere like the pain was all the time.

I guess that's how I'm feeling. The tooth is gone. And I just hit the empty hole. But I have to remind myself that it did hap-pen. And I'm just telling you my story.

My neighbor was crying, telling me that I have to call the detective's office because he was just here at the house, looking for my body, because they thought that Rich had killed me. Of course I said, "What are you talking about, my body?" I had just made a police report on Friday.

This is just too hard to write. I don't want to write about this anymore. This is just all too painful to write about. The strangest thing is that I have told my story lots of times to several different people. So I don't understand why writing this is so hard. Well, to be truthful, I do know why writing makes this so painful. Handwriting makes all your emotions come out. You can even tell in my handwriting when things are hard to write. My handwriting gets bigger. Sheryl says that's common with most people. I want to say normal for most people. When I tell people about my story, it's like telling them facts that I know. But writing makes everything so much more real, just like reading about the detective looking for my body because it was *that bad*. I was living it, yet I didn't know how bad it was.

Talking to Sheryl made me understand why I didn't know (or want to know) how bad things were. With me being DID, when things were bad, I would just switch so the person that was just in a horrible fight or whatever the case may be or the person fighting with Rich would go away because it was *that bad*, and another person would come out to protect the one that was fighting with Rich. Now remember, they were always Cindy. That little spirit that I had, my love for God, the four-year-old little girl that always helped me fight, always kept me Cindy. If not, I would have totally switched and become totally someone else.

This was such a blessing. How would I have had children, let alone take care of them, if I would have totally switched to another personality? And I wouldn't have survived through all this and been able to tell my story so you, as well as myself, can be healed and whole. So one day you can tell your story and give others strength and encouragement to press forward. So one day we all can be healed and whole so that, one day, we all can break this demonic cycle that so many of us have to face day to day. This demonic cycle that has destroyed so many families. Like my family, for example, a huge demonic dysfunctional family. Every single one of them.

I always wondered why I was so different, yet I was the one that had most of the abuse done to me. But you know why. You know about that little girl, a part of me who always wanted to make a difference, to help the pain for everyone. Since you're reading this, I believe that you have that spirit deep down inside of you too that also wants to make a difference, to be healed and whole. So again, I have to thank you for helping me, giving the strength and encouragement to keep writing so that, one day, all of us together can make a difference in all our lives.

When my neighbor was over my house that day, telling me about the detective coming over, at first I didn't believe her. Why would the detective care when nobody else cared? What made him so different? A perfect stranger just doing his job. Why would he care? This is his job; he does this every day. So why would he care?

Jeanette, my neighbor, told me that the detective went to all of my neighbors' houses, wanting to know when was the last time that they saw me. The detective knocked on their doors, asking and looking for me. Wow, for the first time, someone actually cared!

Then Jeanette told me that he was looking in the windows to my house, thinking that he would find my body on the floor. Now how on earth could this be that bad that this detective thought that

Rich had killed me? To me, that doesn't hap-pen in real life; that just hap-pens in the movies.

Well, for me, that's how I survived, believing that it couldn't be hap-pening to me, that it's hap-pening to someone else. And that's exactly what hap-pens in dissociation. It's too bad, it can't hap-pen to me. So let's make it someone else that the abuse is hap-pening to. So then it's the other person that the abuse is hap-pening to. It hap-pens over and over again. Well, it's only honorable to name the person that the abuse is hap-pening to. That person is doing such a wonderful job. It wouldn't be fair not to name that person. I still don't understand where the names come from. But that's how God planned it for us to survive abuse.

So I began to tell Jeanette a little bit of what was going on. Well, you see, I began to tell her.

And here I go again, two days later, still not wanting to write. I'm making every excuse in the world not to write. I told you that I knew that writing this part would definitely be that hardest part, which I still don't get; maybe I don't want to get it. I am so angry. I know it was for the best. But maybe one or more of my parts are mad at me for staying with Rich for such a long time. And maybe my parts are mad at me for telling the truth. I just don't know.

That last day that I saw Mark was like any other day. I got Rich and the boys off to work and school and went to Mark's office for my two-hour session. I began to tell Mark how Rich raped me all weekend long—Friday night, Saturday, and Sunday. I was telling Mark what hap-pened. That in the middle of the night, I was sleeping in bed. It was one of the few times that I slept in the bed. Going through counseling with Mark, I wasn't sleeping in bed. I was sleeping on the love seat. It was safe. That is typical for someone that was sexually abused because the bed was never safe. I don't remember what Rich was doing or why I went to bed, but in the middle of the night, I woke up to find Rich's fingers between my legs. His fingers were trying to go inside of me.

When I woke up, I was freaking out. I don't know what other words to use besides *freaking out*. I begged him to stop. The more I begged, the more violent he got. I was begging and pleading with him to please stop, to please let me get my head together, please let me try to focus. But the more I fought with him, the more violent he got. I remember fighting and struggling with him, begging him to stop. But he was just too strong for me. This must have lasted a good ten minutes. It felt like forever. Rich just kept on saying, "I'm your husband, I'm your husband."

Yes, what a wonderful husband. How could he do this to his wife? How could any man do that to his wife? A wife, a man's precious queen. I guess, in my case, that wasn't the case. How can someone who is supposed to love you do something like that? Thank God I will never know.

Again, I begged and pleaded with him, saying "Okay, okay, just please let me get my head together, let me get a grip on myself." Finally, I was able to jump out of bed. Then he assured me it was over. But as soon as I get back into bed, thinking that he would leave me alone, he attacked me again. As much as I fought with him, he was so much stronger than me. The only thing left to do was to just lie there. As awful as it was, I did what I did when I was little. I picked a spot on the wall and focused on it, trying not to think of anything else. Trying to let my body go numb and pray that he would get done as soon as possible. Rich was getting madder and madder that I was just lying there, not moving, just stiff as a board.

Rich just didn't get it or care to get it. Rich just wanted one thing and one thing only. He didn't care how much I was hurting or how much it was affecting me. The worst part was Rich really saw how bad my parents affected me. Rich saw the aftermath of what these people did to me. But he just didn't care. Abuse was still hap-pening; I was still getting raped. The only thing that changed was the person who was doing it to me.

That was just the beginning of the dreadful weekend. All day Saturday and Sunday, it was the same thing. Rich was trying all weekend to have sex. As much as I begged him, Rich just didn't stop. Saturday night, it was the same thing, waking me up in the middle of the night. Then Sunday, he was mad about Saturday night. On a late

Sunday afternoon, Rich got me on the floor in the living room. Rich got on top of me in a straddle position right in front of the boys. He was trying to rape me. He left bruises on my arms and hickey marks on my breasts. The worst part of the whole thing was that the boys were little, six and seven.

Robby started hitting his dad, telling him, "Please let Mommy go, please let Mommy go." That didn't even stop him. Right in front of his own children that he would do something like that. Then Sunday night, it was the same thing, but I didn't have the strength to fight him anymore. I just lay there—no feelings, no emotions, just lying there. Waiting for it to be all over. At that point, it didn't matter anymore. That Monday morning, the next day, same old routine. Got the boys off to school, then Rich off to work, like nothing was wrong. Another typical day at the Purser household. After everybody left, at 9:00 a.m. was my appointment with Mark. I was feeling so empty that it didn't matter anymore. I didn't know what to do. It just didn't matter. My life didn't matter.

When I got to Mark's, I told him how my week and weekend went. When I told Mark that Rich raped me, Mark said, "What? Did I hear you right? Did you just tell me that Richard raped you?"

It's funny (well, it's not). I just casually told Mark that Rich raped me like it was no big deal. I've been raped for so long and by so many people, at least this time it was my husband. And that's so sick. That Rich was my husband. That he knew everything that had hap-pened to me. Everything. Rich was no better than they were. Even worse. Rich knew exactly what the aftermath of abuse was. He had lived it and seen it.

Mark couldn't believe that I actually used the word *rape*. That was one word that I couldn't hear let alone speak. Now I'm telling Mark that Rich raped me. Mark and I went into detail of the weekend, everything that hap-pened. Mark told me that I had to make a police report that Richard broke the law (again) and things finally had to stop.

I had already worked three years in counseling with Mark. The stronger and more healed that I got, the more Rich lost control over me. And the madder Rich got. Rich finally quit hitting me after he went to jail for the last time he had hit me. Rich was in for thirty days for hitting me and breaking my nose. So he stopped hitting me. Now he started. Well, when he wanted sex, he always got it. You never wanted to make Rich mad. The more I healed and the stronger I got, I realized that no meant no. It doesn't matter, husband or not, no means no!

So I'm sitting there with Mark. He's really strongly encouraging me to go down to the police station and make a report of what hap-pened over the weekend. At that point, I was so out of it that it just didn't matter. After my two-hour session with Mark, I went home like usual. Nothing had changed. It was Monday, so I had to teach catechism. Just going through the motions, like nothing ever hap-pened. As dreadful as everything was, it all hap-pened.

Just thinking of the Friday-night rape, trying to decide if I ever tried to deny that I was raped before that night with Rich, made it all so real. If it never hap-pened before, then why did I freak out so badly? Nothing made sense unless it hap-pened.

That Monday I was numb; that whole week I was numb. I don't remember that week. It was like that week never hap-pened. I don't remember anything about that week. But that Friday, that Friday I will never forget. I don't remember how I got to Mark's, but I saw him at his office later in the afternoon. Lynn was there, an intern that Mark was training. PJ was also there. I don't remember if we drove there together or separately. I just don't remember. I even just called PJ to ask him, but he doesn't remember either. I guess that part isn't that important. Yes, it is important. Everything matters. *It hap-pened.*

Anyways, we were there for three hours. Mark and Lynn were doing everything in their power to convince me that I had to call the police. I'm very stubborn and bullheaded, not wanting to listen very well. I knew I had to do something. Both me and the boys couldn't live like that anymore. It got to the point that PJ didn't even want to come over the house. Our friends didn't want to come over; it was that bad. They didn't want to deal with Rich's mood swings. Rich was drinking more. Rich was in the garage more, doing his own thing.

The boys and I did our own thing. And at some point, Rich and I met in the middle.

Mark suggested telling PJ what hap-pened that weekend. It was so hard to tell PJ, but Mark kept assuring me that this was all in God's hands, that PJ would be able to handle it. Of course Mark was right. PJ wasn't happy about what hap-pened, and his anger was through the roof, but PJ was okay. He even tried to talk me into going to the police department.

After going around and around, they convinced me to go to the police department. It was late at the time and Rich wasn't home from work yet, but he would be soon. PJ followed me to the fire department; that's where our sheriff's department was. Our small township didn't have a police department. We had sheriffs. We got there and I told him that I had to make a report. At that time, that was the hardest thing ever.

When I began to tell the officer in detail everything that Rich did, he acted like it was no big deal or he didn't really believe me because it took me a week to make the report and there was no doctor's report. I told him, "What is a doctor's report going to do? He is my husband, what were they going to say?" I told the officer how violent Rich had been. Just within the last month, he had slammed the bedroom door on me, which tore up my big toenail. To the officer, that was a big deal and they could have arrested him for that. But this? As painful and embarrassing this was, the officer thought it was no big deal.

It took everything I had to make the report. It was getting late and Rich started calling, wondering where the boys and I were. Rich started calling more and more. I told the officer to please do something, that if I go home Rich was going to kill me. I was that scared of Rich. He was such a ticking time bomb waiting to go off.

The only thing the officer said when I told him how Rich had been was "Then just don't go home." I couldn't believe it. Three hours with Mark, Lynn, and PJ talking to me, trying to give me the strength to do this. That once and for all, no means no. But as was the story of my life, no one would listen.

PJ and I left the sheriff's department. I was thinking to myself, *What a waste of time.* I did everything possible; as hard and degrading as that was, I did it. There was nothing else to do.

I picked the boys up at the neighbor's house. I couldn't go home. We went to our cousin's house. Since the boys were little, they didn't understand what was going on, but they loved going to our cousin's house, so the boys were okay with going there.

When I called my cousin and told her what was going on, Kathy was more than understanding. Kathy was glad that I did make the report. Kathy and Will live about forty-five minutes away, so I had a lot of time to think about that day. I didn't know what to do anymore. There seemed like there was no way out.

When we got to Kathy's, she made us dinner or I think we went out for dinner. We all had a nice evening. But deep down inside, I kept thinking about what the officer said. I didn't know what to do. Now I'm scared to go home to my own home with my boys. And I still didn't do nothing wrong. The only thing that I did wrong was try to make a family with Rich.

Saturday morning, we woke up and hung out with Kathy. It was getting late Saturday afternoon and I decided that we better go home. We had to go home sometime. Kathy wanted us to stay with her, but we needed to go home.

Whatever was going to hap-pen when we get home was going to hap-pen.

When we got home, Rich had been drinking. I tried to talk to him, but there was no talking to him. Rich was in his own little world. I didn't know where to go, so I went over to my other friend Kim's house to talk to her. At the time that was Robby's best friend's mom.

She was abused by her ex-husband, and she had been telling me for a long time that Rich would never change. I always believe that Rich was capable of changing and he was capable of change. But it's Rich's choice if he truly wanted to change.

The boys and I stayed there for the night. In the morning we went home. What else was there to do? Nothing.

Rich didn't say much. He didn't even ask or care where the boys and I had been. So Rich and the boys and I all went to church together as a family.

Every week we always sat in the same spot, and Rich and I and the boys sat in the same places. But today was different. I sat at the end so I could look at Rich and the boys. I cried through the whole service, asking and pleading with God to take it. "Please, there's nothing more I can do. God, it's all in your hands. God, please do something. Me and the boys cannot take it anymore."

I just prayed through the whole service. There was nothing more that I could do except to pray.

Sheryl reminded me about a month ago that when people say, "All I can do is pray," what more can anyone do? God, he's God, he can do anything and it's all in his timing. I'm so glad that God doesn't listen to me about how to fix things, that God's timing, of course, is the best.

So I just prayed over and over. And this time, when I gave it to God, I left it in his hands. I love to play Indian giver and take it back all the time. So that day in church, it was all in God's hands. Whatever hap-pens. Whatever. The whole situation, however the outcome, everything was in God's hands.

When we came home from church, I tried to talk to Rich and tell him how unhappy I was and things had to change and that the whole family couldn't keep going on like this. Something had to change.

But Rich wouldn't listen. Why would he want things to change? He had a beautiful wife to cook and clean. I did all the bills, plus taking care of the business side of the tool truck business. The boys were taken care of. And he could have sex whenever he wanted. Why would he want things to change? Rich had it all.

I told him that I wanted a divorce if things didn't change. They had to change. Things were just that bad. Rich wouldn't listen to me. Rich said, "Are you done bitching? I have things to do." I told him yes, I was done, and he made his choice.

So all this I told to Jeanette on that day in November. Jeanette couldn't believe it. She was still crying for me. She was hoping that she could have done something. I told her there was nothing anyone could do. Jeanette handed me the card of Sergeant Timothy McFadden. That man changed my life forever. Jeanette even dialed his number for me because she felt that it was that important.

One day, I hope that he will know how he much such a difference for me. And maybe you will have your own Sergeant McFadden to help you.

When Sergeant McFadden answered the phone and I told him who I was, in one breath he was glad that I was alive and in the other breath he wanted to know why I didn't call him over the weekend. He had left messages on my cell phone.

Well, Sergeant McFadden had to take my report on Rich. I told him that I would be at home for the next two hours, then I had to leave and teach catechism at the boys' school. But Sergeant McFadden said that he just got back to the jail from my house and that I had to meet him there. I told him, "Sorry, I'm not going to the jail. I have been there way too many times because of Rich and I'm not going back to the jail." Believe it or not, Sergeant McFadden said okay and to please do not leave, that he would be back to my house as soon as he could be. McFadden said that since he was coming back, "Promise not to leave." I agreed. After we hung up, I was amazed that he actually listened to me. I believed that he actually believed me. For the first time, they believed me.

Jeanette insisted that she stay with me until Sergeant McFadden got there. Jeanette was still crying, not believing that things were that bad. In her own case, her husband was very abusive, calling her names and hitting her as well. Jeanette had her own stuff to deal with.

We were still talking about everything when Sergeant McFadden and the detective arrived. I had such a bad attitude at this point about the police. We sat down at the kitchen table, and McFadden knew all about us. He knew what kind of car Rich had, my car, way too much information; it was kinda eerie. I kept asking him, "How do you know this?" or "How did you know that?" He just told me that it was his job to know.

Then he wanted to know the details of the weekend when Rich hurt me. I went step-by-step in detail of what had hap-pened. Jeanette asked if it was okay to stay. I didn't care, it hap-pened. I had nothing to hide. As we were going through the details of everything that happened, he asked about the boys, if I ever thought that Rich may have done something to the boys. At that point, anything was possible. There were times when the boys were playing the nasties, so they learned it from somewhere. Their friends, we thought; I never thought Rich. But again, if Rich could do this to me, Rich was capable of doing anything. When I explained that to McFadden, he put his pen down and said, "Enough is enough. You're done with all this abuse, just done."

Then he said that I was the typical poster wife for being abused. I just couldn't believe it. I fought so hard not to be the typical abused wife. Even you know how hard I tried not to be like everyone else. Now here I am, the irony doesn't make sense. When Sergeant McFadden said poster wife, something in me just snapped. I had to make a difference. I just had to. I didn't know it back then, but that four-year-old wanted to make a difference. She must have come out with both guns, ready to fight. There was a drive inside of me not to be that poster wife. I was a poster child for so many years when I was a child; now thirty years later, I'm back here again. Or sadly never left.

So today I had to make a difference; for all of those years in pain, today was the day, the day of the beginning to finally, once and for all, *stop* the abuse.

Sergeant McFadden gave me two options. One, pack a bag for me and the boys for one week and not tell anybody, no one, where we are. The only phone call I can answer is from Sergeant McFadden. Or two, he would send a cop car out and me and the boys would go into police custody until McFadden said otherwise.

Of course I started arguing with him because I had to leave in a few hours to go teach. That week was Thanksgiving and Thanksgiving

Day was Robby's birthday. So this week, we were busy. Not a good time.

Of course, he wouldn't have that. Again, he stated my two choices. There wasn't a third or fourth choice. Either A or B. Well, I chose A. I would pack our bags for a week. McFadden was going to bring a cop car to make sure I left. Jeanette promised him that she would stay with me and help me pack a bag. Jeanette even asked McFadden if she could run home, and he would watch me because she had a couple of really big duffel bags that she was going to let me borrow. When she left, McFadden assured me that I was doing the right thing and enough was enough.

When Jeanette came back with the duffel bags, Sergeant McFadden left. Again, he reminded me that I answer the phone to no one except him. To call his cell phone directly, no one else. I gave him the address and phone number of where we were going to stay. Her house was red flagged. If her phone number called 911, they would know it's an emergency and would come out right away. They wouldn't even have to explain. It was the same way for the boys' school and our house.

Looking back, I guess it was that bad. After I had all our things packed, I looked around the house, thinking of everything that had hap-pened in that house—from beatings to being raped. All the memories going through counseling. I have worked so hard to get to this point. As I was ready to walk out the door, I stood in the doorway for at least five minutes. It felt like forever. I knew that when I walked through the door and locked it that my life would never be the same again. Whatever the outcome was, it would never be the same again. It took everything I had to walk through that doorway and lock the door. The fear of the unknown. How am I going to do this? What's going to hap-pen to the boys? What's going to hap-pen to the business? But most of all, what's going to hap-pen to me?

As I walked through the door with all the questions running through my head, I knew one thing: things were going to change forever. For good or bad. From this day forward, things were going to change. My life, as I knew it, was going to change. My life will never ever be the same again.

So with every bit of strength I had, I walked through that door, knowing that everything was in God's hands and whatever hap-pened, it's all in God's hands. I went through that door, closed it behind me, and never looked back.

When I got to the school to pick up the boys, they didn't understand what was going on. I taught Joey's catechism class and I wasn't there, so Joey didn't know where I was. No one did. But God took care of everything. The boys were fine. We ended up staying at my girlfriend Sally's house, the one that took me to the hospital with PJ.

Sally knew things were bad. Of course, I couldn't go into detail of what hap-pened, but she said we could spend the night there because the boys had school in the morning instead of going to my cousin's house forty-five minutes away. We just spent the night there. The boys didn't question too much. They knew things were bad from the weekend.

That Tuesday, after we got the boys to sleep, Kathy and I talked for a long time. Things were starting to set in. What did I do? What is going to hap-pen? Rich could go to jail for ten years because of all this. Of course I started feeling guilty. Of course I didn't do anything wrong. Actually, I did everything right for the boys and for me. If we stayed, someone was going to get hurt.

Sergeant McFadden called me to let me know that he wanted the boys to be interviewed at Care House. It's literally a big house where kids can get interviewed in a childlike atmosphere to see if they have experienced sexual abuse. Sergeant McFadden wanted to see if my boys had been touched in a sexual way by their father.

Care House has a room with video cameras where the detectives can watch the interview for themselves. That was the worst part, knowing that Rich might have touched the boys sexually. It was my job to protect the boys; now something like this could have hap-pened. It was bad enough it was hap-pening to me. But not my boys. Please not my boys.

I needed someone to go with me. One to watch one boy while the other one was being interviewed. I didn't want my family there. Will and Kathy had to work. So my boss Mick met me up there to help watch the boys.

Robby was so upset that he wouldn't even get out of the car. Mick had to sit in the car with him. When I took Joey in, there were so many mixed emotions, as you can imagine. I was bouncing all over the place. I was hoping with my whole heart that Rich never touched the boys. And that no one else did.

They were nice at Care House, very child friendly. I could go with Joey until a certain point, then they made me leave the interview room. Sergeant McFadden was there to watch the interview. After the interview, they believed that Rich didn't touch Joey. But it was strange that Robby never got out of the car. He never agreed to be interviewed.

After that, we had a meeting in the conference room. Sergeant McFadden, Detective Rolluo, child protective services, the people at Care House, everyone was there. Sergeant McFadden said that they did pick up Rich that day. It took them three days because they wanted to wait until they had a special unit available in case he resisted. They did arrest him and he was in jail. Sergeant McFadden also told me that he himself interviewed Rich and that McFadden did believe me and that he believed that Rich was guilty. But at this point, it was up to me if I was going to press charges or not.

They could hold Rich for when he got me on the floor of the living room for assault charges in front of the boys. But I had to be the one willing to go through with all the sexual charges. They wanted to charge him with three counts of criminal sexual conduct (CSC) in the first degree and also the assault charges. But if I wasn't willing to go through all that and press forward, their hands were tied. It was all my choice. Whatever choice I made, Sergeant McFadden was there for me and believed me.

We got talking about everything that had hap-pened. That thirty years ago, I was a victim, trying to figure out what to do, and now I was still a victim. Everyone else made choices for me before. Now it's my choice to have a say and stop the abuse. The fear of Rich was so bad. I was scared to make the choice. But I kept hearing McFadden say, "You're the typical poster wife." That bugged me more than anything. I tried my whole life not to be the typical poster wife or poster child, but here I am, no question about it. And if I truly wanted all this to stop, today was the day to finally make a difference.

As hard as it was, the fear, the unknown, I told Sergeant McFadden to go ahead and to press charges. I would do whatever it takes to make a difference.

Child protective services told me that my job and only job was to protect my boys whatever it takes. And if they found out that I wasn't protecting them, they were going to take the boys away from me. I agreed to everything. Little did I know what I was getting myself into. If I would have known, maybe, just maybe, I would have made a different decision. I thank God that I didn't know what I was getting myself into. But I thank God that I did it so you can read my story, but most of all, me and my boys are safe and are still trying to heal from all this.

That night when we left Care House, as you can imagine, my emotions were all over the place. For as many times that Rich hit me, called me dirty names, destroyed my stuff, and, most of all, raped me and yelled at my children, all three of them, on the way back from Care House to Kathy's house, we had to pass the jail. Again, my emotions were all over the place. I finally made a difference and the abuse would finally stop.

I called Kathy to let her know what hap-pened and let her know that we were okay. The next morning was Thanksgiving and Robby's eighth birthday. Kathy's family were at her house, helping get things ready for Thanksgiving Day dinner, plus a small birthday party for Robby. I was glad that people were over, trying to help me get my mind off everything.

That night was hard with everything that had hap-pened that week, actually the last two weeks. My life was upside down. But on the other hand, I was starting to heal from all this. That night, I think I hardly slept. That morning was Robby's birthday, one that he would always remember. The boys were starting to miss their dad and were kinda confused about what was going on. It had been a whole week, and they had been home only Sunday night. They were ready to go home. But I wasn't. That was the last place that I wanted to be. I didn't have any presents for Robby, so that afternoon, I went shopping for a cake and presents. It wasn't much. I kinda just walked around the store like a robot.

On Thanksgiving morning, Sergeant McFadden called me. He was so excited. He began to tell me that I was worth over half a million dollars and that, on Thanksgiving morning, they actually called a judge in to arraign Rich. That's unheard of, calling a judge in on a holiday. But McFadden pushed that "it was that important to protect you." McFadden wanted to be sure that Rich couldn't get out of jail for no reason at all.

So on Thanksgiving morning, Rich was set a $500,000 cash surety for three counts of CSC in the first degree and a second bond for $25,000 cash surety for the assault charge in front of the boys. Cash surety means that you have to pay the court the full amount, not just 10 percent. Someone would have to pay $525,000 for Rich to get out of jail. It was amazing that this was hap-pening to me. It was that bad. Murderer's bonds are not even set that high. McFadden wanted to make sure that Rich wouldn't hurt me anymore. I forgot that when McFadden was over my house and I was going back and forth about what I was going to do, McFadden looked at me and said, "Do you want to see the pictures of your face the last time he hit you?" Of course I told him no.

McFadden was so happy and asked me, "How do you feel being worth over half a million dollars?" I felt so empowered. Sergeant McFadden wished Robby a happy birthday and my family a happy Thanksgiving. And he said not to worry about anything as Rich was going to be in jail for a very long time. The boys and I were going to be safe.

After I hung up with McFadden, I told Will and Kathy what had hap-pened. They were both so pleased for the outcome. But on the other hand, we were just at their house two weeks ago as a happy family. My cousin Will and Kathy both liked Rich a lot. When Rich's nice, he's the sweetest guy in the world. But when he's the mean Rich, watch out. No one wants to be in his way. Both of them felt a little sorry for him. Just a week ago, our plans were to all be here as a family.

That morning, Jeanette called me to wish us a happy Thanksgiving and to check on us to see how we were doing. I let her know what was going on. She let me know that she's keeping an eye on the house for me.

During Thanksgiving dinner, I tried not to cry. I was trying to hold it together for the boys. After dinner, we had cake and ice cream, and Robby opened up his presents. For the most part, the boys had a good day. Robby was upset he didn't have much of a birthday. And Joey was upset because he was so worried about what his dad was going to eat for Thanksgiving dinner.

I just couldn't wait for the day to be over. I was so excited that the abuse was going to stop. But on the other hand, I missed him. After all, he was still my husband.

The next day, Jeanette called me to let me know that we lost power at the house. I had a sump pump, and I had to get home to check to see if my basement was flooding. After that long drive home, not wanting to go back to the house, sure enough I came home to a flooded basement. It wasn't that bad, but bad enough to make a mess.

So here I am in the basement, no power, trying to clean up the mess. I asked God what else could go wrong. After I got all that cleaned up and got more of our things, I walked around the house, going from room to room, remembering all the bad memories of the house. I couldn't wait to leave to get back to the boys.

It felt like I would never get back to Kathy's house. I was so tired. I didn't sleep, and I was so worried about the boys. I kept going over and over, "What are the boys going to do?"

Finally, I got back to the house where we spent the rest of the weekend.

When Sergeant McFadden said it was okay to go back to the house and the boys back to school, we packed up our things with so many mixed emotions. As much as I wanted to go back home was as much as I didn't.

Now I had to explain to the boys where Dad was and that they wouldn't see him for a very long time. That was the hardest part to explain to them and that, for our safety, we couldn't be with Dad anymore. Especially Joey. Joey was definitely daddy's boy. Joey was Rich's little shadow. Joey was always doing things with his dad. Robby not so much, Robby was more like me. Robby always did things with me.

That day when we got home, I was ready for bed. I think it was only maybe two or three o'clock in the afternoon. I don't remember for sure. I couldn't even function. I kept asking myself, "What am I going to do? What am I going to do? I have my job, plus the business. What am I going to do?"

That night, I remember sitting on the floor with the boys, Robby on my right and Joey on my left. The house was so empty. I was so empty. A part of me was gone. A part of me that believed Rich loved me. A part of me that wanted to have good Rich around forever. But the biggest part of me knew that the bad Rich, the one that hurt his family so terribly bad, could never come back. I thought that night would never end. Never. It was even harder on the boys. I think we went to bed around seven o'clock in the evening, with Robby on one side of me and Joey on the other. And sometimes Marshmallow, the cat, sleeping between me and Joey.

The next couple of weeks were crazy. Yes, I said crazy and you know how much I don't like using that word. But in this case, it's the only word that fits. I had to drive the boys to school instead of having them take the bus and let the school know what was going on. Like I mentioned before, the boys' school was red flagged for 911 calls. Police would be there as soon as possible if there was call. There was even a letter from the sheriff's department, telling them of the severity of the situation. The office was very supportive of what was going on. They had no idea that things were bad at the house. They all said that if I needed anything, to let them know, reassuring me that the boys' teachers would keep an extra eye on them.

After I got the boys off to school, I came home thinking to myself, *Now what? What am I going to do now?* That next week, I was in contact with Sergeant McFadden a lot. I had to meet with the prosecutor. Kathy went with me that day. Again, we were in a large conference room. The prosecutor was a younger woman, very nice. When we were all in the conference room, I had to go over what hap-pened that weekend in detail. Every detail. How degrading that I had to tell her exactly every detail and relive all those feelings and emotions all over again. It was very painful. But she was so under-standing. She wasn't sure if she was going to bring my past into this or not. She didn't know if it would be painful for me or if it would hurt the case. One way or another, she did choose to bring up my past in order to show that someone being raped is a horrible, horrible thing. Someone that has a past of being abused and then raped again just made everything a million times worse.

After she made her decision of using my past, she was think-ing that I was strong enough to bring up my past. So was Sergeant McFadden. About a half hour later, we went into a small courtroom. I had to get on the stand and testify in closed court. It was just the judge, the prosecutor, McFadden, and the detective. I don't think that they let Kathy in the courtroom. Before we went in, Sergeant McFadden reassured me that everything was going to be okay. When I'm testifying, he said to keep my eyes on him and that when I started to get nervous, or whatever the case, maybe I could just focus on him.

At first they explained the case to the judge, going into detail of what had hap-pened. Then they wanted me to get on the stand. I was extremely nervous. I hated talking in front of anybody, let alone in front of this judge, not to mention what we were talking about.

Both the prosecutor and McFadden questioned me. It was awful telling and reliving all the detail. We were in criminal court because this was a felony because of the CSC charges. If the judge decided to proceed with this, we would go to a jury trial. Then we still had the other charges of assault over in the civil court. What a mess!

After they both got done, I forgot what it's called, asking me questions, then the judge was asking me questions. I felt like I was the person getting charged. I didn't do anything wrong but try to get this madness to *stop*. And I felt like I was the one on trial. Going through all this, that's exactly the case. I was the one that was going to be sent through the ringer and then some.

But the best part of it was I would do it all again in a heartbeat. Then the judge came back with what he was going to charge Rich with. He could have thrown it out of court if (*a*) he didn't believe me or (*b*) there wasn't enough evidence. At this point, everyone is basing this all on what I'm telling them. Before when we went to court, the bruises on my face and body were evidence enough. But rape charges, without a doctor's report from the hospital, and especially by a husband, it's not heard of. Well, I believe that far too many husbands rape their wives all the time. Over and over again. Just no one ever reports it.

That's why I'm telling you my story. If you're ever in a situation that your husband, boyfriend, whatever, and you say no, no does get to mean *no*!

It felt like we were in the courtroom all day. When the judge left to go over all the information that was given to him, we had to wait and see what he was going to do. At that point, I didn't know what I wanted. I just wanted Rich to leave me alone.

When the judge came back, boy, did I have butterflies in my stomach. I really had no idea what the judge was going to say. Bottom line: did he believe me? The judge read out loud every CSC charge McFadden was charging Rich with—three CSC charges in the first degree. The judge read each event and each charge. For Friday night, CSC in the first degree. For Saturday, CSC in the first degree. For Saturday again, CSC in the first degree. And Sunday night, because I didn't fight with him, I just lay there, the judge charged him with CSC in the second degree. The judge believed me. Now the fun really begins. The nightmare hadn't even started yet.

It took a while for the civil charges. Things were just going crazy.

It looked like Rich was going to be in jail for a very long time. Rich was going to be in jail through both cases. The CSC charges alone were going to take months. And we also had the assault charge. Rich was facing ten years in jail. So I had to make a decision. What was I going to do? I had the business to run, but I also had my job. I couldn't do both, so I had to quit my job with Mick. I loved my job. And overnight, I had to quit. No fun at all.

Then the tool truck. I knew nothing about tools. Nothing. But I had to do something. I just couldn't let the business fall apart. I had too much invested in it to let it fail. And at the point, I was the only source of income for the family. I had to pay the bills.

Our business was a mobile tool tuck, just like Snap-on tools. Rich and I were tired of working for someone else, so we had started our own business. We were a franchise for Cornwell Tools; they started the mobile tool business. Rich and I had to incorporate to start our business and purchase a tool truck. We had a territory where we saw people on a regular basis, like Jerry. Anyway, after Rich was gone, either I had let the business fall apart or try myself to make it work.

Scott, our district manager for Cornwell, was wonderful. We became best friends. Scott and his wife Camie and their kids all hung out together outside of work. There were always functions to go to. And a lot of times it was for families. The four of us got along great. So when Rich was gone, Scott was more than willing to help me on the truck. I knew all the business end of it, but the sales part, dealing with the actual tools, I had no clue.

With Scott, I set up plans to go out that first day. My nerves were shot. Being in the tool truck was a constant reminder of Rich. He was on the truck for eight to ten hours a day. That's what he did, the sales. I had no clue.

When Scott came over for us to leave to start going to each of our stops, I wanted Scott to drive the truck. It looks like a potato chip truck, twenty-eight feet or so, a big truck. Anyways, I did start the truck from time to time and I did move it, maybe fifty feet or so. But that was it, never off my street, let alone on a main street. But

Scott wouldn't drive the truck. Scott assured me that if I was going to do this, I had to do all this. That meant driving the truck from day one.

When Scott and I went to start the truck, we had problems starting it. I guess right before they arrested Rich, he was talking to other tool dealers, and they all thought the truck had blown a head gasket, which meant it was a huge job and would cost a lot to get it done. I said, "Great, this is all I need. What else can go wrong?" I should never have asked that.

Scott went over our computer software. We had a laptop on the truck that had all our customers' information on it and the inventory of all the tools on the truck. The whole business was on the laptop; I had never even turned it on. Rich would print out all the info I needed for all of the paperwork. Then I had to get up enough nerve to get behind the wheel, let alone back up. It's a box truck, so you can't see anything behind you. So how in the heck was I going to back up? Scott said you put the truck in reverse, and if you hear a boom, you stop. Ha, ha, ha! Fair enough. So as hard as it was, I put the truck in reverse and headed for our first stop.

Now that brings us to our next biggest issue. What do I tell the customers about Rich? One day, Rich was on the truck. Two weeks later, without warning, here I am on the truck. What do I tell them? I have to tell them something. That was the hardest part. I couldn't tell them the truth. That's just wrong. Do I tell them that Rich went to jail? I just didn't know. Nothing I choose would be the right choice. It was just a mess all the way around.

So here I am, driving this truck that I had never driven before, trying to deal with my customers that I had no idea who they were or, for the matter, they didn't know who I was, trying to run over a quarter of a million-dollar business and I have no clue what I'm doing.

Normally when Scott trains people, they go very slow—a few customers at a time, not 250-plus all at once. Here I have a whole truck full of tools that I had no idea what they are for, sockets for example. I didn't know there were metric or standard, six point or twelve point, quarter inch, three eights and half inch drive. I owned the truck for two years and didn't know that one side of the truck was standard and the other side was metric.

That tool truck, I think, was the worst part. I hated that tool truck when Rich was on the truck. Rich worked all the time. In the morning before he left, he prepped for the run; he was gone for nine or ten hours, came home, and worked some more. I hated the truck when Rich was on the truck and then especially when I was on the truck. I just hated it.

Like I was saying before they took Rich away, Rich and all the dealers thought we had a blown head gasket. Every day I had to check the oil and coolant level to make sure the levels were full because I didn't want to blow up the motor. That would have been very expensive.

Until writing this, I didn't realize how much I really hated that truck. Every time I got mad at the truck and I questioned God, "Why God? Why am I going through all this? Are you sure this is what I am supposed to do?" I would remember how we got the truck

Rich and I were both in management, and I wanted to own my own business. I was practically running Mick's business from the paperwork end.

We thought about this a lot. What could we do? But I always went back to the tool truck idea. Rich got a hold of the district manager for Cornwell tools, Scott, to set up an appointment to meet with him about starting up a franchise.

We talked to Scott over the phone. He was really nice. When we met, we went over everything. It seemed perfect. Just what we both wanted. We both filled out the applications for the franchise. Rich and I both had bad credit from our first divorces, and we were worried about that. But everything seemed fine. A few days later, Scott let us know that we were preapproved if we wanted to become a franchise. He told us how much money we need so we could get a loan. Cornwell was wonderful. Everything was falling into place, except the finances.

By this time, Rich and I built up excellent credit. We both worked hard to build it up. So I tried to get a loan through our banks. But since both of our vehicles were paid off and we had no credit card debt, we had a hard time getting a loan. Seems they would rather loan money to people making payments on other debt than to a couple who paid off all their debts. We were not in debt, so that was a bad thing. Go figure.

Things were moving along. I was working with two banks. Both banks weren't offering the dollar amount that we needed, but I kept trying. Rich quit his job in preparation to begin the business. It was a Friday at three o'clock, we still didn't have the finances and Rich was coming home in two hours with his toolbox. So he was now out of a job. What was *I* going to do?

I was doing the dishes, and I looked at the picture of Jesus that I had on my window. I told God that *I* did everything that *I* could and that if this is his will for us to be in Cornwell, then please take *it* because *I* didn't know what to do anymore. "If this is your will for us to be in Cornwell, then let it be, or not, we'll have to figure something else out." So I gave it all to God.

About fifteen minutes later, a lady called from a bank and said that they were ready to set a date for the loan, but she needed a little more information. I said, "What? You need more information for a closing date for a loan?" I had no idea who she was.

I was working with two other banks. And now she wants to set a closing date? Boy, was that God. All I could think was that a few weeks ago I called other banks for their interest rate, that was all. Now they have all the stuff for a closing date? They were going to loan us more money than the other two banks combined. It still wasn't the dollar amount we needed, but it was so much better than what the other banks were offering. The lady on the phone let me know what she needed and asked if I would please fax over the information. Just fax it. With the other banks, I had to go down there and wait in line to meet with them just to give them the paperwork.

After I faxed the papers that she needed, I called Scott to tell him what hap-pened. We were both so excited that when you put something in God's hands and when it's his will, everything works out. Even when it doesn't seem like it's in God's hands, it is.

We weren't talking long when the other line beeped in. I told Scott that I would call him right back. It was the lady from the bank. She thanked me for faxing the papers so fast; it was everything she needed. We set the closing date and time, and then to my amazement, she told me how much the loan was for. You guessed it, what we needed to the penny.

Every time I hated the truck, everything that God allowed to hap-pen on that truck, it was still in God's hands. I yelled at God plenty of times, saying "Okay, this is in your hands, and you think I'm handling this?" Of course, it was all in God's hands.

So there I was, with the truck that I hated that God gave me. At night when it was cold and snowy, I had to plug in the block and plug in the batteries. I know it doesn't sound like much, but the extension cords were frozen. I had to unwind the cords, stretch them out, and plug them in, and in the morning, I had to use a screwdriver to unplug it, then wrap the cord back up. They were frozen and full of snow. It was not fun trying to wrap them up and put it back up on the hooks. I know it sounds silly, but trust me, it was a pain in the butt. And checking the oil and coolant, I had to climb up on the bumper to check to coolant. Again, in the snow, sliding on the bumper, trying to hold myself up, falling, slipping, sliding, trying to get the truck ready. I remember crying and crying and telling God, "Why, God, why? I didn't do anything wrong! Why am I having to go through all this? It's just not fair." I hated it, just hated it.

I had to order more tools two or three times a week. When they arrived, I had to carry the big boxes on to the truck from the garage. They were so heavy that I couldn't carry them on the truck, so I had to open up the boxes and take an armful back and forth from the garage to the truck. Then I had to check all the tools in. That's one thing that I had done for Rich before, so that part wasn't so bad. At least I knew some of the part numbers so that made it a little easier on me. But that was all, just a little easier.

I just remember how much I hated it day after day. I knew I should be thankful for the business, and I am. I had to pay the bills, but I still hate it with a passion. Now the customers, that was awful. Stop after stop, customer after customer. I had to explain something. Where was Rich? Good question. Over and over and over again. Where was Rich? What did I do with Rich?

I was very naive. I told them that Rich was detained, which could mean lots of things, but most of them thought that he was in jail for drunk driving. And most of them were okay with that. A lot of the mechanics drank, so they were okay with that. But I wasn't. He hurt me, and now I'm picking up all the pieces because of what Rich did to me. Here I have to explain to the customers something I don't want to talk about at all, wanting to tell them the truth of what he did to me and our family. But for the sake of myself and the business, I had to be professional about it. Now that I was running the truck, they had to see me week after week. I had to be a professional.

The first week was horrible, just horrible, trying to run a full business that I don't know enough about. I had printed out receipts for the customers, but I didn't know who they were. I just wanted to go home, but I also didn't want to do that. Then I would be going home to an empty house and take care of the boys who missed their daddy and wanted him home. So all day long, all I heard is Rich this and Rich that and daddy, daddy.

As much as I was mad at him, I missed my husband too, the little things, coffee in the morning, him setting the alarm clock. You figure I hadn't set the alarm clock in fourteen years. Silly things like that I missed. When I was freezing at night, when my feet were so cold, I would cuddle Rich tight and place my feet in between his legs and warm up my feet.

As for the business, if Rich had died, life would have been much easier. The next week, when Scott and I went out on the truck, my neighbor across the street called me to let me know that my minivan had been moved. She was confused because I had a rental car for the last week and a half, right when all this started.

The Friday night before, we had been at my cousin Kathy's house when my cousin Will backed into my van. So not only was I dealing with all this but I also had to deal with my van and the collision shop, which was also one of our customers as well as good friends from church. We used to go to their house as well as they were coming to our house. So since they were mostly Rich's friends, they also wondered what hap-pened to Rich.

On that Sunday in church, I cried through the whole service, asking God to please, please take care of this business, that I couldn't take it anymore and neither could the boys, all three of them. So the very next Sunday, when the boys and I went to church, God took care of everything.

Rich was out of the house. He was in jail with a very high bond. There was no way he could get out. I didn't think anybody had $525,000 to loan him. Added to that, the boys and I were safe. The boys were back home in their house, and as much as I hated the truck, I was still able to provide for the boys. So I could never question all this because it was all in God's hands. All of it. So every time I questioned it, I could remember that whatever God started, he will always finish. When someone told me that, I think that it was Sheryl, that when something's in God's hands and he starts something that God wouldn't get two-thirds of the way and say, "Okay, I'm done, you have to finish this yourself. You're doing a pretty good job," and leave you alone to figure it out yourself.

God's a good God. God's not going to start something and it's not all over with until God says it's all over—from the beginning to the end when it's in God's hands, no matter what the outcome is! Remember, that it is God's will; when it makes no sense no sense at all, trust me, I've lived it. When it's in God's hand, the biggest thing you have to do is trust him. Trust God like you have never trusted him before. When everything seems to be falling apart and you look at the situation and you say to yourself, "There's no way, absolutely no way, so how this can be God?" But you always have to have strength and courage, the courage that only God can give you. When everything seems wrong, nothing makes sense, but all this is in God's hands. I can honestly tell you that yes, it's all in God's plan—God's perfect plan. And when it's all over, you can thank God for being with you, holding your hand, wiping all the tears that you have shed, always with his hands, loving you unconditionally, just as you are, for just being you and not being the person that everyone wants you to be no matter what anyone says or tries to convince you differently. But when it's in God's hands and you believe with your whole heart and soul that things have to change, you and you alone with God can make all the difference in the world.

All you have to do is believe Philippians 4:13: "I can do all things through Christ which strengthens me." It doesn't say some things or most things or some times. It says all things. Nothing is ever too big for God. The biggest thing that got me through all this was there's not a testimony without a test. It was maybe a year or so before all this hap-pened, and I filed the rape charges that God put on my heart that I would one day be writing a book. This book that you are helping me write.

CHAPTER SEVEN

> I can do all things through Christ,
> because he gives me strength.
> But it was good that you helped
> me when I needed it.
> —Philippians 4:13–14

I REMEMBER, LIKE IT WAS YESTERDAY, going through the drive-through window at the bank. It was so clear, hearing from God. And of course I didn't want to believe it. I'm just this small girl from Detroit. What do I know? It didn't make any sense. What do I have to write? But God knew; God knew all along the choices that I would make. God knew when I was four and the desires of my heart way back then. When I was four, God knew I would be writing this and all the good and not so good choices that I've made that brought me here. God always knew my heart. Sometimes my head wasn't always in the best frame of mind. But my heart always was. God knew I was mad at him, and my parts were mad too. God knows all that. God's *god*!

You always have to try with everything. You have to press forward when you don't want to. When you want to climb under the covers and never want to come out, when the anxiety is 5,327,243,927 and you want to quit. When you're going second to second, just trying to survive, you have to believe that God's with you and will never leave you. *Never!*

When my neighbor called and told me that my minivan was moved, I was confused. I just brought the van home that day from the collision shop. How and why did my van move? Magic? I just didn't know. No one had the keys except Rich. And Rich was in jail, or supposed to be in jail. So how would it move?

If Rich did, for some reason, get bonded out, I was supposed to get a phone call to let me know that he would be getting released within twenty-four to forty-eight hours with a tether on so they could watch him to make sure that he didn't come around the house. If it was Rich that moved the van and he was out, why? How? I didn't get any phone calls.

I asked her over and over again, "Are you sure my van moved?" She said, "I know it did. That's why I'm calling you!" I hung up with her, told Scott what had hap-pened, and right away I called 911 to let them know that someone was at my house and moved my minivan. The officer on the phone could tell how upset I was. I explained how my husband was in jail and all the circumstances behind it. I told him to please get in contact with Sergeant McFadden right away. The officer on the phone began to tell me that Rich did get released. I said, "What? I wasn't notified." How could that be? Who could have given him that kind of money? It just didn't make sense.

I jumped in the tool truck to fly back home to see what was going on. On the way back to the house, Sergeant McFadden called me to tell me in detail what had hap-pened.

Last week, when I went in front of the judge and they formally charged Rich, Rich, at some point, knew that this time he was really in big trouble. Rich got an attorney—Mr. Ronald Goldstein, one of the biggest, meanest attorneys in the area.

After the court formally charged Rich, his attorney talked the court into lowering his bond to $100,000 cash surety and $25,000 case surety. Then the jail released him out on bond with the stipulation that Rich could not come to the house, see the kids, or have contact with me. He was to leave me alone.

After Rich got released, a peace officer brought him back to the house. That's right, they brought him to the house to get his clothes and some belongings. When Rich went into the house to get his things, he also took all the money in the house, around $2,000, and our safety deposit box where all our important papers were, along with the key to the box. Then left with his truck.

I just couldn't believe it. Rich was out of jail. Now what? What am I going to do? I'm not safe anymore and neither were the boys.

When I got into the house and checked everything, Rich's clothes were gone from the closet and the safety deposit box and key were gone. What else was gone? And yes, my husband! My husband was gone and my children's dad was gone. I was starting to lose everything, or so I thought. That same day, I picked up the boys from school. At this point, I had to be so careful when it came to the boys. I just didn't know what was going to hap-pen next. So much had hap-pened in these last few weeks.

The boys were still confused about all this. Daddy's truck was here for the last couple of weeks, now Daddy's truck is gone. So then I had to explain to the boys where Daddy was. Both of them wanted to see their dad, especially Joey. Joey so much loves his daddy. Joey was Daddy's little helper, always his daddy's shadow.

I was so mad at Rich, especially when the boys missed their dad. And they were crying and crying, wanting to see Rich. I would just hold them and tell them how much I loved them and how special they were. At night, Joey would cry and cry, wanting his daddy. Robby too, except he would get angrier about everything. Robby was my little adult that always took care of everything.

At night it was the worse. I did what was right. And here I am, having to take care of everything.

When I picked up the boys from school, I went into the office to let them know that Rich got bonded out and to please don't let the boys go with their dad or anyone else except for me. They had the letter from the sheriff's office, but the office said they needed something more. I don't remember just what all they wanted.

I drove the boys to school in the morning to make sure that they got into the school okay. After that, I was talking to Scott, my district manager. And he suggested I go to the bank and switch the bank accounts just to be safe.

Well, I called the bank manager and let him know what was going on just to give him the heads-up and to try to get things ready for me. I knew him pretty well through where I used to work because that's where they did their banking. It was convenient for me to bank there as well. When I got to the bank, the manager told me to have a seat at his desk. I thanked him and sat down, thinking he was finishing up with someone else's paperwork. Well, on his desk were copies of bank statements with a balance of zero dollars and five cents. I still didn't think anything of it. Then I looked at the top of the statement, and I couldn't believe it. It was my accounts. All of them had a zero balance. Well, zero dollars and five cents. My heart sank. I just couldn't believe it. All the money was gone. And I had just written $18,000 worth of checks for bills that didn't clear the bank yet. It was all gone.

My heart was pounding. I was sick to my stomach. I couldn't believe it. Just couldn't believe it. Here I did what was right to stop the abuse and here I am, trying to deal with all this, and now all the money is gone!

When the manager got back to his desk, it must have been obvious that I saw the statements. Right away he took me back in the conference room so I could get my thoughts together. He called Mick, my old boss. They were friends and the manager wanted to let him know what was going on. He didn't think it was a good idea for me to be by myself.

I remember calling the sheriff's department and telling them what Rich had done—everything from what hap-pened at the house to what hap-pened at the bank.

I did what was right, the hardest thing to do. And now, look, this is what hap-pens. Life just wasn't fair. I remember crying and screaming at the sheriff, "You told me that I was doing the right thing. Now look what's hap-pened!" They had no answer. Really, what could they say?

With everything that had hap-pened in the last few weeks, this was it. This was too much. It took me over the edge, and I lost it right there at the bank.

I called the boys' school. The secretary, Mrs. Fletcher, answered. I was pretty hysterical at that point, just begging and pleading with her, "Please! Please don't let Rich take the boys. That's all I have left." Rich had all that money now. Rich was capable, at that point, of doing anything.

Mrs. Fletcher, I will never forget her. She's always so quiet and soft-spoken. I heard a side of her that I had never heard before. Mrs. Fletcher assured me that the boys would be safe. I had to tell her what their dad looked like. They told the maintenance man, who used to be a policeman, to lock the doors behind the boys when they were in each classroom, protecting the boys from their own dad. The school doors were locked, protecting my boys from their dad.

Mrs. Fletcher told me not to drive, that she was going to pick me up. She told me that she was going to leave the school to come get me. Mrs. Fletcher was so sweet. She barely knew me. I was just Mrs. Purser, Robby and Joey's mom. And she was just going to get up and leave work to come get me so that I could be safe. Not only was she going to make sure I was safe but the boys too.

All I could think of was that Rich had all this money and that he was going to get the boys from school and take off to Florida to stay with his parents. And I would never see my boys again. At this point, I couldn't say what was going to hap-pen next. I never thought in a million years that Rich could have done anything like this.

I assured Mrs. Fletcher that someone was coming up the bank to sit with me. She still wanted to come get me. I asked her to please just protect my boys. She agreed. I let her know that I was going to pick them up, no bus today.

When Mick got to the bank, I just cried and cried. I was doing what was right, and everything was falling apart. When I told Mick what had hap-pened, Mick reminded me that I had another bank account at another bank. We said, "Oh my god." Mick took me right over to the bank, just praying that there was some money in that bank.

When Mick and I got to the bank, I could hardly talk. Everything just hit me at once. I asked Mick to talk to them for me because I was so upset. The people at the bank knew me really well and could see that there was something wrong.

They told Mick and me to have a seat while they pulled up my bank statements. You could see that they all were talking when we were sitting at the desk, waiting for them. I could tell by their reaction that all the money at this bank was gone too. All of it.

When the gentleman came back to the desk, he was shaking his head. I knew for sure that it was gone. Just a couple of weeks before Christmas and the money was all gone. This was Wednesday. Rich had taken the money out yesterday, Tuesday. All the checks that I wrote on Monday were going to bounce. There was no money.

That day just pushed me over the edge. Now what was I going to do? Things just got worse and worse. All this was in God's hands. But it just wasn't funny anymore.

I started calling all the places that I wrote checks to and explained the situation to them. Over and over again, I had to tell them what hap-pened. Some of them were nice and kind, others very understanding, and some of them were just rude.

What a mess! Cornwell needed money too. Their check bounced as well, and they wouldn't send me more tools until they got their money. And I needed tools to sell to make money.

Now I really didn't know what to do. I did what was right, and look at me now. Rich took all the money out of both banks. The money out of the house safe. The deposit box was gone. All the bills, all of the responsibility, even for the boys, were still mine. Their two little lives were turned upside down.

What was Rich thinking? I guess he wasn't. Or Rich was just thinking about himself. Ten years would be a long time in jail, and he had to do something. So he did something and this was it.

Everyone couldn't believe that Rich got bonded out, let alone took all the money and left me in the negative so badly. When I look back at all this, it's still hard to believe that I lived through all that. Just thinking about it makes me sick. Just the stuff with the boys not seeing their dad day after day, night after night. They both wanted to know what hap-pened to Dad. Everyone wanted to know what hap-pened to Rich.

The irony is, as much as I didn't want to talk about Rich or what hap-pened, now I'm telling my story so everyone is going to know.

I had one of my customers one day tell me that so-and-so was talking about me. I started crying again. Why? Why was everyone talking about me? I couldn't stand it anymore. Will people please stop talking about me! Then my customer said, "Why are you so upset that they are talking about you? Don't you realize the strength and courage that it takes to do what you're doing? Men that have been doing the tool business for years are intimidated by you." He also told me that I should be honored and happy that they are all talking about me. That it's a positive thing, not a bad thing.

When I was little, everybody always talked about poor little Cindy. Everything was Cindy, Cindy, Cindy. I hated everyone talking about me. I knew things were bad, but I didn't want to hear about them all the time. And no one ever did anything about it; they just talked. I tried to be as normal as I could—at least my normal.

As much as I hated the tool truck, I had no choice but to drive the tool truck now. For the first few weeks, Scott was on the truck every day with me, helping me with the computer, learning the tools, just helping me out all the way around. But after Scott left me to do it all on my own, I really hated it.

I remember one day, it was on a Friday, a customer wanted a socket be given a warranty. It took me ten minutes to find the socket to warranty it. I was so frustrated. Only God knows how many hours and hours I would cry on the truck, trying to figure things out. The customers would ask for tools that I had no clue what the heck they were talking about. All day long, I was trying to figure things out. I hated it, just hated it.

The boys went from coming home off the bus to Mom, always being there to the boys being in latchkey every night, most of the nights not picking them up until six. They were the last ones to be picked up. I always felt so bad having them stay so late, then coming home trying to cook dinner.

I remember picking the boys up one night after latchkey and going to the corner store to get lunch meat. That was the boys' dinner, ham sandwiches, when we got home in the tool truck. I was always so tired, so mentally tired.

I was glad I had the boys. They were always so good for the most part. They were still little. But we managed as best we could.

After Rich got bonded out, I had to go to court again. This time, we were in court to . . . I don't remember for sure.

Well, Rich was there and the judge was going to figure out something about the charges and to make sure that Rich didn't come around us. That day in court, Rich wanted the business back and his cell phone. I had his cell phone because it was the business number. And I had my phone still because that was my personal number. If that phone rang, I knew to get it right away because it could be an emergency with the boys or something.

They were going to give everything back to Rich, but when I explained everything to the judge of what was going on, the judge told Rich to leave me alone. I got to keep the cell phone and the business, and he was not allowed back into the house. People were starting to listen to me.

After that, things got worse. One day, when I got back from court, the side of the tool truck was scratched up, like somebody took pruning shears and dug into the side of the truck. The steel was actually rolled up into little balls from digging in so deep. Another time I was on the truck billing out a customer, and guess who jumped on the truck? You guessed it, Rich. I was so scared of him. Out of all the times we fought and he beat me, that time I was the most frightened of him. He was so mad that I believed that if he would have had a gun he would have shot me right in the head. He walked away, drove off, and seemed to think nothing of it.

Rich was used to having total control over me. Now that he wasn't in control, Rich was getting more and more angry. After Rich left the truck, I was really shaken up. The customer who was the owner of the business I was selling to came out to the truck afterward and asked me if I was okay. Of course I wasn't okay. I really thought that he was going to kill me. My customer saw everything through his office window. When I asked him why he didn't come outside to help me, he admitted that Rich seemed so upset that maybe he would have hurt the customer. A grown man, go figure. After that I had to make a police report. Rich was breaking his bond by seeing me and being on the truck. Rich was told to leave me alone.

When my customer and I called the police, they instructed us to go to the police station to make a report. They wouldn't come to the customer's shop. When I asked them why, they said because Rich had already left. Why didn't I call 911 when Rich was on the truck? Why did I wait if I was so scared? And why didn't the customer come outside or call himself if it was so bad? I explained that I was too scared to call, afraid that I would just have made him madder.

When we got down to the police department to make the report, I asked them to go find Rich and arrest him for breaking his bond. I was explaining everything to the officer. The officer explained that he could not arrest Rich, that we would have to have a court date and then the judge would decide whether to have him arrested or not. I asked, "Why is there a bond if it has no meaning? Rich was on the truck. Rich broke his bond. I had enough courage to make another report. Now you're telling me that you're not going to do anything!" The officer told me to fill out a report and they would take it from there. He suggested getting a personal protection order (PPO). I was shaking my head. I'm doing everything to protect myself and the boys. What's next?

I had to quit asking that question about what else could happen! Things just kept getting worse and worse. Rich started to stalk me. Rich kept showing up on the truck. I made report after report. The police never did anything. Rich started going to the shops, telling the customers all these horrible things about me—shop after shop, customer after customer.

The owner of one shop hated me from day one. The owner said everything he could to call me a b—— without actually using the word. He would tell me that I don't believe in family values, that Rich was my husband. What are you doing to him? How could I be so greedy? What about my boys? How can you be such a horrible Mom to keep them away from Rich? It took everything I had and then some not to explode at him. Holding back the tears, I asked him was there anything else he needed and that I would be back with a receipt. Scott was with me that day, and when I got on the truck, I threw the cell phone across the truck and screamed out loud. What about the boys? I'm not thinking of the boys! Little did he know that I was the one protecting my boys from their dad, keeping them safe from their dad. When the boys are crying every night that they miss their dad, I was there. I was the one that was holding them, trying to tell them that it was going to be okay. I was a great mom. I was putting up with buttholes like this customer to put a roof over the boys' heads since their dad left us in the negative. Yeah, what kind of person am I? *A great one.* Then I had to pull myself together and walk back in the shop, smiling and saying thank you and see you next week. Stuff like that hap-pened over and over again.

Another customer was so mean, telling me that he felt sorry for my parents and that since I did this to Rich, my family had to watch the boys for me and they were paying my bills. What kind of person was I? I wanted to slap him in the face for saying such a thing. If he only knew the whole story. No family was helping me. They were the reason my picker was broke! Again, I thanked him and walked out. But that shop I never went back to.

Yet another shop I went to. The same thing. But this time, the customer asked me, "What Cindy are you today?" That was totally out of the blue! What Cindy was I? Meaning dissociative. Come to find out Rich was breaking into the house. He found my journals from counseling with Mark, made copies of them, and was showing them to my customers! How sick was that?

Everything that Rich did. How could he make copies of my journals? Rich knew how hard it was to write them. Rich saw everything that I was going through. How could he do that? This was my husband. How could he have done that? Rich did it because he could. But that didn't stop me from working. I had to support the boys. The customers of that shop started saying, "How could you be crazy? You have never said anything bad about Rich or what was going on? Why do you have the truck?" I was there every week.

Then the customers started to question Rich. Cindy seems normal. She has the truck, Rich doesn't. Rich was talking bad about Cindy. And the customers started to put two and two together. Over a period of time, the customers started telling Rich to leave me alone and to never come back to their shops. Over and over again, my customers were telling me that they kicked Rich out and that if he came back to their shops that they were going to kick his butt (although probably not said so nicely). People all over were believing me, and I really didn't say anything. That saying that actions speak louder than words, it was true in this case.

Even that one customer who made me cry, talking about family values. One day, he asked me to come inside to his office. He said that if I ever needed anything to please ask. I guess Rich was coming into his shop a lot, talking bad about me all the time and never letting it go. The customer said, "You never told us anything. You don't talk bad about Rich. You're here every week and you're taking care of business." He actually apologized to me for the way he had acted and made me promise if I ever needed anything, anything at all, to please ask. I couldn't believe it. I was in shock. This customer that was the meanest from the beginning was now so nice. The other employees that worked there also said that they all told Rich that if they ever heard that Rich hurt me they would find him and hurt him.

My customers were starting to protect me from Rich. It was just amazing! But my family was totally different; they all believed Rich.

Right after the money was gone, I figured I better call Grandma and let her know what was going on. I still hadn't told them. When I told Grandma everything that hap-pened, she said, "Why did you do it? Look at the mess you're in." *Thanks for the confidence*, I'm thinking to myself. That's why I didn't call her in the first place. I asked her if I could borrow money for my house payment. I was already a month behind because the check had bounced, and now another payment was due. Grandma told me no, figure it out. That was pretty much the last straw for Grandma. Just finding out all the stuff while in counseling with Mark, my emotions were very torn when it came to Grandma. Even Will and Kathy became more distant. My neighbor across the street, and we had been close, was believing Rich. What was going on?

When Rich made copies of my journals, showed them to my customers, and didn't get the sympathy he wanted from them anymore, he started on my family. Rich started going over to Will and Kathy's house all the time. And they actually let him in. They were having Rich over for dinner. Poor Rich; he lost his home, business, phone, kids. Cindy took it all. Rich's story was that I plotted all this. I schemed this all up. None of this was true, he was saying. I wanted a divorce, so I made all this up.

I talked to my neighbor across the street. She was a Christian. I told her how I prayed on Sunday for God to please help me and the boys, that we couldn't take it anymore, and for God to please do something. And I told her how the next week in church God took it all, and the boys and I were now safe (or so I thought at the time). She twisted it and told Rich. I don't know why.

But that was Rich's story—that I made all this up to get the business, the house, and the boys. Why couldn't people get that I didn't want any of this? I wanted my husband to be healed and to be a family. That's all I ever wanted was family.

So that's what Rich did. Told everybody I made all this up and "look at her journals, she's crazy." The worst part of all this was that my family and friends believed Rich. My own flesh and blood believed Rich.

After leaving Sheryl's today, we had such a good session. I felt so empowered. Looking back at all the hard work with Mark, Anna, and Sheryl, that was really paying off. Even like talking about family. I *should* (I know Sheryl doesn't like that word, so I'll try *could*). Maybe I could feel differently about my family. I don't really miss them anymore. I don't even really miss having a big family anymore. Why would I want a family that wasn't ever really there for me? Okay, we got together for birthdays and holidays. But not really a true family. Like talking to Sheryl tonight. My true family are the boys, Sara, Brandon, and even Sheryl herself. I have learned differently that there is true family and bio-family.

Will and Kathy, I think, hurt me the most. Kathy more so than Will. Kathy was my best friend. When I was going through counseling with Mark and I had my really, really bad days because I was having an anxiety or panic attack, I would call her to help me focus and try to get through the day. Kathy, more so than anybody, knew exactly what I was going through. She saw and heard a lot—all the stuff in counseling, all the memories, and everything she knew. I would have thought that she wouldn't have changed her mind like that.

Rich went to my grandma's house and tried to convince her that I was making all this up. Rich even tried calling my uncles and going over to their houses to turn them against me. This was the first time that I thought of this: if Rich was so innocent, why was he trying so hard to make me look like I was crazy?

After Grandma told me no, she wouldn't loan me money and Will and Kathy would have nothing more to do with me and even my neighbor was siding with Rich, well, let's just say I was having a hard time with all this.

My other neighbor from across the street told me to watch my mail because she saw Rich going through it. She also told me that

Rich's truck was at my other neighbor's house, Sara, the one that was supposed to be my friend. Rich was at her house all the time.

Rich always knew when I left the house in the morning, when I came home at night, and who came over and when. I was constantly being watched. The fear was always there. What else was going to hap-pen?

Rich did a lot of things, constantly calling me, trying to get back together. He would stalk me on the truck. I would be in a shop or going back into the tool truck and Rich would call me and let me know what color of clothes I was wearing or what I was doing. What a horrible feeling that he was watching my every move. Thinking back, he was actually stalking me.

Rich was always doing stuff to me—dumb stuff to make my life miserable. Rich called the cell phone company to have the bill put online so I wouldn't get the bill in the mail. When I realized that I hadn't received a bill in a while, I ended up with a thousand-dollar phone bill. Anything that could make my life miserable, Rich would find a way.

Every time I thought things were starting to settle down, Rich must have got bored and started something else.

A couple of months after all this started, I was thinking of starting a divorce with Rich. I didn't really want a divorce. I wanted to save my family. I wanted my boys all the time. After all the stuff that hap-pened with PJ, not waking up with him every Christmas morning, that kind of thing, I wanted to be with my boys all the time. But after everything that hap-pened with Rich, how could I have stayed with him?

Rich did everything to change my mind. About a week or so after he got bonded out of jail, one Sunday when the boys and I were in church, I cried through the whole service. Okay, I cried through the service every week. Once a week I didn't have to be strong. I could just sit there and cry and cry, knowing that this was still in God's hands.

So on this particular Sunday, while I was sitting there crying, someone touched my shoulder. And there he was, Rich, sitting right next to me. I didn't know what to do. I missed him so much even with everything that had hap-pened. I missed him dearly. Here Rich was sitting next to me. Rich held my hand, told me how much he missed me. I didn't know what to do. I missed him so much; even with everything that had hap-pened, I missed him dearly. Here Rich was sitting next to me, holding my hand, telling me how much he missed me and that he loved me and wanted things to work out.

There was a part of me that wanted that last month to go away. But there was also a big part of me that had enough of the abuse. I was still very confused. I still wanted everything to work out. But things had to change and Rich didn't want things to change. Why would he?

After church, we talked. I so wanted to believe him. Everything he was telling me I wanted to believe. But I knew I couldn't. Things would never be the same again. But that was the good thing; they would never be the same.

When I knew that I really didn't have a choice to get a divorce, well, that was wrong. I had a choice to leave things the way they were or had the choice to make things much better. I couldn't live that way anymore. I already made that choice a couple of months before, so the next step was filing for a divorce.

My attorney, what a wonderful person. She was also Christian. I got her number a few years before when I got Mark's number. Around the same time. Anyway, my spirit led me to call her.

I remember our first meeting. She was so nice. She got our his-tory of how things were going. I told her everything that had hap-pened those last few months. She told me from day one that divorces are 95 percent emotions and the legal is only about 5 percent. Boy, was she right.

I thank God for my attorney. She was more wonderful than anybody could ever imagine.

After our first meeting, she asked me to think about what I was going to do. With everything Rich did, why did I still not want a divorce? Nobody knew. When I started to tell her about all the years we were together and everything that had hap-pened, she didn't understand why I didn't want a divorce.

Talking to Sheryl made me realize that some type of affection, once in a while, was better than no affection at all. Or so I used to think.

Thinking about everything, I knew it was the best choice to start a divorce. I thought, for sure, that Rich would be devastated over divorce papers. But that wasn't the case. Rich was like no big deal. Rich's divorce attorney was also his criminal attorney, Ron. The first couple of times when we went to court for the divorce, since criminal charges were pending, they weren't really sure how they were going to proceed. Rich's attorney (or was it the prosecutor?) wanted a plea bargain with the criminal charges.

The plea bargain for Rich was the next step. Either we offered a plea bargain or the case was going to a jury trial. I couldn't believe it. Everything that hap-pened to me was going to trial.

I don't know how many times I went to court over all this. Every time Rich broke bond or the PPO, he got away with it. There was always something. One time, the courts moved their location and his file got lost. The judge wasn't there. Always some kind of reason that Rich got away with it. Or so I thought. One of the times that got me the worst was my minivan. I got home one day from court, I don't remember for what, but when I got in the garage to leave, my whole van was keyed. The gouges on the van were deep, like someone took a pair of pruning shears and scratched the van. It was deep, just like the tool truck. The metal was rolled up into little balls.

The police came out to the house again to make a report. When they came out, of course the suspect was Rich. But since he still owned the house and van, fingerprints were not helpful. There was no forced entry. They said to go down to the jail so they could take pictures. You know how much I hate to go down there. But here I go again. When I got down there, a lot of them knew me, asking, "What did your knuckle-head husband do now?" They all knew it. But what could they do? They came outside and took pictures. They said that whoever did this was very angry. I was thinking, *You think? That's why I'm here.* I went home in disbelief.

When I got home, the boys were still in school. While I was waiting to go get the boys, the police officer called. She began to tell me that they believed that it was Rich that did this to the van and that there was nothing that they could do. It's still his property. Until we went through the divorce, he could do whatever he wanted to his property. And again, even with his bond and PPO, the police still couldn't do anything because nobody saw him do anything. When I hung up the phone, I just couldn't believe it.

I did all this. I lost so much. I'm in this stupid truck, hating every day on the truck, working way too many hours, especially since it kept me from the boys. And when I was with the boys, I was so tired and burnt out with everything. I was doing what's right to keep Rich from hurting me anymore. For him not to destroy any of my things. And he still is! Rich's not working, just doing whatever, and I'm busting my butt to take care of everything. Where is the justice?

The courts kept going back and forth with a plea bargain. It was all my choice. One choice was to go ahead with a jury trial and be the main witness. I would literally go through hell and back again. Everybody thought that I had been through enough. The courts put the divorce on hold because the situation was just too confusing, and whatever the outcome was of the trial would impact the divorce settlement. If Rich was going away for ten years, that makes the outcome of the divorce different. Then Rich wouldn't need a house, money, and the boys. What would hap-pen to the boys? So the courts put the divorce on hold, waiting for the outcome of the CSC charges.

I don't know how many times I talked to Mark about going to trial or not. Back and forth. If we went for a plea bargain, at least Rich would get some type of consequences or punishment for what he did. But every time I tried to settle for a plea bargain, I wasn't comfortable with that. Something inside of me just didn't want to settle. Rich would have got a slap on the wrist for what he did to me. To all the parts of me. That would have been such a dishonor to my parts. I had worked way too hard, been through way too much for

Rich to get a slap on the wrist. Everyone my whole life had gotten away with everything—my dad, my mom, everyone in the occult, everyone. Hurting me was no big deal. Even when I was just a little girl. Everyone knew about the abuse from my mother, and everyone just let it hap-pen. Did anyone really care?

Back then, I was just another case. But now it was time for me to stand up for myself and say enough is enough. No more abuse. I'm tired, I'm tired of being the poster wife when I was the poster child for years.

Talking back and forth with Mark, I wanted him to tell me what to do. But Mark never would. He would just listen and try to guide me as much as he could. I remember being outside one day, talking to Mark, going over everything in those last few months, Mark assuring me that everything is in God's hands.

Right after I started the truck, I was telling you about the head gasket. Well, I needed $1,500 for the repairs. As you know, there wasn't any money. When I prayed, "God you know I need the money. Where am I going to come up with the money? God, if it's your will for me to drive the truck, you need to come up with the money." There was a pipe bender in the garage. God's like, "You need to sell it." There was couple of different people who came and looked at it, but they said it was too much money or it wasn't what they were looking for. Then when I knew I couldn't drive the truck anymore, there was a gentleman right out of the blue who wanted to look at it. I'm like, "Okay, God, you know how much money I need. Please let this be the one."

He was the nicest guy. He knew exactly what he was looking for. I was asking more than the $1,500. It was worth a lot more. When I told him how much the price was, he told me that he would take it right now, but he only had $1,500. He could pay me right now and leave with it. Just like that, I knew it was God's will. Right to the penny. God is so amazing. I could have gotten a lot more. But when it's God's will, what you need now, God gives. It's all God.

The first Christmas that Rich was gone after the rape, we didn't have any money, and I was telling the boys that we weren't going to have a really good Christmas. When Robby said, "Yes, we are, Mom. We're going to have the best Christmas ever." At eight years old, even Robby knew that this was all for the best.

Robby's teacher, Ms. Page, called me right before school was over and asked if I was going to be home. I told her yes; she said thank you and hung up. About a half an hour later, Ms. Page and Mrs. Lenked showed up at our door. Ms. Page was the boys' teacher. Robby had her for two years. This was her first year for Joey. So the family has been with her for going on three years. Mrs. Lenked was the teacher in the classroom I used for Bible school. So they both knew what the boys were going through. I think that it was Mrs. Fletcher that started it, that they would be a secret Santa and brought a whole bunch of presents for the boys. The school knew that the money was gone. One of the moms even bought me presents for Christmas. She said that moms needed a present too. They all showed me the true meaning of Christmas.

Over and over again, God has shown me that this was all in his hands. Trust me, most of the time I don't like it. It's in God's hands. God knows what's best for me more than I know what's best for me.

Going back to the whole plea bargain thing, to the outside world, I had been through enough. Rich would take the plea bargain. The divorce would be over, and I could move on with my life. But could I really? No. A part of me, all of me, just couldn't settle. I had been through so much. I'm still standing stronger and healed more than ever. If I've been through so much already, why can't I go through this? But they're also telling me that Rich could be acquitted and get away scot free. But what are the odds of that? But if I don't go through all of this, it was my choice to let him get off scot-free. This was my choice. One hundred percent my choice. I was the one being raped all weekend. It was me and my children living all this. It was my choice to call the police. It was my choice to talk to Sergeant McFadden when all this hap-pened. And it was my choice if this was going to trial.

Not only would it be an injustice not to go through with all this but it would also be an injustice to you. You have given me the strength to keep going forward. You are the one who gave me hope when there was no hope at all. You were the one that gave me the courage to go forward, knowing that one day you would be reading this, knowing that I could thank you for giving me all that. That one day I could thank you for giving me so much. That I would tell you my story. That maybe from your reading this, that by reading my story, I could give you the same encouragement that you have given me. That one day I could make a difference in your life just the way you have for me. Again, I thank you!

Still going back and forth with the courts and talking with Mark. It came down to the last day of court. Again, we were in a large conference room. Sergeant McFadden was there, the prosecutor was there, and the victim's rights advocate was there. She was very helpful, but she didn't really get why people stayed in abusive relationships, going back and forth with McFadden and the others. Rich was there with his attorney. I was trying to put an end to all this.

Everyone knew how tired I was and that I wanted and needed all this to be over. They just didn't want me to go through a trial because they knew how difficult it was going to be. They truly had my best interest at heart, especially Sergeant McFadden. When he told me enough was enough, when he pulled up the pictures of my face from what Rich did to me, enough was enough. The Lord only knows what I have really been through. Even though my head was telling me that I should just go for a plea bargain, my heart was telling me different.

At least with a plea bargain, Rich would get something. Hopefully he would get the help that he needed. Against my better judgment, I finally agreed to the plea bargain. This would all be over that day. I would be putting all this behind me and I could move on. I wouldn't have to testify. It would all be over.

When McFadden and the others went to talk to Rich and his attorney to try to end this that day, I just sat there. I didn't know what to think. When they came back into the room, I was so anxious, waiting for the outcome. The prosecutor told me that they set a date for jury selection. I said, "What? Jury selection? You told me when you left the room that you were going for a plea bargain."

Then he began to tell me that his gut instinct was that I truly wanted a jury trial and that since I had come this far, I had nothing else to lose. So we're going full force with the trial.

Jury selection took a very long time. It's unheard of for a husband to be accused of raping his wife. I know it hap-pens all the time, but nobody ever reports it. The prosecutor knew that he had a hard road ahead of him. But he believed me and wanted justice to be served.

I wasn't there for jury selection. I don't remember if Rich was there or not. I was just trying to get through the day. Sergeant McFadden kept me up-to-date on what was going on. I was so numb at this point. I just wanted things over with. My life was in limbo.

I had so many mixed emotions. What if Rich goes to jail? How is that going to affect the boys not seeing their dad? Did I really want Rich in jail? But none of those things were my choice. What Rich did to me was Rich's choice. The outcome of this was all in God's hands. I know with my whole heart and soul that I made the right choice. It was God's choice. I was at peace with it. As much as it hurt, as much as I hated everything, I was at peace with everything. Does that make any sense? I hope so.

The prosecutor had to get things ready. He had to get witnesses. The witnesses that we were going to use on my behalf were going to testify for Rich. My friends and my family were on Rich's side. That just made me feel so warm and fuzzy. Ha ha. I just couldn't believe it. The only support I had was the courts and Mark. Nobody else. I was doing what's right, and I was all alone. Over the years, I've learned that I'm better off being alone and happy then being with people that betray me. The story of my life. Everyone has betrayed me.

Nothing would have ever prepared me for what was about to hap-pen. Nothing.

The trial was awful, just awful. As much as I prayed, as much as I tried to focus, it was just awful. Again, Sergeant McFadden told me to focus on him. Just thinking about going over everything again and being on the stand, I had to defend myself, like I did something wrong. I distinctly felt like I was on trial. As painful as it was, I knew that I was doing the right thing.

When I got on the stand, my anxiety was through the roof. I was going to tell my story to twelve people. It was up to them if they believed me or not. At the time, it felt like it was up to them what my future held. But whatever hap-pens, I already stopped the cycle that *no* means *no*.

When I got on the stand and sworn in, Sergeant McFadden, the prosecutor, and even the victim rights advocate were all in suits. They were right in front of me so I could focus on them. Then to my right was Ron and next to him was Rich. And they were, of course, in suits—a picture that I never thought I would see. I took a deep breath. The prosecutor asked me questions first. Over and over again, questions after questions. I was up there forever. At times it felt like I was reliving it all over again.

Then Ron started asking questions. What that man put me through was unbelievable. At times the jury was crying. It was so bad that both men and women of the jury were crying. Even at times a jury member told Ron to stop. Even Sergeant McFadden, at one point, had tears in his eyes. Ron was trying, of course, to make out that I was crazy, that I was making this up, that it couldn't be Rich doing this to me, that it was my memories of my dad. Ron went through the occult stuff and the DID and PTSD. He had researched what's out there about DID and PTSD, but he was not looking for the truth. He said that I did all this because I wanted the house, the business, and the boys and that now I could get a divorce and I could get everything. That was his story.

Ron made Rich out to be a wonderful husband, father, and businessman. Very involved in the church and the Knights of Columbus. Rich was such a hero putting up with his crazy wife. Sounds familiar. My dad was the really crazy one but made Mom out to be crazier than him. History repeats. How funny.

But the difference is that I loved myself and the boys enough to get healed and whole from what my parents did to me, not allowing myself to be in the system anymore.

That morning, I was on the stand for at least three hours, and after lunch, they had me on the stand again, I think, for at least another two hours or so. It was such a long time. They even brought the copies of my journals, trying to say I was crazy like my mom. The whole thing was awful. But as I think back, whatever the outcome was going to be, I would do it all again. Not only was I on the stand for myself, I was also on the stand for every other wife, girlfriend, and significant other, anyone who was raped by their partner. *No* means *no*.

Mark had to testify. That wasn't fun either. They were all talking about me like I wasn't even a person. The whole dissociation was their big focus.

That was one of the hardest parts. With what my parents did to me and all the abuse that hap-pened to me, the only way I could live and not literally go crazy was to dissociate. Since my picker was broke, with a lot of other things, I went to Mark to help heal from all the abuse. Now the last step was to stop the abuse from Rich. I was doing a good thing.

Ron turned everything around and used what I worked so hard to heal from against me. The hardest thing I had done was to write those journals, and they were using them to make me look like I was crazy. Go figure. Where was the justice? I'll tell you. Me going up there for no one ever to touch me like that again, that I will never ever be raped again.

Poor Mark. Ron ran him through the mill too. Mark was up there forever, question after question. Ron was trying to twist things and even get Mark confused. This whole dissociation thing. Everyone puts such a bad stamp behind it. Even I still have a hard time with it. The abuse was so bad that my brain couldn't handle it and literally gave the pain to someone else. So sad.

After Mark was done testifying, I think they called Sergeant McFadden to testify. He was just wonderful. He really believed me and wanted the abuse to stop once and for all. Obviously he knew that I was strong enough to go through all this. I think that's all that testified on my side. Then it was Ron's turn to call his witnesses.

I couldn't believe it. Well, I should have. I knew my girlfriend from across the street was testifying for Rich. My girlfriend who was supposed to be my friend, the one I put my confidence in, she was going back to Rich and telling him everything that was going on. I couldn't trust anyone.

When she was on the stand, the prosecutor was trying to get a feeling of our relationship. She told them how we were best friends. That I was the first person she told when she first found out she was pregnant and that there were problems with her pregnancy. How I was always there for her. And after the baby was born with all the complications afterward, how I always was there for her. Our sons were best friends. We weren't fighting. But Rich was a nice guy, and she didn't want him to go to jail. Her husband and Rich were good friends. You could tell that the prosecutor was confused. If we were such good friends, why was she testifying against me?

She told Rich what I had told her about when I had been in church that Sunday, telling her that God's a good God and God's taking care of everything, that things were so different than my divorce from Timothy. Rich's whole case was based on that. So that's when Eva told the courts what I had told her. Again, a good thing that happened, the enemy was trying to use it against me.

I talked with Sergeant McFadden after Eva was done testifying, and he told me that things were going wonderfully when I made the jury cry and then the jury was telling Ron to stop that I had had enough. Even how things sounded so crazy, what my friend was saying. Things were going much better than planned.

After days of testimony, they brought in a surprise witness. Rich himself. It was unheard of. The defendants in cases like these rarely testify. Ron decided to have Rich testify. For me that was horrible. I cried through all of it. The judge said that if I didn't stop crying, they would have me removed from the courtroom.

After months and months of all this, I started to cry and just couldn't stop. Rich was up there telling the jury all these lies. I was thinking about everything that he did to me—being on the truck, the boys not being with their dad, a single mom overnight dealing with everything, then him stalking me all the time. Now this. It was overwhelming.

But the hardest part of all this was that it could have been avoided. We were seeing Mark. If Rich truly loved himself enough to get the help that he needed, none of this would have hap-pened. We would have been at home like a family, a family that I so desperately always wanted. And at times, Rich, I did have it. I really did have my family, the one I always dreamed of. But was it real? At times it seemed it was. On Sunday mornings, during church and after church, for some hours, I had my family, my perfect family. Or so I thought. If it was real, would I have been there in court?

After the testifying, there was a recess.

I went outside. I wanted to be alone. I stood there, just looking around, looking up at the sky so blue, like the blue it was the day Rich and I got married, looking at the buildings with all the people walking by. It was a warm day, the sun warm on my cheek, and a calming relaxing breeze went through my hair.

To this point in my life, I have never felt so empty. Just empty inside. I can't explain the emptiness. But at the same time, I was never more at peace. The peace was through me head to toe. I felt like I was the only person there. I knew at that moment that whatever the outcome was, good or bad, there was peace. I really didn't even know what I wanted the outcome to be. It didn't matter at that point. I know that I did what I was supposed to do. And whatever the outcome, it was in God's hands a million percent. I was at more peace about that than anything in my whole life.

When I went back to the courtroom, both sides gave their closing arguments (statements, whatever you want to call it). The prosecutor's closing statements were just wonderful. I couldn't have said it any better; he got it. He got how I was feeling and how everything was at home, in my past, everything. He got it. He told the jury how

I was feeling. Someone got it! After all those days in court and all those months, when it came down to the bottom line, all this was about me. It was me. And the prosecutor got it. I couldn't tell the jury any better myself. My story was out, and the jury heard it.

After closing statements, the judge gave the jury their instructions. How actually she wanted things thought out. There was to be no reasonable doubt. I don't know or even remember for a fact; all that really mattered was that the trial was over. I did what I had to do. The prosecution ended wonderfully. But the most important part was the outcome was in God's hands.

It was a Friday afternoon. The jury went back to their room to discuss things. I forget the word you call it. Then Sergeant McFadden told me what's going to happen next. When the jury reached their verdict, they will call everyone back into the courtroom and give us the verdict. Sergeant McFadden suggested for me to go home for a while, that I needed a break, and that I had gone through enough. Go home and spend some time with the boys. The boys needed me as much as I needed them.

When I was going to my van, guess whose truck I saw? When I saw Rich's truck, I started to cry again. It was still so hard to believe that we had gotten to this point. I still had mixed emotions of him going to jail. Even Mark did. Everyone did. Even PJ. The boys not seeing their dad for ten years, was that really the best for the boys? Only God knows.

I sat in the van for a long time before I left. I still couldn't believe it was over and I did it. And for the most part, I was doing so good.

I literally went through hell and back that week, and I was functioning just fine. I just pretty much went through my life story this week—everything about Mom and Dad, the occult stuff, and my life with Rich. I finally left the parking lot to go home. Jenny, PJ's girlfriend at the time, was there watching the boys for me.

It felt like such a long drive home. I thought that I would never get home. But the other part of me didn't want to come back home to reality. As much as I wanted to see the boys, I also needed to see them. And thank God that I had them at home with me.

If Rich does go to jail, what are the boys going to do? They both love their dad very much, and it would be devastating for Rich to be totally gone.

As you can imagine, my emotions were all over the place, just sitting here thinking about that day—the sadness, the pain, the anger, the uncertainty of the whole situation.

Just hoping that none of this was true and my husband would be coming home to me. Just wishing that I could put all this in a box, put the cover on it, and wish that all this didn't hap-pen. But the truth was that all this hap-pened and that my husband raped me and hurt me and the boys, and I had to suffer because of Rich's choices. I know with my whole heart and soul that I did make the right choice, the only choice. But I still miss Rich.

Writing about this stirs up so many emotions. The boys had a snow day today. I couldn't wait to get home to them. Last night when I came home from work, the boys were so happy to see me. They are eleven and thirteen now. I will take all the hugs and kisses that I can get from them. It still amazes me how God works. I'm writing about the boys' feelings about their dad, thinking that I'm sure I did the right thing. And not only did I do this for myself, I did all this to also protect the boys. Even if it's from their dad. My one and only job is to be mom and protect them and guide them so they grow up to be strong, healthy men.

So when I start thinking about how all this affected the boys, when I came home last night and they wanted mom, especially wanted to cuddle, I took it. I cuddled with Joey and he fall asleep. Even stranger, Robby wanted to cuddle instead of playing video games. I cuddled Robby and he fell asleep in my arms.

And the strangest part of all is PJ's now twenty-four. He's doing just wonderful. I am a mom and couldn't be prouder of her oldest son, that I am. PJ came over, which he never does. PJ jokes that he sees me too much at work.

So last night, I fed him dinner, joked with him for a while. He even let me hug him goodbye. PJ hugged me for a long time, the hug that lets me know that he loves me. This all proves to me that yes, I did the right thing. PJ is growing up and doing so good for himself. The boys are doing awesome. Yes, I did make the right choice. My boys, all three of them, want mom. Still want to cuddle me and love me after all this. Yes, no doubt in my mind. Yes, I made the right choice for everything.

I couldn't write all day yesterday. I was stuck again. After cuddling with the boys and seeing PJ last night, I came home tonight, and to my surprise, instead of wanting to play video games, the boys both wanted to watch a movie with mom. And to make things all the better, we all three cuddled on the floor with our pillows and blankets. They wanted me in the middle so both of them could cuddle with me. What more could a mom ever want?

After cuddling with the boys last night, it gives me the strength to keep writing.

So here I go again.

CHAPTER EIGHT

> God, your thoughts are precious to me.
> They are so many!
> If I could count them,
> They would be more than all the grains of sand.
> When I wake up,
> I am still with you.
> —Psalm 139:17–18

When I pulled down my street, wanting to see the boys, they were playing outside with Melissa. To my surprise, PJ was there too. That's all I had left, well, the only thing I needed. All of them were home. Before I left, Sergeant McFadden said, "Have a good weekend" and that I wouldn't hear anything until, at least, Monday. "So go home and try not to, ha ha, think about anything." The trial was almost over. I got out of the van with a smile on my face, now going to be mom. I need the boys and they need their mom.

I got in the house, changed my clothes, and told PJ and Melissa what had happened and that we just have to wait now, that it's all in the jury's hands. Well, it's really all in God's hands.

PJ, Melissa, and I were all sitting on my front porch, talking about what happened, when the phone rang. I didn't feel like talking to anyone on the phone, but PJ said, "Mom, you really need to answer it." It was Sergeant McFadden on the phone. He told me that the jury reached a verdict already. I was amazed. So soon? They said that it would be days. I told Sergeant McFadden that I would be right down. I was supposed to be in the courtroom when they read the verdict. I told him that I would get dressed and be there in less than half an hour.

Then Sergeant McFadden began to tell me that they already read the verdict. I asked him, "How is that possible? I was supposed to be there. You, the judge, everyone was supposed to be there. What hap-pened?" The judge had to leave; she wouldn't be there on Monday. Why make the jury wait? It was just more convenient for them to read the verdict right away. But it was my life. I was the one that went through hell and back again all these months. I was the one that was raped over and over again. I am the one that had to tell my boys what hap-pened to their dad. I was the one that had the strength and courage to go through all this. It was my life for the rest of my life, and what the verdict was, was going to affect my life. Whatever the outcome, this is what I had gone through counseling with Mark for three years for. All the times Rich hit me, broke my things, yelled at me, and everything else I could remember and they already read the verdict? When he told me yes, I just couldn't believe it.

I took a deep breath, held PJ's hand as tight as I could, and waited for the verdict. Then Sergeant McFadden asked, "Are you ready?" Whatever the outcome was, I would never be ready. I still wasn't ready. Rich was found not guilty. I just couldn't believe it. At first I was so angry. But initially, I looked up to the sky and asked God, "Why?" But then I had to stop myself. I thought about when I was outside, with the peace that all this was in God's hands. As much as there were so many emotions, the verdict was all in God's hands and he knows best.

When I started to ask Sergeant McFadden why they didn't call me, he said it hap-pened 1, 2, 3. McFadden said that it was probably for the best that I wasn't there.

At least I was home with the boys and especially with PJ there. I asked Sergeant McFadden what Rich's reaction was. Of course he was excited. But Sergeant McFadden strongly recommended to watch myself. That Rich was a free man, there were no more bonds. Like it even mattered in the first place. But since he's a free man, Rich thinks he won and that he can get away with anything. Sergeant McFadden told me that if Rich was to come over to the house, I was to ask him to please leave or that I would call the police.

Sergeant McFadden was right. The very next morning, Rich came over to the house like he owned it. I did exactly what McFadden told me to do. I asked Rich what he was doing there and what he wanted. I told him that he had to leave or I was going to call the police. That's exactly what I did. Rich said that he was coming home, that he lived there, and that he was a free man and he could do whatever he wanted.

When Rich refused to leave, I asked him again to please leave. Rich told me no, that he wasn't going to leave and to please call the police. So I did. The boys were outside, and I never wanted the boys to see the police take their dad away. So far, they never had and I wanted to keep it that way. The boys had been through enough. When I called the police, there was no fear about what Rich would do to me. He's done enough, and he can't hurt me anymore. Rich heard me call the police, and when I mentioned Sergeant McFadden, Rich did leave.

When the police came out to my house, I explained the whole situation to them and showed then my PPO. It was still in place. To my amazement, the police listened to me and did something about it. I thought since Rich already left that they wouldn't do anything. I thought all they would do was to make him leave had he still been there since he got away with everything else. No, they actually found him, arrested him, and impounded his truck. PJ offered to drive it back to the house since Rich was still in the neighborhood when they found him. When the police came back to my house and told me that, tonight I can rest in peace because Rich was back in jail for breaking the PPO order. Well, how amazing was that! Rich was found not guilty; he was a free man, and he told me that since he was found not guilty that he could come back to the house to harass me. Things were starting to change. Even though Rich was found not guilty, Rich still had choices, and that meant even Rich couldn't break the law anymore without consequences.

Since that was Saturday, the courts weren't open till Monday. Poor Rich had to stay in jail. Poor baby.

The boys were pretty upset about their dad. I couldn't blame them, but the boys, as well as their dad, needed to learn about choices. Life is all about choices. Rich made a choice; that was why he was back in jail. Everyone had told Rich, even his attorney, "Be thankful you're free. Please, just leave her alone." But he wouldn't. The boys had to learn, even if it was painful for them, that Daddy has a choice to make.

The boys were pretty upset. It was a warm day, and after that, I really didn't want to be at the house; so much had hap-pened there. PJ and Melissa were also at the house, so I asked everybody if they wanted to go to a hotel with an indoor water park. Of course they all agreed to that.

I just packed a bag for me and the boys. PJ said that he and Melissa would come up there for a night too. They had stuff to do, so the boys and I just left to go to the water park.

When I got to the hotel, got our room, and got everybody settled, I called Anna. I started seeing Anna a few months after Rich got out of the house. My attorney said it would be a good idea for me to see someone, and since I was on the truck all of the time, Mark was too far away for me to continue seeing him. Anna's office was right by my house; it was ideal. It worked out so perfect. Anna was just what I needed to get through all the stuff that was going on with Rich. And

I was just trying to be a single mom overnight and dealing with a business now all by myself, my job and Rich's job with the business.

Anna was just great. She helped me with everyday life, just trying to get through the motions of the day. Many days were a lot longer than others.

There have been so many times through all this that I have thought of Anna. Even though she was with me for such a short time, Anna was my foundation. She taught me that when things were unbearable, God wants me to be a strong tree—so very tall and strong that nothing or no one can ever knock me down. When I want to quit, when I feel like I can't take it anymore, I think of that tree. When the winds blow, whatever hap-pens, nothing can bring me down. My roots need to grow deep into the ground, strong and deep like a solid foundation. The bigger the roots grow, the stronger my faith grows. The water that keeps the roots growing and strong and healthy is the Holy Spirit building and growing inside of me. No matter what hap-pens, God is continuing to grow in me, keeping me healthy and whole, and with God in me and through me, one day I can stand here and tell my story. I can get through anything knowing that I am this strong, healthy, and healed tree; and nothing, I mean *nothing*, will ever bring me down.

I thank both God and Anna for that because, with everything that has hap-pened, a lot of days I couldn't have survived without thinking of that tree.

When I called Anna, she couldn't believe that Rich was back in jail. And instead of me crying and crying, thinking that it was all my fault, worried about now what was he going to do to me, here I am, in a hotel room with my boys, all three of them. Just to top things off, not even twenty-four hours had gone by since Rich was a totally free man, he was back in jail.

Now my emotions were totally different. Even though I thought that, in some way, justice wasn't served, now I have to laugh. You have to admit it's funny. It was all Rich's choice that he was back in jail.

The next few weeks were very interesting. Since the trial was over, we could start the divorce back up again. We went through the friend of the court, and Rich got visitation for the boys. I had the business, and he wasn't working. Rich hadn't worked since the tool truck. He was living with one of our friends; the boys always called him Uncle Ernie. He was always there for us. When Rich got to see the boys, they were with Uncle Ernie too.

When we went back to divorce court to start things back up again, the courts actually let Rich move back in the house. I couldn't believe that Rich would be moving back into the house. What amazes me more is that he would want to move back into the house after everything that had hap-pened. Why on earth? If I'm this horrible person as he claimed in the rape trial, why would he want to move back in with me? God only knows.

My attorney said that since Rich was acquitted, there was nothing legally that we could do to keep him out of the house. Everything that I had gone through, everything, now I have to live with him and support him since I was the one that was running the tool truck. Yep. And this is still in God's hands? I still had the PPO on Rich, so if anything hap-pened, I could still call the police.

So Rich was back at the house. I felt like nothing was going to change. I went through so much, just during the trial alone. And Rich went back to jail after the trial was over. When I found out that he got bonded out and who bonded him out, I just couldn't believe it. It was my cousins, Will and Kathy. Talk about betrayal.

The next few months were very different. I worked on the truck every day. Rich played Mr. Mom. We did get along for the most part. It was strange going to divorce court and then coming back to the house and seeing each other. The boys were kinda confused. Dad was out of the house, and they didn't really know why, then he was back in the house. They knew things were bad, but they didn't need to know details. But as much as I tried to protect them, they found out anyway.

Guess how they found out? Their dad. Rich showed the boys my deposition from the very beginning of the trial when I went to court for the first time. How could a father do that to his kids? So the boys were mad at me. Rich wanted to turn even the boys against me. Even PJ, Rich tried to turn against me. But PJ didn't want to be in the middle. With everything that was still going on, I just kept going forward.

Anna got really sick, so out of the blue one day, she was out of my life and I had no one again.

During all this, my attorney suggested that the boys start seeing someone. And that's how I started seeing Sheryl. Both Anna and Mark said she was wonderful. Boy, were they right. Sheryl had been an angel and then some. Sheryl has been my backbone, trying to help me write this for myself, but she always encourages me to write for you. Both of us want to make a difference in your life.

The first day I met Sheryl, I really liked her. She is so soft-spoken, and she got along with the boys. I knew this was exactly what all three of us needed. I never really knew how to raise kids, and since I didn't have the best examples in the world, Sheryl was my parenting coach. Sheryl taught me so much. Living with Rich again, the boys were so confused, and Sheryl helped balance everything out. Thank God for Sheryl.

When it came time for custody for the boys, we had to go through the friend of the court. At first Rich was not fighting for full custody. I never thought he would, but after that last year anything was possible. Sure enough, my attorney called me in to her office to let me know that Rich was fighting for full custody of the boys. I couldn't believe it, or shouldn't believe it. But yes, Rich was fighting for full custody. I'm thinking to myself, *God, here we go again. I have had enough fun, ha ha. God, let's do this again.* The friend of the court makes an investigation for full custody. After everything that had hap-pened, I'm amazed that they would even consider letting my boys be with their dad full-time. Anyways, we both had to meet with a counselor and investigator.

My interview was first, and I had to bring the boys. They had to interview them also. The gentleman was different. He kept answering the phone during the interview, which I thought was totally unprofessional. He reminded me of one the psychiatrists at Holy Cross. He kept talking about different patients over the phone in front of me. He sounded like he needed a counselor.

The interview was long. He wanted to know my background about Mom and Dad, the occult, the abuse when I was a kid, then Timothy and my relationship with him, then Rich and why on earth was I still with this man after everything he had done to me. I told him that I wasn't strong enough to get away from him, but now I was doing everything that I could to protect myself and the boys. When I told him about the trial, he couldn't believe that Rich got acquitted. I couldn't either, but I knew it's all in God's hands. After the interview was over, he encouraged me to stay strong, that everything was going to be fine. Then he met with the boys one at a time. It didn't take very long. Maybe ten, fifteen minutes each. I felt pretty good when I left. He understood how I was feeling and why I stayed with Rich for so long and that now I was able to get out of the relationship.

He met with Rich a couple of hours later that same day. So it shouldn't be that much longer before we got the outcome of his report.

About a week or so later, my attorney called me into her office. You could tell in her voice that something was really wrong. She told me that she got the friend of the court recommendation back and I needed to see her right away. I'm thinking, *Oh no, what now?*

I met with her right away. I knew from the sound of her voice that something was bad. When I got there, my anxiety was through the roof. I lost so much, but not my kids. I had joint custody of PJ because Timothy was so mean and he said that I was crazy, just like my mom. And I got PJ for four days with me, and then he was four days with Timothy. It was crazy. And every time I took Timothy back to court, he always used that "I'm crazy" bit. Timothy's parents had money, so Timothy always had the best attorney. Everything always went wrong.

Now here I am again with the boys, a million times stronger than ever. I cannot lose my boys.

When I got to my attorney's office, she sat me right down. She started reading the recommendations. I just couldn't believe it. If I didn't see it with my own eyes, I wouldn't have believed it.

They wanted to give Rich full custody of the boys. The report went on to say that I needed to be locked up in a mental ward for long-term psychiatric treatment. And then after months of treatment, I could see the boys for a couple hours once a week, supervised, with a friend of the court professional. I said, "What?" I couldn't' believe it. How? Why? I just couldn't' believe it. Lock me up? After everything that Rich's done to me and the boys? Now I'm the crazy one? And this is all in God's hands?

So my attorney and I sat down and went over all this. Since the boys and I were seeing Sheryl once a week, we needed letters from her. I had been seeing Anna, so we needed letters from her. What a mess. I was really, really pushed to the edge. Now I had to go home and see Rich at the house and pretend like everything was okay. God, please give me strength because I really need it now.

My attorney was getting all the stuff ready for court. She got everything she needed from Anna and Sheryl, with Anna speaking as my counselor and Sheryl as the boys' counselor. But my attorney needed an outside report. I had such a hard time with that. That I needed to see someone and pay him a lot of money to tell me if I'm crazy or not.

Pretty much. Bottom line, my attorney said that we really needed this. I felt like I was on trial again. So here I go. The psychiatrist was different. But my attorney said he was the best, so I had to trust her. We had to meet a few times. The first time was a consultation to get my background. Again, going over my past with Mom and Dad, the occult stuff, and the abuse, my relationship with Timothy, then Rich and everything that hap-pened with him. When people find out that Rich was acquitted, they immediately think that I really did make all this stuff up. But I have to remind myself that no, all this is in God's hands no matter what.

Then after the interview, he gave me a bunch of papers to fill out and bring back. There were all sorts of different questions on there. Then he brought me back for a couple more sessions. What fun.

He did his report and called me back for the results. He told me that I was not crazy, but I did have signs of PTSD (post-traumatic stress disorder). I'm thinking to myself, *You think? Did you not hear my story?* I was getting a pretty bad attitude. I was really getting tired. I just wanted all this to be over and live my life, the life that I was working so hard to have.

Living with Rich and going through all this was so hard. I tried not to fight or argue with him. Just trying to get through the days. Going back and forth in court, things were upside down. There seemed like there was no end. I couldn't give up. Rich either wanted to stop the divorce and try to work things out on his terms, meaning not going to counseling, or he wanted to go through with all this.

Everybody involved just wanted all this to end. We had another court date. Either the judge was going to end this and had made up his mind or this would go to trial. Another trial, that's just what I needed. How on earth could I go through another trial? This time, the boys would have to be dragged through the trial too. What a mess. I kept reminding myself this was all in God's hands.

That day on the way to court to find out which way the judge was going to go, I remembered how I hadn't been strong enough to go to trial with Timothy, so I got him PJ half the time. If I went to trial with Timothy, I knew I could have lost PJ full-time.

But so many years later, I was so much stronger. I had to plant both feet and fight for what's right and try to put the fear behind me, remembering that with everything I have and then some that this is all in God's hands.

I remember right before I left for court, God gave me a scripture in Romans, I believe. Sorry, I don't remember, but it went like this: I am the judge, the jury, and the lawyer. I thanked God more than you know. I repeated it all the way out the door, into my van, and the drive to court. I kept saying it going up to the courtroom, "God, it's all come to this." And just saying it over and over again in my head.

I saw Rich and just dug my heals in deeper, saying the scripture over and over again.

When I saw my attorney, she assured me that everything was going to be okay. But nothing would have ever prepared me for what was going to hap-pen next. Nothing.

Ron, Rich's attorney, came over to my attorney to let her know that Ron was done fighting, that I had been through enough and Ron wasn't going to put me through a trial again, that the boys had been through enough, that they're not going to trial, that enough was enough, and that we were going to end this now. Ron wasn't even listening to Rich at this point. Ron asked my attorney if we could meet in her office tomorrow, if that wouldn't be a problem. Not to inconvenience her. And Rich was telling Ron, "I'm not meeting at Cindy's attorney's office." Ron told Rich to be quiet. Ron told Rich to call his office and get directions to her office for tomorrow.

Ron wanted to make sure that everything was okay with my attorney, that all four of us were meeting at her office the next day to end this. Ron left, saying, "Thank you. I will see you tomorrow."

My attorney and I just looked at each other with amazement and said, "See ya tomorrow."

Now that's God. Only God.

When I woke up the next day, I just couldn't believe it. Everything was almost over. God showed me how much that everything, everything was in his hands. When I got to my attorney's office the next day, in a beautiful house that she made into her own private practice, we talked for a while. Couldn't believe so much had hap-pened. And now it was almost over. The divorce was almost coming to an end.

A part of me still wanted things to work out, but I knew in my heart of hearts this was the last choice to make. Rich arrived first, then Ron. In the middle of her office, my attorney had a beautiful wooden table. Little did I know that the end of this dream would be at that table.

When Ron got there, my attorney made coffee and had soft drinks there. It was so much more comfortable than being at a conference room at the courthouse. As comfortable as we could be. The four of us went over everything—the business, the house, all our personal belongings. For the most part, Rich and I agreed on everything.

Now for the boys, the most important part of all this. What were we going to do with the custody arrangements? I'm still amazed. Everything that my attorney asked for, Ron said okay. He didn't even ask Rich what he wanted. Ron just kept on agreeing with her.

Rich ended up with every Wednesday. Rich would pick the boys up after school and take them to school the next morning. He and I didn't even have to see each other. And Rich would have them every other weekend from Friday after school until Monday when he would take the boys to school. Again, we wouldn't see each other.

My attorney split the holidays and vacations. Again, whatever she thought was fair, Ron just agreed to.

Then the debt. The credit card debt for the tools that Rich bought before all this hap-pened, the checks I wrote that bounced, I became responsible for them because they were for the business and I got the business. That's a good thing, right?

Going through all this in my attorney's office was still really hard. When Rich looked at me, we were across from each other and I knew that he still loved me. Well, loved me as much as he could love someone. Remember, Rich doesn't love himself enough to get better, not even for himself.

After we settled everything, the guys left. My attorney and I talked for a few minutes. She knew I was sad. She knew, for the most part, everything that hap-pened over the past year and a half. It was September; in November, it would be two years since all this had started. She knew how tired I was and how much I wanted all this to be over. But a part of me still wanted my marriage to work out.

I thanked my attorney again for everything. Just thinking, a little over twenty-four hours ago, we were all going to court, with the recommendation that Rich gets full custody and for me to be locked up in a mental ward. Now here I'm leaving my attorney's office and I have the boys. It's my job to protect the boys, and I'm really doing it.

My attorney said that she would draw up the divorce papers, and it would be just a few more days before it was final.

I think I beat Rich back to the house. For the next couple of days, we really didn't even talk to each other. We both knew that this was for the best, but it didn't make it any easier. The divorce was final on September 14. We had gotten married on September 16. Almost eleven years we were married.

The morning of court, the final day of all this, I thought it was strange but I put on my wedding rings. I don't know why, but I did. When my attorney and I were waiting to go in, I even told her that I felt funny putting my rings on but that I needed too. She told me that's normal. Putting an end to anything is painful, if it's good or bad. The end is the end and it's a loss.

My attorney told me of one couple that she had. They were separated for years and years. When they finally got a divorce, they both were very sad. And that wife had also put her rings back on that day.

When Rich and Ron got there, all four of us had to sign the divorce decree. My attorney faxed over a copy to Ron's office, and he told her what a fabulous job she did with the divorce papers, that he couldn't have done a better job himself. When Rich was trying to change things in the divorce decree again, Ron told Rich to shush. Ron told Rich to just be quiet and sign the papers.

Was this the same man that had me on the witness stand for hours during the rape trial? That put me through the unthinkable? It still amazes me what hap-pens when everything is in God's hands.

We went in front of the judge, and he couldn't believe it himself. That just a few days before, this couple was going to trial and now everything's resolved. Only God could do that. I wasn't sure how I was going to feel—cry, be happy, angry, or what I was going to feel. All that mattered was that it was over.

When my attorney and I left the courtroom, she told me congratulations, that I did it and now I could start my new life.

Since I got the house, Rich had thirty days to move out and find a new place. That was interesting too. Rich didn't want to leave. Again, he didn't make anything easy. Even though he had thirty days to get out of the house, there was nothing legally that I could do to get him out of the house. Now we're divorced, everything's over, and Rich's still there. I just couldn't get rid of him.

I had to refinance the house to give Rich the money that I owed him, which was half of the value of the house and half of the value of the business. That wasn't fun. Since I was already in a financial mess, trying to refinance wasn't fun. My credit was bad now since all the bills had bounced and I didn't have the money to pay them. My credit was bad. I was working with my attorney and a mortgage broker, going back and forth. I was having such a hard time with it. This was the part that I really didn't want to do. When I found out how much my mortgage payment would be, I knew that I could never afford it, but I had to do what I had to do.

I kept stalling this because I knew down deep what the outcome would be. I was still upset because the money Rich and I put down on this house was the money I made from the sale of the house I had before I met Rich. And a part of me was mad because none of this should have hap-pened.

I was really struggling with all this, but I had to do it. At this point, I had no choice. I did refinance and my house payment doubled. Now what was I going to do? I couldn't make my house payment before, so how was I going to pay it when it's doubled?

I had to keep reminding myself that it was all in God's hands. Just thinking about when I gave Rich that huge check still makes me upset. See, I still have to remind myself today that it is all in God's hands.

Rich did eventually move out. That was such a hard day. As much as I wanted him to move, I did not want him to move.

Rich had a buddy to help him move out. Watching my furniture leave, the furniture that I picked out and bought, that we, both Rich and I, struggled to make payments on, watching my family room become empty, then slowly the rest of my stuff, pictures, videos of the boys (Rich took the video camera, so I guess he got the videos too), just watching all my stuff leave was hard. Rich and I fought over stuff. It was a long, hard day. Then he left. The house was upside down. Rich was gone, half of my stuff was gone. What was left was this empty feeling. Why did all this have to hap-pen?

Rich bought a house with the check I had to give to him. I knew I would be losing my house because I still couldn't pay all the back bills. Where was the justice? And the crazy part was I helped him move some of his stuff with the tool truck. When I was helping him, well, you can imagine all the emotions, looking around, seeing all my stuff at Rich's new house that I paid for, knowing I would be losing mine, and here I am helping him.

A part of me still loved Rich and wanted to believe in him. Rich told me that we all could move into this new house. Imagine that, after all of what had hap-pened, now he wants me and the boys to move into his house. That wouldn't be the smartest thing to do. A couple of days later, Rich was being Rich again. Things really would never change, and that's why we're divorced.

For the most part, things had settled down. I was still on the tool truck, hating it more and more. Rich still got moody back and forth. When he was nice, I would take it. When he was being Rich, I pulled back again. I knew it wasn't the smartest thing, but it hap-pened.

Over the summer, I got court papers. Rich was taking me back to court for full custody of the boys. I got the papers the day of Joey's birthday party. PJ was there, thank goodness. Those papers pushed me over the edge. At that point, I was trying to survive and I was tired.

The boys and I were still seeing Sheryl. Of course I had to call my attorney and let her know what was going on again. I just couldn't believe it. Here we go again. Will it never stop?

My attorney responded to the motion, and then we were back in court again. Ten months later, back in court. The judge referred the case back to the friend of the court. I'm thinking, *Oh no! Here we go again!* I was thinking, of course, about what hap-pened last time.

I went for an interview with the friend of the court, but my attorney went with me. Things were so much different. I was so much stronger and healed. The fear of Rich was less and less. What was he going to do now? It's all in God's hands. The interview went well. Now we had to sit back and wait again for the outcome. The only thing I could do is love my boys and keep the faith that all this was still in God's hands.

When my attorney got the recommendation, she called me, saying that she had to see me right away. Oh no, here we go again! Anxious and nervous. What's going to hap-pen now? I didn't think I could take much more. When I got there, my attorney was so happy. This was a good thing! The investigator did his job. He went back through all of Rich's history, went and pulled everything up, including police reports. Come to find out Rich had just had a drunk driving incident and his license was suspended. And a lot of other things too. The recommendation was that things stay the way they were and that if Rich kept pursuing changing the custody, then he would get less custody. Wow! Things were really changing.

All three of the boys were doing good. The boys were on a regular schedule. They were doing good at school. Rich had left us alone for the most part. Rich will always be Rich. I had taken care of everything, but I was really tired, beyond tired.

One day, when I was on the tool truck, one of my customers started yelling at me about a flashlight that "if Rich was here, he would take care of it," that "Rich went out to the truck and called me to take care of it." That was it, I lost it. I'm standing there yelling at him about Rich, telling him that it was me that took care of the flashlight, standing there with tears in my eyes, fighting them back with everything I had. I was done. I couldn't take it anymore.

I left and parked the truck in the driveway. I was done. Mentally, emotionally, whatever you want to call it, I was done. I stopped working on the truck. It just sat there. I wouldn't call Cornwell or Scott, my district manager. I wouldn't even open up the shades to the house. I was living in the house. I was getting judgments for the credit card bills. I even got calls from Cornwell that if I didn't start rolling in the truck, I would lose Cornwell too. But it didn't matter. I was tired. I was done. I did what I was supposed to do. Now I was done.

Sheryl knew everything I was going through. The boys and I were seeing her every week. Now it was time for me to start totally healing from all this. Time to start integrating all my parts that have helped me go through all this. It was time for them to heal and to catch up to speed with me. All the parts needed to be me.

I remember when Mark told me that one day I would look back at this like I was sitting down, looking at the water flowing and watching all the memories float by. I lived through them, felt them. There would be no more body memories to go with them; they wouldn't hurt me anymore, if that makes any sense. It does make sense to me now. Hopefully I can help you to understand too.

One day, when I took the boys to school, I was having a horrible day. Anxiety was through the roof. I went down to the water. As I have told you, the water calms me. That day was a beautiful day. Nice and sunny, blue skies, spring in the air, warm enough to take my coat off. I sat down by the water, going over everything in my head. Things were bad for so long. It was like a light switch and someone turned it on and I said, "What hap-pened? Everything in my life is what hap-pened!" That day was the start of the final phase of healing.

All my parts could heal. One at a time they could start to heal. That all my memories were true, that it did hap-pen, and that we all could heal. I remember calling Sheryl while I was at the water, explaining everything to her. She was so excited for me. Things weren't going to be easy, by no means, but what's new? Had anything or any of this ever been easy?

So slowly parts of me started healing. I was becoming a stronger mom. I'm not sure if I told you before, Sheryl reminds me of this all the time, and even to this day, it upsets me. The first day, Joey, Robby, and I walked into her office (at the church where Mark had his office too). Sheryl said that two children and one adult walked in. Guess who the adult was? It wasn't me, it was Robby. After three years of counseling with Mark, and after everything that had hap-pened, Robby was the adult. Every time I hear Sheryl say that, I get angry, even writing it now. Mom and Dad messed me up so bad that I didn't know how to discipline my kids. They were walking all over me. I knew I was a wonderful mom; I love my kids dearly, but in the discipline area, I lacked. How would I know? Now I even amaze myself at how good I am with the boys. Sheryl's even amazed at how good I am with the boys.

With PJ, there was only one child. There was no fighting or arguing. He was always an angel baby. He never really got into trouble. PJ was always really good. And when I saw him, since it was fifty-fifty, my time was precious with him, so we always had fun. But with Robby and Joey, they were always fighting. Even at a young age, they saw how Rich had total control over me, so they learned to have the control too. They learned it, and now I had to teach them a new healthy way. All three of them. Every time I told them no, no had to mean no. By the example of my actions, the boys are learning healthy ways and habits. I'm so proud of myself. I even amaze myself.

After that day down by the water, I want to say I was depressed, but I really wasn't. I was tired. Forty years of abuse. I was tired. Working with Sheryl and the boys was very tiring, day after day, healing, integrating, knowing that this was all real and that it happened. The more that I healed, the more integrated I was.

I remember one day when Sheryl came over to the house. The one personality that knew everything was Helen. She didn't think that I could handle knowing everything. Helen was the meanest. She was the one that was going to protect me from knowing everything. It was her job to protect me. Gosh, even today it's hard to think about. But I'm really at peace because that's the only way I survived any of this.

When we were in my bedroom, I started crying and crying; the pain was so bad. I was starting to feel the pain that Helen kept inside of her for so many years, trying to protect me for so many years, trying to protect me from knowing the whole truth that I couldn't handle all the pain from the occult. I had to assure her that I needed to know everything because we all needed to be totally whole and healed from all this.

It was almost like a battle going on inside of me. Actually, it really was a battle going on! The parts that wanted me to know and the parts that didn't. Of course, my parts didn't want me to know. If it had been okay for me to know back then, I would have never gotten the parts in the first place. Does this make sense to you? I hope so. After years of counseling, it makes sense to me. That's why I'm able to write this. I believe that there are other people like you and me that feel the same way. We all need to be able to make sense of what has hap-pened to us.

That summer, I did so much healing. As much as the outside world was falling apart, every day I was healing more and more and getting stronger and stronger. One day, when Rich came to pick the boys up, he was arguing with me. I don't remember what it was about. All I remember is that I told the boys to get in the house. Rich was parked in the driveway. I remember just telling him that my job was to protect the boys. Rich asked, "Protect them from who?" I told Rich I was protecting the boys from him. Rich looked at me like I had five eyes, but he didn't say a word. He stopped arguing. He was nice to the boys and left. Another time we were arguing about the boys, and I told Rich to stop, that I was protecting my boys. He was at the house again, and he was where I usually park my van. He knew that was where I always park; he just did it to get me upset. I told him that he needed to move, that this was private property. After that, he always parked on the street and wouldn't even get out of his truck.

There was another time that we had to go to the friend of the court because Rich wasn't paying his child support. When we went up to the counter, he started saying bad things about me. Rich told them about what hap-pened over Thanksgiving.

It was a Wednesday, which would be Rich's day with the boys. But it was the Wednesday before Thanksgiving, which was my holiday that year. I wasn't going to give Rich the boys overnight because they were supposed to be with me the next morning. Rich called the police on me, so the police were at the house again, and they told me that I did have to give the boys to Rich. And Rich told them that I was the crazy one. The police made the boys go with Rich even if it was just for a few hours. I kept telling the officer that Rich wasn't going to give the boys back to me as he was supposed to. The officer didn't care. Rich promised the officer that I could pick up the boys. And sure enough, I was right. Rich wouldn't give the boys back to me. It was Thanksgiving, and you know how hard Thanksgiving is, being when Rich was arrested for raping me. Well, I called the police and went back and forth with them until I got the boys back.

Well, Rich told all this to the friend of the court. They were so upset with Rich that he would call the police and that the boys had to deal with the police twice. And again, the courts told Rich to leave me alone. They also told him to get a job within the next thirty days or he would be in contempt of court.

Believe it or not, he did get a job. And he has never called the police again. As much as I was going through, things were changing for the good. Day after day, I was healing more and more. Good days and bad days. Every day I was healing and getting stronger.

Sheryl's rule of thumb regarding dishes in the sink: if it's over seven days, maybe a problem. If it's under seven days, that's okay.

That summer, I wasn't working on the truck anymore. I was getting letters from Cornwell. I knew that was over for me. I just couldn't do it anymore. The house was a problem. I mixed up the days for contacting the mortgage company so the house went into foreclosure. I lost the franchise for Cornwell. Credit card companies were taking me back to court. But none of that mattered anymore. The only thing at this point was to heal from all this.

That whole summer, I didn't do much. I did start rolling on the truck again as an independent tool dealer. I did that for about six months, but that didn't last long. There was still that attachment with Rich. After three or four months, some of my customers would still say, "What did you do to Rich? I was Rich's customer. I want to know the truth." Customer after customer. I couldn't do it anymore. I parked the truck, and that was that.

I'm sitting here getting ready to write, knowing that I was able to tell you my story. I'm crying because I can't believe that I went through all this. I thought that I would be doing the happy dance because this book, my story, is almost over. That I did it, that I have accomplished so much. That you too can tell your story. I can't believe that I'm lying here crying like a baby over everything. That I did it.

PJ's doing wonderful. I'm so proud of him. The boys are doing just great. Rich is even being nice; we are finally co-parenting. We are both working together for the boys. I just can't believe it's almost over. But the rest of my life is just beginning.

That summer I was just surviving. I got a part-time job at the front counter at a repair shop. One of my customers owned it. We became friends, and PJ started working there. I got to spend time with PJ. For all the time I didn't get to see him, I got to make up for it.

Now the house. I knew it was all in God's hands whatever the outcome. I lost the house. I didn't know what to do. I just kept surviving one day at a time.

One day, out of the blue, the mortgage company sent me a letter, stating the actions that I could do to save the house. I said to myself, "See, it's all in God's hands." The outcome of the house was in God's hands, but I really didn't know what the outcome would be. What was really the best for me and the boys?

I went back and forth with the mortgage company. I had to explain my story over and over again. They were going to put me through as a hardship case. There was a date that I was waiting for, the Fourth of July. Since that was a holiday, they gave me until the next Monday, I think. I got the approval from two different people that they were going to lower my house payment and give me my new amount, which would be due on August 1.

Still waiting for the outcome of the third person who had to give it the okay. My emotions were all over the place. I loved my house. But what was really the best for all of us? There were just too many bad memories there.

God knows what's best for me and the boys; it was all in his hands.

Rich took me back to court again for lowering his child support and paying him for a credit card and money for the business. When we went in front of the judge, it was my attorney and I and Ron.

Rich wasn't there yet. The judge wanted to start. Ron said okay; he didn't care that Rich wasn't there yet. The judge started without Rich. And again, the judge sided with me. Even Ron did.

The last time I saw Ron, it was quite amazing.

Over the summer, I had a customer over my house. He and his wife were having problems, and I was telling him my story to give him encouragement. We talked late into the night. Anyway, in the middle of the night, around two thirty, we heard a noise outside. I looked out my bedroom window because I thought I heard the sound of Rich's truck. It couldn't be Rich because he had the boys that weekend. But when I looked out the window, it looked like Rich's truck. I couldn't tell because it was so dark. I heard all this noise. It sounded like air was coming from the tires, then I saw a pickup truck drive down the street. When my customer went outside to see what was going on, sure enough, all four tires were flat. I called the police and made a report. Guess who the first suspect was? Going back to court several times for this, Rich wanted the boys to testify that he was home. Being the boys' mom, I said absolutely not, the boys had been through enough. The courts listened to me. After going back and forth with this, the customer didn't come to court that day, and they dismissed it. That was okay; as you know, I was so tired of going back to court anyway. But the best part was when Ron came up to me and said that I could go home, that they dismissed the case. Ron asked me how I was doing and if the boys were doing okay. I told Ron how good we were all doing. That the boys were doing good in school, that we were all still seeing Sheryl. And Rich was leaving us alone.

You could tell that Ron was genuinely concerned. Then I thanked him for everything. God put it on Ron's heart how the divorce ended up. I thanked him again, sincerely, for everything. Wished him well because he was retiring, so all the court stuff was over with Ron. And then I gave Ron a big hug. When Ron wished me well, I thought Rich was going to faint. After everything that's hap-pened, here I am hugging Ron and he's wishing me well. And Rich was paying for this. God is such a good God. I had to laugh all day just thinking about what God said to me way back at the beginning that he was the judge and jury.

Waiting for that third person to call back felt like it would take forever. Then the phone call came, but I missed it and they left the answer on the voice mail. The third person denied me, meaning that I only had two weeks to get out of the house. I couldn't believe it. Two weeks! Where were we going to go? What was I going to do now? I thought that I was staying, but now I had to be out and I only had two more weeks. God, now what? I was in disbelief. But I still have to believe that it's all in God's hands.

I started to look at apartments. I had no other choice. I looked at one close to the house. It still would be near the boys' school. I went to go look at it. It was really nice, but it was small. I explained my situation to the man at the apartment complex. He told me of an apartment complex that was nice and much bigger. It even had a washer and dryer in the apartment itself. It was their sister complex. Then he told me how much they were. I couldn't even afford the apartments I was just looking at, how on earth could I ever afford the larger, nicer ones? When I left the apartments, I was so discouraged. God, how could you allow all this to hap-pen? I did what was right, went through all this healing, now I've lost the house. And still all this is in your hands?

When I left that apartment, something told me to go to the other apartments. I kept fighting the feeling. But it became so strong that I had to go look.

When I got there, they were so beautiful. The outside clubhouse. Everything. I could tell it was a very expensive place. The lady was so nice; she took me through the floor samples. They were beautiful at 1,250 square foot. Bigger than my house. Then she told me the price. I laughed to myself. Okay, you had me come here, showed me these beautiful apartments. Why? For what? God, this isn't even funny.

She asked me for how long would I need the apartment. I had enough money to pay for three months from the mutual funds.

THE LIGHT THROUGH MY EYES

When Rich and I were going through the divorce, I forgot about our mutual funds. They were never brought up in the divorce. A couple of months before looking at the apartments, out of the blue, I remembered about the mutual funds. No reason. It just popped up in my head (or so I thought). When I called the bank to inquire about them, the gentleman on the phone said that my husband was already on top of things and we should have the check shortly. I said, "My husband? You mean my ex-husband. I don't have a husband." Then the man on the phone started to explain to me that the funds had already been sold and processed and there was nothing that I could do to stop it. The check was already made out, and it was going to be mailed to Rich's address. I was shocked. As Sheryl would say, why should I be shocked? Remember what he's already done? I still keep reminding myself of this.

Anyway, I explained to the man on the phone that we are divorced and half of the money belonged to me. He said that both of our names were on the check and that we both would have to sign it. If Rich signed my name, would that be forgery? I thanked the man and hung up the phone after stating that I would call my ex-husband and set something up.

When I called Rich, he couldn't believe that I found out what he was trying to do with the mutual funds. He couldn't believe that I found out. I didn't believe it was hap-pening at all! Just out of the blue, I hap-pened to think about it. I just hap-pened to think of it on that particular day and placed a call on that particular day. If I had called a couple of days later, I would have missed out on the money. God knew what I needed. God knows the outcome of everything, and he knows everything that I need. Over and over again, I question God. I ask him all the time, "Why?" Most of the time, it seems so unfair that nothing's going my way. Nothing makes sense out of all this. But I'm sure glad that God knows what he's doing and doesn't listen to me as much as I want him to.

I guess God always knows best.

After I hung up with Rich, obviously it didn't' go very well. I called the gentleman back at the bank to set something up. He suggested that we could go to a branch to receive and sign the check, that he could have the check sent there instead of sending it to Rich's address. Then we could both sign the check, cash it, and divide it in half. I told him that it sounded like a wonderful idea, especially since I knew the people at that bank branch.

God took care of everything, but I only had money for three months' rent until I could get back on my feet. But it still did not make things easy or simple or make sense.

When I left the apartments, I was so distraught, as you can imagine. I got to work and explained everything to my boss. I sat down on the ground and yelled at God, literally yelled at God, "Okay, God, the house is in your hands. I lost it. Now I need a place to live!" Just like that, I yelled at God. I needed a place to live; it was all in God's hands. "God, you need to figure it out."

Not only ten minutes later, a perfect stranger called me and said that she heard that I needed a place for three months. I was so excited. She told me who she was; her name was Rochelle and she lived in the last apartment that I looked at, the one that was 1,250 square feet. Well, anyways, she bought a house and needed to sublease her apartment.

I got so excited. Everything was perfect. Then she told me how much it was going to cost. Then boy, did I get bummed out. I couldn't afford it. She asked me what I could afford and I answered. She told me, "I'll take it." What? I was thinking to myself. She'll take it? Okay, this really is all in God's hands.

We made arrangements to meet. I saw the apartment; it was beautiful. She had painted it blue, not my favorite color, but it was still beautiful. Now all we had to do was go to the leasing office and set everything up. Well, I didn't make enough money to qualify for the lease to be all in my name. So the leasing office gave us some suggestions, and the only way was to put me on her lease. I'm thinking to myself, *I'm a stranger to her. There's no way she is going to do that.* But she did. I was able to pay for the rest of her lease. I couldn't believe everything that she did for me. But she did. It was all God.

Within a week, I lost the house and didn't have a place to live. Now I'm good for the next three months. That was August first.

The mortgage company set up a court date to see if I could get another thirty days in the house because I had so much stuff and was dragging my feet. When I went to court, it was the same court where Ron and Rich and I were last. It made me smile of how far I had come.

When I was waiting to be called, I started talking to people. There were so many. They all had a story to tell. When I was talking to the people there, no one thought that I was there because I lost a house. They thought I was there as a property manager or even an attorney. That was truly a compliment. Everything that I went through and I was doing so good no one could tell. When I met with the mortgage company, they did give me an additional thirty days. I was grateful for that. Packing was not fun; it was so hard on me. It was just a couple of weeks ago with Sheryl that I figured out why it was so hard.

After the PJ thing (my part seeing PJ for the first time since he was a baby) and the four-year-old me, well, now we know why that part was so important. It was her prayer that got me here. Now there were other parts that were stuck, and it was about throwing things away.

At Christmastime, I won't throw the wrapping paper away even if it was in the garbage bags. I have to empty out the garbage bags and go through all the wrapping paper to make sure I didn't throw anything away that I would need.

When I met with Sheryl, I knew there was something left in the pot. There was. I had to deal with Mom throwing my things out. I remember when my toys were outside in garbage bags. But I forgot that Mom and Dad got me a bike for my fifth birthday. I remember looking back at the pictures from my party and my memories. I was really, really sad. Anyway, they bought me this bike and kept it in my bedroom. I was not allowed to ride it. They kept it in my bedroom. I couldn't even touch it. If I did, I got hit.

Sheryl was helping me with that. It's funny how she helped me heal from that. Because I still was stuck to the house. She explained that everything has its purpose. My clothes, they only last for so long, then they either don't fit or go out of style. Even furniture lasts for a season to serve its purpose. And food, sorry about this one, but it fits. You can laugh at this. Even food has its purpose; you eat it, it serves its purpose, then you get rid of it. Ha ha!

When she explained it to me like that, I was able to have a much better time of letting things go. For the most part, I'm at peace with the house. It served its purpose. Now the apartment has to serve its purpose here.

I was able to get most of the big stuff, the important stuff out of the house and into the apartment. For the most part, the apartment was fixed up. The boys didn't even want to go back to the house. They had had enough there. The apartment had a really nice pool and hot tub, so they were, for the most part, happy. I was going back and forth between the apartment and the house, trying to get rid of stuff, going over memory after memory of stuff.

My neighbors came over and were helping me go through things and moving things. They were all so helpful. There were just a couple of days left before I had to totally be out of the house. I still had a lot of stuff left. I didn't have anywhere to put the stuff. I was just moving it from the house to the garage. I gave a lot of stuff away. But I still had a lot of stuff. Over twenty-five years of stuff.

I remember sitting in my garage, going over boxes of stuff with my neighbors. Some stuff was easy for me to go through, other things were hard. I still had that emotional attachment to them. After the other day with Sheryl, it just made me so mad. For three days, all I did was walk around and say, "My parents were sick, just sick."

If the boys had a bike in their bedroom they could never ride or got hit if they even touched it, they would look at me like I had five eyes or something. With all the occult stuff and everything that they did, even the bed in the living room and the bicycle in the bedroom just made me sick. The next week after that, when I saw Sheryl, she couldn't even believe it. Out of everything, that was just sick.

I had a nice time with my neighbors. They were such a big help. Since all this started, I really didn't talk to any of my neighbors, but they were all there for me when I really needed them as I was packing up the house. The next day was the day that I was supposed to be out. But so much stuff was going on, I mentally and physically couldn't do it.

The boys were at the apartment when I ran back to the house to check on things. There was the sheriff at my side door, reading my note that I put on the door, explaining everything that was going on. Then I saw who it was—Ted, the sheriff that I had known at the courthouse all the times that I was there.

When he said, "Cindy, I knew that name. It sounded familiar," but he couldn't believe that it was me.

Since it was me and since he had a whole crew with him, believe it or not, they helped me move the rest of my stuff out of the house. Here I had nobody to help me, now God sent people to help me. Even though it was the most degrading thing in my life to see all my belongings on the grass, again, God turned everything out for the good. I asked God for help, and here God brought me all these men. Just like an assembly line. I had my keep pile and a garbage pile.

I called PJ at work. His boss, my friend, had let him go and get a U-Haul to help me. I asked this friend if he would come and help because I really needed him. Again, I was told no. Here I've learned who my true friends are. PJ called his girlfriend to come and help. All my neighbors who were home came out to help me. It was amazing to see the whole neighborhood come out and help me.

That day was so long. We had people coming and going. Just in a few hours, it was all done.

The house was empty; everything was in the U-Haul. I had a place for the tool truck. God was good; the worry and anxiety were over. I was out of the house, and God again took care of everything.

Since so much stuff got thrown away and there were so many people, Ted said he would hold off on taking the dumpster away. Ted had ordered a huge dumpster for all the debris since they had to totally empty the house. The next day, I went dumpster diving for the things I was missing. Again, the neighbors were laughing when we were all in the dumpster. Just trying to get in was funny. Just four of five women, dumpster diving. It was raining to boot!

I couldn't do anything but laugh. And we were all laughing. We are going to look back at this and laugh and laugh.

The part with Sheryl, the other week about letting things go, I was still holding on to the house. God knew that I never could have written this book there. And now I'm at peace with that because God knew that I would be writing this book here in the apartment and that he supernaturally literally put me here at this apartment.

Sara and Judie have been my backbone to help me write this. Judie is one floor down and Sara is two floors down. We live in a cat building, and we have Marshmallow, the cat. Everything fell into place more than I will probably ever know.

I started this book in October. It was right after the first three months of being here at the apartment and when the original lease was to end. I needed to do something about the lease and rent. I got to know the people in the front office really well. They helped me out so I had my own lease. "Great, God figured out how to get my leased signed. Great, but now how am I going to pay for it? Hello, God. Please if this is your will, I need a job."

I was just working part-time that had been okay because the rent was paid for three months. I was starting to write; now I just needed a way to pay for it.

I was casually talking to my girlfriend Lisa. I had to run to the bank for my boss. We were laughing and joking around. "Okay, God, I need a job. I need full-time. I have to pay for the apartment." I talked to Lisa on the way to the bank and on the way back to the shop. We had a great laugh talking about how good God is. When I was getting ready to walk back in the door, I told Lisa goodbye and that I would talk to her later.

As soon as I walked in the door at work, I mean literally two steps into the door, my boss looked at me and asked me if I wanted to work for him full-time—forty hours, double my pay. He began to tell me that his tech quit and that if I wanted full-time, if I wanted the job, it was mine. I just looked at him. What hap-pened? This isn't even funny. I just went to the bank. I wasn't even gone thirty minutes. Everything was fine when I left. This wasn't funny at all. My boss told me, "Go look. He's gone. Ask the guys if I'm serious or not." I looked for the tech and asked the guys what hap-pened. I just went to the bank, shaking my head in disbelief.

Lisa and I were just joking around about me working full-time. We weren't in serious prayer. But God knew what he was doing. Two or more in agreement, when you give it to God, God takes care of everything. Everything.

CHAPTER NINE

> Lord, listen to my words.
> Understand my sadness.
> Listen to my cry for help, my King and my God,
> Because I pray to you.
> Lord, every morning you hear my voice.
> Every morning, I tell you what I need,
> And I wait for your answer.
> —Psalm 5:1–3

THAT'S MY STORY. AS YOU KNOW, I started this book in October. It is now February 13, over a year later. It's been such a long year and a half trying to get it written. I knew for years that I would be writing this. You reading this have given me the strength and courage to go on. I hope my story has given you strength and courage to keep going on. When it seems like tomorrow will never come, you're right. You have to live for today because you will never get today back again.

All the days that I have struggled to get through, only God really knows. All the pain and hurt that you have gone through, only

God knows that too. I hope that my story gives you hope that, one day, you will be healthy and whole and can tell your story too. From the bottom of my heart, I thank you for helping me through my story. If it wasn't for you, I would have no one to read it.

The day I stood at my side door for the very last time, I looked at all my neighbors, Ted, the people that were helping him. All the love and compassion on their faces. For everything that I had lost from that day so long ago, when Sergeant McFadden said enough was enough, that day I had I stood in that doorway, knowing that my life would change forever.

The irony was that the last time I stood there, I was all alone. I had no clue at all what was going to hap-pen. Thank goodness I can't tell the future.

And here I was, in the doorway again. Gone through hell and back again way too many times. God has shown me over and over again that when I walk through the door and close it for the last time that what hap-pened is over and what a beautiful future I will have. I have a beautiful apartment to write my story in. God took care of that and everything else.

Scared to not want to walk through that door again, looking at all their faces, I was pretty much crying out of control.

I see the love on PJ's face, the love that I fought so hard for. Now my amazing son was telling me that it's okay to go. And that he loves me so much. With tears in his eyes, PJ is telling me it's okay.

Never looking back, I took a deep breath and walked out the door. Never to look back again. To never need to look back again.

Or so I thought.

ABOUT THE AUTHOR

C INDY KUPINSKI IS HAPPILY MARRIED and lives in a suburb outside of Detroit with three dogs and two cats. She has always wanted a big family. She has been blessed with three boys and three daughters overnight, an amazing daughter in-law, two sons-in-law, and five grand-babies. Cindy has been truly blessed.

Since her heart's desire is family, she wanted to dedicate her life to speaking to people on domestic violence and mental health issues, about how much your childhood affects your adult life, and the choices you make because of it. For families to also heal from abuse from their childhood.

CPSIA information can be obtained
at www.ICGtesting.com
Printed in the USA
BVHW030020150220
572386BV00001B/2